RAGS-TO-RICHES BRIDE

Mary Nichols

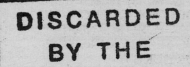

◎™ MILLS & BOON®
Pure reading pleasure™

First published in Great Britain 2008
Harlequin Mills & Boon Limited,
Eton House, 18-24 Paradise Road, Richmond, Surrey TW9 1SR

© Mary Nichols 2008

ISBN: 978 0 263 86273 7

Set in Times Roman 10½ on 12 pt.
04-0808-93473

Printed and bound in Spain
by Litografia Rosés S.A., Barcelona

RAGS-TO-RICHES BRIDE

Chapter One

1837

'Papa, you will make yourself ill if you do not take some nourishment,' Diana said, leaning forward to take the half-empty glass of cognac from her father's hand and put a plate of food on the table in front of him.

'Not hungry.'

'No, I am told strong drink dulls the appetite.' She put his glass down on the table and sat down opposite him. He had once been robust, weatherbeaten from years at sea, a loving husband and beloved father who made their lives carefree and interesting, until four years before when his left arm had been amputated after a skirmish in the Indian Ocean and he had given in to his wife's pleading to leave the service before it killed him. The loss of his arm and what he termed a life of uselessness on shore had started the downward slide, but while her mother was alive he had still been the father she knew and loved. Since Mama's death he was not the same man at all.

'We cannot go on like this, Papa. Something must be done.'

'What about?'

'How we are to manage.'

'I have a pension.'

She sighed. 'I know, but it is not enough.' She was tempted to add that he drank most of it, but that would have been cruel and she desisted. Together with the tiny pension, he had left the service with a small accumulation of prize money but that had disappeared very quickly trying to keep up their hitherto comfortable way of life. They had been forced to dismiss their servants, sell their furniture and move into smaller accommodation, and when even that proved too much to maintain, to these two rooms in a boarding house in Southwark. These were poorly furnished; though Diana did her best to keep them clean, the grime seemed ingrained in the fabric of the tall, narrow tenement. It was difficult to maintain standards, but she was determined not to let them slide even further into poverty.

Her mother had made ends meet by taking in fine embroidery from a dressmaker in Bond Street, but now Mama was gone, worn out with the stress of it all, Diana knew she had to do something herself to keep the wolf from their door. She had no one to turn to, not a relative in the world that she knew of, and her father was becoming more and more hopeless.

If only he would rouse himself, he was not beyond a little light work, but he did not seem able to drag himself out of the pit he had dug for himself. In the two months since Mama's death, he had spoken only briefly and then only when necessary, and he had hardly eaten at all. His diet consisted almost exclusively of strong liquor with which he hoped to achieve oblivion.

'I must find work,' she told him. 'The rent is due and there is very little food in the larder.'

'Do what your mama did.'

'I tried that yesterday. Madame Francoise told me I was not skilled enough.' That had rankled, considering she had been doing most of the work since her mother became too ill to do it herself, though they had never told Madame that. 'Plain sewing, perhaps, but they had nothing to offer me; in any case, the wages for that make it no more than slave labour.'

'We will manage.' He reached for his glass and she gave up. It was up to her to do something. If she did not find work soon, she would have to sell her mother's necklace. Mama had given it to her just before she died and Diana treasured it as a lasting memory. Its stones were a pale greenish colour, which she thought were opals, set in silver filigree. She doubted it was valuable—her father had never been wealthy enough to indulge in expensive trinkets—but it would be a dark day indeed when that had to go.

Swathed in mourning black in spite of the heat of a summer's day, she left their lodgings and set out with a handful of advertisements culled from the newspaper, determined to find something, but everything she tried—lady's companion, lady's maid, governess to small children—all required her to live in and that she could not do. Who would look after her father if she did not come home to him every night? She thought of teaching, but her education had been so unconventional that she was not considered suitable, except at dame-school level and the pay for that was barely enough to feed her, let alone her father. Besides, she knew their landlady, Mrs Beales, would not allow her to use their lodgings for the purpose.

The man in the employment agency she tried was disparaging. 'I could try for a position as a domestic servant,' he said, 'but I doubt you would suit. You need to be properly trained and experienced, and have excellent references...' He paused to shrug his shoulders and look over his spectacles at her with a certain amount of compassion. This applicant had obviously been genteelly brought up, not in the highest echelons of society but high enough to exclude her from menial tasks. Beneath her large unbecoming bonnet, her complexion was unlined and unmarked, her hands were smooth and white; her clothes, though not the height of fashion, were well made in a good bombazine. 'And in any case, you would need to live in.'

'I cannot do that,' Diana told him. 'I have to look after my invalid father.'

'Then I am afraid I cannot help you.'

She had known before she entered that it was hopeless. She thanked the man and set off she knew not where. Unwilling to go home with her mission unaccomplished, she walked down Regent Street and turned into Burlington Arcade. Perhaps she could obtain some plain sewing from one of the many fashion shops that traded on that busy thoroughfare— low pay was better than no pay at all. The shops were all high-class establishments, catering for the elite. Surely someone would employ her?

She stopped to look into the window of a shop displaying costly silks, ornaments and trinkets imported from India and the Orient. She had seen items like that on her travels being sold in noisy bazaars and market places, at a time when she had been happy and carefree. Better not dwell on that, she decided, turning away. And then her eye was drawn to a ticket in the window. 'Clerk wanted,' she read. 'Conscientious and quick at figuring. A good hand essential. Apply within.'

Diana knew perfectly well they wanted a man; ladies simply did not do that kind of work, but she did not see why they could not if their skills were appropriate. She and her mother had often travelled abroad when her father had been posted to some far-off station and she had been taught by her parents, augmented by her own curiosity, about the sights and sounds of foreign places they visited, as well as through her reading, which was wide ranging. Surely that must count for something? She pushed open the door and her nostrils were immediately assailed by a mixture of spices and perfume, which had once been so familiar to her.

A tall gangly youth came towards her, a smile of welcome on his face, assuming she was a customer. It was no good stating her errand to him; she would be laughed off the premises. She drew herself up to her full five feet five inches and faced him squarely. 'I would like to speak to the proprietor.'

'Mr Harecroft?'

'If that is his name, yes.'

'Do you have an appointment?'

'No, but he will see me. My name is Miss Diana Bywater.'

She made herself sound so confident that he did not doubt her. He asked her to wait and disappeared into the back of the premises, while she looked about her. The shop was spacious and well laid out. There were shelves full of bolts of silk, muslin, gingham and chintz in a rainbow of colours, and others displaying ivory ornaments, snuff boxes, fans and tea caddies. Towards the back were larger items, stools and intricately carved chests. These were the source of the exotic odours. She had not noted the name of the establishment and remedied the omission by going to the door and reading it from the facia. 'Harecroft Emporium' it said in gold lettering. She had barely returned inside when the young man came back.

'Please follow me.'

She was conducted through a labyrinth of rooms, all packed with merchandise, and up a flight of stairs along a corridor lined with closed doors, then up a second flight and along another corridor to a door at the end, where the young man knocked and ushered Diana in. 'Miss Bywater, sir.'

Diana walked into the room, trying not to let the man who rose to greet her see that she was shaking. He was in his middle years, his hair the colour of pepper sprinkled with salt and his eyes piercingly blue. He wore a dark grey frock coat and striped trousers. His collar was tall and stiffly white, his cravat slate grey. 'Miss Bywater,' he greeted her, holding out his hand. 'How do you do.'

'Very well, sir.' She shook the hand and allowed herself a quick look about her. The room was large. The desk from which he had risen to greet her was in its centre, facing the door. One wall was covered in shelves containing ledgers and boxes, a large window occupied the middle of another wall and there were several upright chairs and two small tables. She was favourably impressed by its neatness and the fact that there was a square of good-quality carpet on the floor surrounded by highly polished boards. 'You are the owner of this establishment?'

'I am its proprietor. It is one of several under the Harecroft banner. Please sit down.' He resumed his own seat behind his desk and steepled his hands on it, waiting for her to state her business.

'I see from the card in your window that you are seeking a clerk.'

'We are indeed.' Again he waited.

'Then I am that clerk.'

'You!' He made no attempt to disguise his amusement. 'You are a woman.'

'So I am.' She looked down at her skirt as if to confirm this, but really to renew her courage, before raising her eyes to meet his gaze. 'Would you prefer a man? I could dress up in a man's clothes and cut my hair. Would that make a difference?'

'No, certainly not. Miss Bywater, you surely did not think I would entertain such a preposterous idea? My employees are all men, we have never employed women in the business—'

'Now, that is not quite true.' The voice came from behind Diana and she swivelled round to face a very old lady who had that moment entered the room. She was tiny, but very upright. Her snow-white hair was pulled up under a black bonnet with a purple feather curling round its brim. She wore an old-fashioned gown in purple taffeta and a short black cape. Her face was lined, but her eyes were the blue of a summer sky.

Diana realised almost at once that she must be related to Mr Harecroft and this was confirmed when he sprang to his feet and exclaimed, 'Grandmother! What are you doing here?'

'I have come to see you, since you have not been anywhere near Borstead Hall for months.'

'We have been extremely busy, as you must know. Visitors to London are more numerous than usual what with all the goings on at court, foreign dignitaries arriving and everyone wanting black for the late King. Some are even buying material for their coronation clothes. They have money burning a hole in their purses, and who was it who taught me that the business must come first?'

The old lady laughed. 'I did and I am a woman. So what is this young lady asking of you?' She turned to Diana for the first time, a smile on her face. 'Am I right in thinking you are here looking for work?'

'Yes, ma'am.'

'I am Lady Harecroft. The dowager, of course,' she said,

blue eyes twinkling. 'But I once worked alongside my husband in this enterprise and helped build it up from nothing, which is why I said my grandson was not correct in saying the company has never employed women. One of its instigators was a woman.'

'That's different,' Mr Harecroft said.

Her ladyship ignored him. 'Tell me, child, why do you need to work and what can you do?'

'My father is an invalid and my mother died two months ago,' Diana answered her. 'I need to earn a living that will allow me to live at home and look after my father. As for what I can do, I can write in a good hand, I am familiar with adding, subtracting, fractions, decimals and computing percentages. Items such as you have displayed downstairs I have seen and handled in India and the Far East.'

'You are very young to be so well travelled.'

'I am eighteen, my lady, and my father was a sea captain. Mama and I often travelled to distant parts to be with him.'

'What will he do when you are at work?'

'He is not so incapacitated that he cannot amuse himself, my lady. He has lost an arm and that has weakened him, but I am hopeful he will improve day by day. The demise of my mother affected him badly.'

'Have you no relatives?'

'None that I know of. Both my parents were without siblings and their parents long dead.'

'Then you do indeed carry a heavy burden.' She turned back to her silent grandson. 'John, give Miss… Oh, dear, I do not know your name.'

'Diana Bywater, my lady.'

'Good Lord!' The smile faded suddenly, her eyes opened wide and she put her gloved hand to her mouth with a little cry before sitting heavily in the nearest chair.

Diana started up in alarm. 'Ma'am, are you not well?'

Whatever it was that had disturbed her, the old lady recovered quickly and the smile was back. 'I am extremely old, my dear, you must forgive my little lapses.' She opened her fan and waved it vigorously in front of her face. 'It is so hot today, I am quite worn out with it.'

'You should not have attempted the stairs,' her grandson said. 'If you had sent a message, I could have come down to you. I will send for Stephen to take you home.'

'Very well. But give Miss Bywater a trial. If she is as good as she says she is, it will not matter a jot that she is a female.'

'Grandmother,' he protested, 'women cannot be expected to do such meticulous work. They do not have the constitution for it, nor the mental ability…'

'Nonsense! You forget the country is ruled by a woman now.'

'The new Queen will no doubt be guided at every step by her ministers and advisers. There is no comparison. And how can I put Miss Bywater in a room full of men? I will never get any work out of them.'

'Then find her a corner to herself. I am sure she can deal with any unwarranted attention.' She turned to Diana and scrutinised her carefully, her gaze ranging from her sensible boots, her simple black dress and three-quarter-length coat to her wide-brimmed bonnet, which hid most of her face. 'Take that bonnet off, girl.'

Diana did as she was told, to reveal lustrous red-gold hair which she had attempted, not very successfully, to drag into a knot at the back of her head. The old lady gave a secretive little smile, which puzzled Diana. 'You will hide that under a suitable cap when you are at work, my dear, and you will wear a plain gown, long-sleeved and buttoned to the neck, otherwise you'll do. John, you may send for Stephen now.'

Mr Harecroft picked up a bell from his desk and gave it a vigorous shake. Almost at once the young man who had conducted Diana upstairs entered the room and was told to find Mr Stephen Harecroft and ask him to come. He looked at Diana as he turned to obey and gave her a smirk, which told her he had been listening on the other side of the door. Lady Harecroft had said she could deal with unwarranted attention and she must demonstrate that she could. She gave him a haughty look and replaced her bonnet.

She was wondering if she ought to leave, but she had not yet been appraised of her duties or told her hours of work and remuneration. She was not even sure that Mr Harecroft would give her a job after Lady Harecroft had gone. He had certainly said nothing that indicated he would, had said very little at all, leaving the talking to his grandmother. She sat with her hands in her lap and waited.

Stephen Harecroft was a younger version of John, in his early twenties, Diana guessed. He had similar clear blue eyes and a shock of pale gold hair with just a hint of red. 'You sent for me, sir? I was busy checking that last consignment of silk. It's not up to the same standard as the last batch. We shall have to have words with our suppliers.' He turned to the old lady, his face lighting up with pleasure. 'Great-Grandmama, you here? How are you?' He bent to kiss her cheek.

'Perfectly well, boy. I want you to escort me back to Harecroft House. I will stay with you tonight and go home tomorrow.'

'A pleasure, but who brought you?'

'Richard, but he's gone to a meeting. He will join us for dinner.'

'A meeting?' Mr Harecroft queried. 'With whom?'

The old lady shrugged. 'I don't know. He didn't say.'

'Something to do with his book, I dare say,' Stephen said.

Suddenly seeing Diana, he stopped. 'I beg your pardon, ma'am.' This with a bow. 'I did not see you there.'

'Miss Bywater is coming to work here,' Lady Harecroft said.

'In what capacity?'

'Clerk,' his father said.

The young man did not trouble to hide his astonishment. 'But—'

'No buts, Stephen,' her ladyship said. 'Miss Bywater is in every way suitable and she needs to work, so you will do all you can to help her.'

He looked from his great-grandmother to his father, one eyebrow raised in a query. His father shrugged. It seemed to Diana that the old lady's word was law and, however much they might disapprove, they dare not go against her. She watched as the young man escorted his venerable relative from the room, then turned to face Mr Harecroft.

'Ahem…' he began, twiddling a pen between his fingers. 'I assume it is no good asking you for references?'

'No good at all, sir, but I am willing to demonstrate my ability.'

He reached into a drawer and drew out a ledger, opening it at random. 'Add that column of figures, if you please.' She did so. After he had checked her accuracy, he asked her to work out seven and a half per cent of the total. This done, she was required to copy a column of figures. If he had hoped to catch her out, he was disappointed. The speed with which she came back with the correct answers startled him. 'My father set me practising on the bills of lading on the ships he commanded,' she told him. 'I also worked out the percentages of the prize money for each member of the crew. It was Papa's way of teaching me mathematics.'

'It seems to have worked,' he murmured. 'What else did he teach you?'

She was relaxed enough to laugh. 'Oh, so many things. How to steer by the stars, the tides and ocean currents, the geography of the ports where we called, what they imported and exported, what it cost and what it fetched when it arrived in England, some of the culture. He is a very knowledgeable man.'

'But now unable to work himself?'

'That is correct.' She shut her mouth firmly on expanding on that. She did not want him to know about her father's drinking. It was something of which she was ashamed, ashamed most particularly because she could not coax him away from it. And bullying him only made him angry. He was her father, he would tell her, she had no right to question what he did.

'I will give you a month's trial. Your pay will be thirty-five pounds per annum and you will work from eight in the morning to seven at night from Monday to Friday and from eight until two on Saturdays. The men are given an allowance for a suit of clothes, so you shall have enough for two gowns. Grey, I think. Is that agreeable?'

'Yes, thank you, but I would like to be paid at the end of each week, considering I am to live at home.'

'Very well.' He smiled suddenly. 'You can no doubt compute how much that will be yourself.'

'When shall I start?'

'Tomorrow.' He opened a cash box and extracted three guineas which he offered to her. 'For your dresses. They will remain the property of the company.'

She rose to take the coins and put them in her purse, then thanked him again and left. He did not ask anyone to escort her off the premises, assuming she would find her own way down to the shop floor. Only when she was safely out into the arcade did she let out a huge breath of relief and allow herself to smile. She had done it! Sheer effrontery had paid off. At least for a month. She had no doubt Mr Harecroft expected to be able to say at the end of that time that the experiment had not worked and he must part with her. She had to disappoint those expectations, which meant not only being as good as the men he employed, but better. At the end of the month she must have made herself almost indispensable.

And she did. At the end of the trial, he was obliged to admit she had earned her pay and told her she could stay. She was still there a year later.

So that she would not distract the men she worked in solitary splendour in a little cubby hole on the second floor. Luckily it had a window which looked out onto the street at the back the shop, which she could open to let in a little air. She was doing that one hot day in June 1838, when she spotted the Harecroft carriage drawing up outside. She leaned out to see who had arrived and saw Lady Harecroft being escorted into the building.

Diana had not seen her ladyship since she joined the company the year before, and assumed her great age had precluded any more uncomfortable coach journeys from her home in Berkshire. But here she was. What had prompted her make the trip, especially in the heat of summer? There was no need for her to come shopping; anything she needed could be sent to her.

In the time she had been working at Harecroft's she had discovered a great deal about the business and the hierarchy of the family who ran it. At its apex was the redoubtable dowager Lady Harecroft. Her husband, plain George Harecroft then, had made his fortune in India where he worked for the British East India Company. Returning with his pockets jingling, he had not only married Lady Caroline Carson, the seventeen-year-old daughter of the Earl of St Albans, but, when Britain's textile manufacturers forced the end of the East India Company's monopoly of trade with the subcontinent, had set up Harecroft Importing and Warehousing from premises on the docks, which still belonged to the company and still figured largely in its affairs. Two years later his uncle died without issue and he became the second Baron Harecroft and inherited Borstead Hall near Ascot in Berkshire.

'Everyone expected him to give up the business and live the life of an aristocrat, but he chose to continue building it up,' Stephen had told her soon after her arrival. He had overcome his initial shock at her being employed and had assiduously obeyed his great-grandmother's injunction to help her all he could. 'I am told it caused no end of gossip, but he was never one to listen to tattle and he was encouraged by my great-grandmother who was, and is, a very unusual woman. Now we have a thriving import-and-export business and several shops besides this one. Great-Grandfather died some years ago and my grandfather took the title. He left the business then to concentrate on the estate where he breeds and trains race horses. My father took over here. One day, the warehouse and shops will be in my hands. Richard, of course, will eventually inherit the title and the estate in Berkshire.'

'Richard is your brother?'

'Yes. He is older than me by three years, but he disdains working in the business. He and Papa fell out over it years ago. He was in the army for a time, but now he says he is writing a book, though what it is about I do not know.'

'Is he married?'

'No. I do not think he is the marrying kind.' And then he had abruptly changed the subject, talking about the estate and his grandfather's love of horses and his great-grandmother, who would be ninety the following month.

That same almost ninety-year-old was even now being helped into the building by a young man Diana supposed was Mr Richard Harecroft. She hurried along the corridor and knocked on her employer's door. 'Mr Harecroft,' she said, when he bade her enter. 'The Dowager Lady Harecroft has just entered the building. I saw her from my window.'

'Good Lord!' he exclaimed, looking up from the paper-work on his desk. 'How did she get here?'

'By carriage, sir. There is a young man with her.'

'Richard, I'll be bound. Go down and make sure she is comfortable in the staff dining room. We cannot have her wandering all over the shop. Do not let her attempt to climb the stairs; the last time she did that, it nearly finished her. I will be down directly.'

Diana turned to go downstairs. At the bottom of the stairs was a full-length mirror and she paused long enough to check her appearance. Her grey dress was plain except for a few tucks down the bodice. It had tight sleeves and a high neck as her ladyship had dictated. Her hair had been drawn back under a white cap. She smiled at herself; she had obeyed Lady Harecroft's instruction to cover her head, but it made her look almost matronly. What she did not realise was that her flawless complexion and neat figure gave the lie to that and her wide intelligent grey eyes made everyone, young and old, want to smile at her in a kind of conspiratorial way as if they knew she was playing a part.

'Peaches and cream,' her father had said, when he was in one of his more affable moods. 'Just like your mother.' Her mother had been slightly taller and her hair had been dark, but Diana was like her in other ways, intelligent, doggedly de-termined not to be beaten and sympathetic to other people's problems without being soft. She had fitted into Harecroft's well and though her male colleagues had been wary at first, most had come to accept her and sometimes brought their troubles to her sympathetic ear. Even Mr Stephen Harecroft.

She could not make up her mind about him. It had not taken her long to realise that Stephen idolised his father and would do anything to please him. At first he had talked to her about her work, but then they had gone on to speak of other things: what was happening in the world outside the business; the coming coronation of Queen Victoria, which had the whole country in a ferment of excitement; the recent publication of a People's Charter, which had the nation split down the middle; the great technological advances being made; music, literature, the things they liked and disliked. Their little talks led to strolls in the park on a Saturday afternoon after work had finished for the day, and the occasional visit to a concert or a lecture. Only the day before he had asked her to accompany him to a Grand Ball to be held at Almack's the evening following the coronation.

Was he just being kind or was he seriously courting her? Flattered as she was, she could not think of marriage while her father needed her. He had been much better of late and she was hopeful he was over the worst, but she was still careful not to give him any cause to relapse. One day she hoped they might move out of the shabby rooms they now occupied into something better; in the meantime, her address and her father's affliction were secrets she guarded carefully. If Mr Harecroft were to learn about either, she was quite sure his attitude towards her would change; he might even find the excuse he needed to dismiss her. She must find a way to discourage young Mr Harecroft, meanwhile, there was his great-grandmother to deal with.

She found the old lady sitting in a gilded chair in the front of the shop, surrounded by fabrics, talking to Stephen. There was no sign of Richard. It appeared he had done as he had the year before: brought the old lady and left her.

'Good afternoon, Lady Harecroft,' Diana said.

The old lady turned to survey her, a wry smile lighting her features. 'Good afternoon, young lady. Have you come to keep me in order?'

'Oh, no, my lady. Mr Harecroft senior bade me greet you and make you comfortable in the staff dining room. He will join you directly.'

Her ladyship chuckled. 'And I am to be prevented from wandering all over the shop, is that not so?'

'My lady?'

'Oh, you do not need to answer me. I know my grandson. But tell me, what do you think of this silk?' She plucked at a length of the material to show Diana.

'It is very fine.'

'That may be so, but is it worth the exorbitant price I believe was paid for it?'

Diana was in a quandary. The desire to give an honest opinion did battle with her need to be diplomatic and she strove to find an answer that would satisfy both. 'I think it might be a little overpriced, my lady, but in today's market, with everyone vying to be seen to advantage for the coronation, it is selling well.'

'Exactly what I said,' Stephen put in.

The old lady smiled and pulled herself to her feet. 'Escort me, Miss Bywater. We can have a little chat before my grandson joins us.' She took Diana's arm and together they made their way to a small room at the back of the ground floor that had been set aside for the staff to eat the mid-day meal they brought with them. It also had a fireplace and facilities for making tea. Once her ladyship had been seated, Diana set the kettle on the fire and stirred the embers to make it blaze.

'How do you like working for Harecroft's, Miss Bywater?'

'Very much. I am grateful to you for affording me the opportunity to do something interesting.'

'My grandson tells me you are quick to learn.'

'I try to be.'

'And Stephen sings your praises constantly.'

'Does he?' The kettle boiled and Diana used the distraction of making tea to cover her confusion. What had Stephen been saying? 'My lady, I hope you do not think I have set out to…' She stumbled over what she wanted to say.

'No, of course not. Ah, here is John.' She turned to her grandson. 'John, you are paying far too much for your silk these days.'

'It is the going rate, for the best quality, Grandmother. I cannot afford to drop standards. Besides, people are prepared to pay good money to appear in the latest fabrics for the festivities.' He sat down next to her. 'But you did not come here to talk about the price of silk, did you?'

'No, I did not. I decided I had mouldered long enough in the country. I came to attend the coronation and to give you notice that I intend to have a house party.'

'Oh?' One bushy eyebrow lifted.

'I am to reach the grand age of ninety next month, as you know…'

'You won't if you insist on racketing about town.'

His grandmother ignored him and continued as if he had not spoken. 'And I wish to mark the occasion with a party.' She accepted a cup of tea from Diana, who also put one in front of John and turned to leave them. 'Stay,' the old lady commanded, waving an ebony walking stick at her. 'Pour a cup for yourself.'

'Grandmother, what are you talking about?' John asked, answering Diana's questioning look with a nod. 'You cannot possibly have a party. It will be too much for you.'

'I decide what is too much for me. Besides, we have a houseful of servants at Borstead Hall, idle half the time—it won't hurt them to stir themselves. Alicia will arrange it. I want all the family to stay the weekend. Friends and acquaintances will be invited for the Saturday only.'

'Why?' he asked, mystified.

'Why? How often does a woman reach the age of ninety and still be in possession of all her faculties? I fully intend to be a hundred, but just in case I do not achieve it, I will have my celebration on Saturday, July the twenty-first.'

'What does my father say about this?'

'Nothing.' She smiled mischievously. 'He knows he will lead a much more peaceful life if he humours me. And William does like a peaceful life, looking after the estate and his beloved horses.'

'And Aunt Alicia?'

'Alicia too. I mean to have a really big day, with my family and friends around me, plenty to eat and drink and fireworks to round it off.'

'It will kill you.'

'Then I will die happy.'

Diana was beginning to feel uncomfortable; she did not want to be a witness to a family argument, and she did have work to do. She stood up to leave, just as Stephen joined them. 'Good, there's tea,' he said.

Diana fetched another cup and saucer from the cupboard and poured tea for him.

'Great-Grandmama, will you ask Miss Bywater to your party?' he asked, making Diana gasp.

'Of course. The young lady will be welcome.'

'You knew about it?' his father asked him.

'Great-Grandmama told me when she arrived. I am looking forward to it.'

'And who is going to look after the shop if we all dash off to Borstead Hall?' John demanded. 'Miss Bywater has to work on Saturdays and so do you.'

'On this occasion, I expect you to make an exception.' This from Lady Harecroft.

'Oh, no,' Diana put in. 'You must not do that. It would set a bad example.'

'Do not tell me what I must not do, girl,' her ladyship snapped.

Diana blushed furiously. 'I beg your pardon. I did not mean to be rude.'

'Do you not care to come?' Stephen asked, aggrieved. 'I am sure you will enjoy it.'

'I am sure I would, but I cannot leave my father while I go into the country.'

'Bring him too,' her ladyship said. 'It is time we all met him.'

'I am afraid he is not well enough, my lady.' Diana was beginning to panic. Her father was not yet stable enough to pay calls, and a party where there was bound to be wine and punch might set him off again. Flattered as she was to be asked, and much as she would have liked a break from routine, to dress up, live in a little splendour and pretend that her life had never had that treacherous downhill slide, she could not risk it.

'Miss Bywater's father is an invalid,' John said. 'She explained about that when she first came to us.'

'So she did. But no matter, we can arrange for him to be looked after for a day or two. Problems like that are not insurmountable.'

'I am sure he would not agree,' Diana said. The old lady's family might defer to her, but on this matter she was going to find herself thwarted. She would not subject her father to the indignity of being looked after, as if he were a child packed off to the nursery when his presence became inconvenient. And she did not know why Stephen was so anxious she should be one of the party.

'I think you must allow Miss Bywater to decline without bullying her, Grandmother,' John said. 'And you know, we are very busy and it is not altogether convenient for me to drop everything to take you home when you arrive unexpectedly.'

'You don't need to.' Her voice held a note of asperity. 'Richard brought me. He has gone to the House of Commons and then he is coming back for me.'

'House of Commons?' Mr Harecroft senior demanded. 'Since when has he interested himself in politics?'

'You must ask him that. I am not his keeper.'

Diana had been inching her way towards the door in order to escape and was reaching for its handle when it was opened and she found herself half-hidden behind it, sucking a little finger that had been caught in the handle.

The newcomer turned to shut the door and saw her. 'I beg pardon, I did not see you hiding there.'

She met his blue-eyed gaze and something inside her turned a somersault. He was a much bigger version of Stephen; he was taller, his shoulders broader, the red-gold of his hair more pronounced—a characteristic she concluded all the family had to a greater or lesser degree—his eyes were bluer and his mouth fuller. She realised with a little stab of guilt that he made his brother look drab and colourless, particularly as in contrast to Stephen's grey suit, he was wearing a brown frock coat, light brown trousers and a pale fawn cravat. It was not only his size and his clothes, his presence dominated the room. He exuded power and self-assurance. She could easily imagine him as a serving officer, in full command of his men. 'I was not hiding, I was about to leave,' she said, finding her voice at last.

'Oh, please do not leave on my account.' He stopped suddenly, unable to take his eyes from her face. She seemed so familiar he felt he ought to know her. She was plainly dressed and wore an unbecoming cap that hid most of her hair, but her complexion was flawless and her eyes reminded him of the plumage of a dove, a soft blue-grey. Her lips were pink and firm and at that moment were sucking a little finger; it was an incredibly sensuous act, made more so because she appeared totally unaware of the effect she was having. 'Does it hurt?'

She took it from her mouth to answer him. 'No, it is nothing.'

'Richard, may I present Miss Diana Bywater,' Stephen said, stepping between them. 'Miss Bywater, my brother, Richard.'

'How do you do?' he said, wondering why Stephen found it necessary to introduce someone who was so obviously a servant. It did not bother him, but his family were sticklers for form.

She bowed her head. 'Mr Harecroft.'

He nodded towards the table where the teapot and the used cups and saucers were evidence of the refreshment they had been enjoying before he arrived. 'Are you going to pour me a cup of tea?'

'I am afraid it must be cold by now. I will make a fresh pot if you like.'

'Miss Bywater, you have those accounts to complete before the end of the working day,' John reminded her.

'Accounts?' Richard queried. 'Oh, you must be the young lady who had the temerity to apply for a man's job. I heard all about it from Great-Grandmother.'

She smiled. 'Yes, though why it should be called a man's job I do not know. It is mental work and does not require strength. I do exactly the same work as the gentlemen clerks without concessions to my gender. Now, please excuse me, I must return to it. Good afternoon, Lady Harecroft.' She turned to go and Stephen sprang to open the door for her.

She thanked him and escaped to the sanctuary of her own room. Arriving breathless, she shut the door behind her and stood leaning against it. The encounter with the elder of the two brothers had shaken her. She did not know what she had expected, but she felt she had been buffeted by a whirlwind, and all in the space of a few fleeting minutes.

She crossed to the window just in time to see her ladyship being handed into her carriage by Richard. He was taking enormous trouble to make sure she was comfortable before getting in himself. She watched as the carriage made its way down the busy street and disappeared round the corner, before returning to the ledger she had left an hour before.

It was difficult to concentrate. Quite apart from that strange encounter with Mr Richard Harecroft, the invitation to the party, the assumption that she would foist the care of her father on to someone else in order to enjoy herself with a group of people who were materially and socially way above her, vexed her. She cared too much for her father to do that to him. She would have to be firm, but would that cost her her job? She could not afford to lose it, for where else could she find something so congenial and so well paid? Without her wages, she and her father would sink even lower in the social scale.

Stephen came into the room and sat on the corner of the table at which she worked. 'Do not let my brother upset you, Miss Bywater.'

'He did not upset me, whatever gave you that idea?'

'Good. Every family is supposed to have a black sheep and I suppose he is ours.'

'He did not look like a sheep to me.'

'No, perhaps I should have said wolf.'

'Not that either,' she said, though when she remembered those blue eyes almost devouring her, she did wonder. 'More like a lion with that mane of golden hair.'

'Hmm.' He seemed to consider this and then dismissed the idea. 'Whichever it is, we do not need to see much of him at Borstead Hall. He lives in the dower house.'

'He lives with your great-grandmother?'

'No, Great-Grandmama lives with my grandfather in the big house. He says she is too old to live by herself and he needs to keep an eye on her, so she told Richard he could use the dower house. He shares it with a couple of penniless artists and his mi—' He stopped suddenly, his voice so twisted with bitterness, she looked at him sharply, but he quickly recovered himself. 'I do not suppose we shall see anything of them.'

She wondered what he had been about to let slip; it sounded as if he were going to say mistress, but surely his brother would not live with such a one so close to the family home? 'What does your great-grandmother think of his friends?'

'Oh, she does not mind them. She has a soft spot for Richard.'

'He seems very fond of her.'

'Yes, she is the only one who can get Richard to do what she wants.'

She realised suddenly that he was jealous of his brother, even though he enjoyed more of his father's favour. It was all to do with the old lady. 'I wish you had not asked her ladyship to invite me to her party,' she said.

'Why not? We will have a splendid time.'

'We will not, because I cannot accept the invitation.'

'Why not?'

'I have to work. And I cannot leave my father.'

'He is an invalid, isn't he? I did not know that until you mentioned it today. Are you always so secretive?'

'I am not secretive,' she said, feeling the colour rising in her face. 'Your father and great-grandmother knew and there has been no reason why I should make a point of telling you. It did not come out in the course of conversation, that's all.'

'What is the matter with him?'

She took a deep breath. 'He was invalided out of the navy five years ago when he lost his arm and then my mother died and his nerves have been badly affected.' It was not really a lie, she told herself, just not the whole truth.

'Father can hire a nurse in for him or arrange for him to go into a comfortable nursing home so that he is looked after. If he does, you will come, won't you?'

'I do not think so. I cannot put Mr Harecroft to the trouble and it upsets Papa if his normal routine is changed.'

'You are just making excuses. You heard my great-grandmother say she expected us all to go and my father will not go against her. The Dowager Lady Harecroft angry is an awesome sight, I can tell you.'

'I do not see why she should be angry with me. I am not family.'

'I am hoping that in the fullness of time you will be.'

She looked up from the ledger on the desk and stared at him. 'What do you mean?'

'I had intended to give you time to get to know me properly before proposing, but Great-Grandmama has precipitated it. But surely you guessed?'

'No.' She felt as though she was being carried along, tossed about like a leaf on the wind, as if she had no will of her own and it annoyed her.

He left the desk, walked round behind her and took the pen from her nerveless fingers, laid it down and clasped her hand in both his own. 'Miss Bywater—Diana—would you consider a proposal of marriage from me?'

It was a very roundabout way of asking her, she thought,

almost as if he were not altogether sure that was what he wanted. He had said nothing of his feelings towards her. Did he love her or was he simply looking for a helpmate in the business? Did she love him? He had not even asked that crucial question. If he had done so, she would not have been able to answer it. But it did not matter; she could not, would not, leave her father and she could not see the Harecroft family taking him to their collective bosom.

'Mr Harecroft,' she said, 'I am an employee, I need my job and you are putting me in a difficult position.'

'I do not see why. If you accept me, then you need work no longer, or only as long as you wish to. You have fitted into the business very well—in fact, I sometimes think you know more about it than I do—and fitting into Harecroft's is more than half the battle.'

'I do not want a battle, Mr Harecroft, I want to be left alone to do my job. And now, if you please, I must get on with it. I am lagging behind today.'

He let go of her hand and straightened up. 'Very well, but I shall ask you again, perhaps at Great-Grandmother's party. Yes, on reflection, that will be the ideal time. I will say no more until then.'

'I have said I cannot go.'

'Oh, you will,' he said with infuriating confidence. 'The Dowager Lady Harecroft will brook no refusal.'

Before she could reply, he was gone and she was left staring down at a column of figures that seemed to dance about on the page so that it took her three attempts to total them correctly.

Chapter Two

'Well, what do you think of Miss Bywater?' her ladyship asked Richard as their driver negotiated the traffic in Bond Street.

'Should I be thinking of her?' he asked mildly.

'I am intrigued by her,' the old lady went on. 'Her situation is strange. She is educated, well spoken, deferential and neat in her appearance, but there is something secretive about her and I should like to know what it is.'

'I cannot tell you.'

'I wonder if it has anything to do with her father,' she went on as if he had not spoken. 'She says he is an invalid and is very protective of him. It is because of him she needs to work.'

'But if she does her work well, is her private life any of our business?'

'It is if Stephen wants to marry her.'

'Good Lord! Does he?'

'I think so. He asked me to invite her to my party.'

'And did you?'

'Yes.'

'And what did she say?'

'She protested she could not leave her father and when I said bring him too, she began to make all manner of excuses.'

'Then perhaps you should leave well alone.'

'I do not want to. I need to know more. You could help me. Find a way of meeting her father, talk to him, discover all you can about his antecedents. I want to know about his family and his childhood, where he spent it, where he was educated, what happened to his parents, his mother's maiden name. If either had any siblings, if Miss Bywater has brothers and sisters.'

'To what end? To find out if Miss Bywater is a suitable person to marry Stephen?'

'If you like.'

'Then ask Stephen to do it. He is the one who will have to decide.'

'Stephen does not have your finesse, Richard. He might alienate the man and that is the last thing I want.'

'And is Miss Bywater to know of this inquisition?'

'I would rather she did not. Not yet.'

'Great-Grandmama, I cannot approve.'

''Tisn't for you to approve or disapprove. Just do as you are told. Be easy, I bear the child no ill will, but I need to be sure.'

'Is there something you are not telling me? I am very busy, Great-Grandmama, and acting the spy is not to my taste…'

She looked sharply at him. 'Busy doing what?'

He smiled wryly. Why did everyone assume that just because he was not seen to go to work like his father and brother, that he was idle? Six years in the army had taught him many things. Serving with men from all walks of life had opened his eyes to his privileged position. Rubbing shoulders with the educated and the abysmally ignorant, those who knew no other life than soldiering and those who had enlisted as a matter of patriotism or because they were out of work or needed to escape the law, had taught him to judge a man on his merits, irrespective of his position in what his parents chose to call society. Unlike most of his fellow officers, who would not have dreamed of associating with the men under their command, he had taken the trouble to find out about their homes and their families. And what he had learned had horrified him and made him determined to do something about it.

He soon realised his attempts to help the poor and lame were too piecemeal: a good deed here, a generous donation there; taking poor artists into his home and providing them with pleasant conditions in which to work; writing articles that the more die-hard newspaper proprietors refused to publish, so they found their way into the more radical publications, which were frequently being shut down by the government on the grounds that they were seditious and encouraged unrest. He risked imprisonment himself every time he fired a broadside at those who ought to have been helping and did nothing. He had come to the conclusion that it would be better to work within the establishment. Hence his visit to the Commons.

The old lady tapped his arm with her fan. 'Well? Will you do this for me?'

He had always found it difficult to deny her anything, but on this occasion he was adamant. 'No, ma'am, I will not. It is an infringement of the young lady's privacy unless you have reason to believe she is up to no good.' He paused to study her lined face. 'Do you?'

'That's what I want to find out. If you will not oblige me, I must find other ways of discovering what I want to know.'

'And what happens if you find out she is not all she seems—what then? Will you expose her?'

'I do not know; it depends on what turns up.'

He knew her well enough to realise she was up to something and it was more than a desire to protect Stephen. Did she already know more than she was telling about Miss Diana Bywater? It intrigued him, but not enough to comply with her request.

They turned into Grosvenor Square and drew up at the door of Harecroft House and he jumped down to lift her out of the carriage and help her into the house and up to her room. He had a feeling he had not heard the last of Miss Diana Bywater.

Diana was still at work at eight o'clock, when Mr Harecroft came into the little cubby hole where she worked. 'Still here, Miss Bywater?'

'I have been trying to catch up on lost time.'

He smiled. 'Grandmother can be a little disruptive. But stop now. I have my tilbury outside. I will drive you home.'

'Thank you, but that will not be necessary. I can easily walk.'

'It is the least I can do. It was not your fault you were behind with your work.'

She smiled suddenly. 'Would you offer to drive one of the men clerks home?'

'No, certainly not.'

'I do not wish to be treated any differently. It was part of our bargain when you took me on.'

'So it may have been, but circumstances have changed. I am wholly converted to lady clerks.' He smiled as he spoke. 'At least to one of them. You have proved yourself more than capable and I take back any reservations I might have had.' He picked up the ledger she had been working on, made sure the ink was dry, and shut it firmly. 'Now come along, I will accept no argument. I would have asked Stephen to take you, but he has already gone home.' He bent and put his hand under her elbow to raise her to her feet.

They were standing close together, his head bent towards her, his hand still under her arm, when Richard came in. He had changed into a black evening suit, which, even more than the clothes he had worn earlier in the day, emphasised his strong lean figure. He stopped on the threshold, his blue eyes taking in the scene.

Thoroughly embarrassed, she drew her arm from his father's hand and he, following the line of her startled gaze, turned to look at his son, watching them from the doorway.

'Richard, what are you doing here?' His voice sounded pleasant enough, but Diana thought she detected an undertone of annoyance.

'Looking for you. You were not in your office…'

'Well, now you have found me. I suppose there is a reason for you to set foot on the premises for the second time in one day.'

Diana sank back into her chair, feeling awkward. She wished she could leave the tiny room and find fresh air.

'Great-Grandmother is a little truculent. She says she expected you home hours ago, she wants to talk to you. If I had not promised to come and winkle you out, she would have commanded Soames to get out the carriage and come looking for you herself.'

'I had business to do and it was her fault, taking up so much of our time this afternoon.'

'Are you ready to leave now?'

'I must take Miss Bywater home first. She has been kept late on company business and I cannot allow her to go home alone at this time of night.'

'Oh, please do not trouble yourself,' Diana said. 'I can walk and Lady Harecroft is waiting for you…'

'Yes,' Richard put in, looking down at Diana, unable to make up his mind about her. His great-grandmother had triggered his own curiosity, heightened by the sight of his father's apparent intimacy with Diana. Was she up to no good, worming her way into the company in order to take advantage of an old lady? But his great-grandmother, though old, was not vulnerable or simple; she was as astute as they come, so what was it all about? 'She will wait up until you get home, Father, you know she will, and she has had a tiring day. Besides, Mother is expecting you and she is not very good at coping with the old lady in one of her moods. I will take Miss Bywater home.' He realised, as he said it, that he was doing exactly what his great-grandmother wanted, that she had probably guessed if she sent him back to fetch his father something of the sort might happen. He almost laughed aloud.

His father sighed. 'If Miss Bywater agrees, then it might be best.'

'But…' Diana began again. She did not want either of them seeing how she and her father lived.

'No buts,' Richard said firmly. 'It will be my pleasure.'

'How did you arrive?' his father asked him.

'In a cab. I have kept it waiting. Great-Grandmama's instructions were to make sure you came home.'

'I will take the cab. You take Miss Bywater in the tilbury.'

'Please do not trouble yourselves, either of you,' Diana begged, reaching for her bonnet and light cape from the hook behind the door and following the two men from the room. 'I am quite used to walking home alone.'

Neither listened. They seemed to be having the conversation with each other over her head; it was almost as if she were not there.

'Are you staying at Harecroft House tonight?' father asked son.

'Yes, but I will probably be late back, so do not wait up for me.'

'I gave up waiting for you years ago, Richard. Do not wake the household, that's all.'

They reached the ground floor and left the building, while Mr Harecroft senior locked the premises, Diana tried once again to say she could manage on her own.

'You are very stubborn, Miss Bywater,' Richard said. 'But rest assured I can be equally obdurate. You are not to be allowed to walk home alone and that is an end of it.' He led the way to the tilbury and helped her into it, then unhitched the pony and jumped up beside her, the reins in his hand. 'Now, you will have to direct me. I have no idea where you live.'

'Southwark. I usually walk over Waterloo Bridge, so if you let me down this side of it, you will avoid paying the toll.'

'Miss Bywater, I am not so miserly as to begrudge the few pence to take you across,' he told her, setting the pony off at a walk.

The streets were not quite as busy as they had been earlier in the day and the vehicles on the road were, for the most part, those taking their occupants to evening appointments. A troop of soldiers were rehearsing their part in the coronation parade, a man with a cart was hawking the last of the flags and bunting he had set out with that morning. A flower girl was offering bunches of blooms that were beginning to wilt and a diminutive crossing sweeper stood leaning on his broom waiting for custom. The evening was like any other, but for Diana it was different. She was riding and not walking for a start and, instead of thinking what she would make for supper, her whole mind was concentrated on the man at her side and how to persuade him not to take her all the way home.

The prospect of him seeing the run-down tenement in which she lived, and, even worse, her equally run-down father, was enough to make her quake. She could imagine his disgust, the tale he would carry to his father. And they would say, 'We cannot have a person like that working at Harecroft's. It lowers the whole tone of the establishment and who knows what pestilence she brings with her? I knew it was a mistake to employ her.' And she was quite sure Lady Harecroft would not intervene on her behalf a second time.

'Do you enjoy working for Harecroft's?' Richard asked her, breaking in on her thoughts.

'Very much.'

'It is a strange occupation for a woman,' he said, as they turned down the Strand. 'How did you manage to persuade my father to take you on?'

'If you are implying that I—' She started angrily, remembering the disapproving expression on his face when he had entered her office and seen his father's hand on her arm.

'Heavens, no!' He lifted one hand from the reins in a defensive gesture. 'There was no hidden implication in my question, do not be so quick to rise. I was simply commenting on the fact that I have never heard of a female clerk and I am sure the idea never entered my father's head of its own accord.'

'I saw the advertisement for a clerk and applied.' She laughed suddenly. 'I do not think he would have even considered me but for your great-grandmother, who arrived while I was talking to him. She told him to give me a trial.'

'That sounds like Great-Grandmama. How long ago was that?'

'A year.'

'And now you are an indispensable adjunct to the business.'

'Of course not. No one is indispensable, but I pride myself that I have justified Lady Harecroft's faith in me.'

'She has rather taken to you, you know. I gather she has invited you to her party.'

'Yes, it was kind of her, but of course I cannot go.'

'Why not?'

'Saturday is a working day, besides, I cannot leave my father for long. He is an invalid.'

'And your mother?'

'She died fourteen months ago.'

'I am sorry to hear that. Is that why you must work?'

'Only the rich can afford not to work.'

'True,' he said. 'But could you not have found something more suitable than becoming a clerk?'

'What's wrong with being a clerk?' she asked defensively.

'Nothing at all, for a man, but it is evident you have had an education, you could perhaps have become a teacher or a lady's companion.'

'I think, sir, that a companion's lot is harder than a clerk's. At least with Mr Harecroft my work is clearly laid out and I do have regular hours and can live at home.'

'Except when you decide to work late.'

'Sometimes it is necessary. It is best to be flexible.'

'And what do you like to do when you are not working?' Having stopped to pay the toll, he steered the tilbury on to the bridge, but she would have known where they were even with her eyes shut; the overpowering smell of the river assaulted her nostrils, a mixture of stale fish, sewerage, damp coal, rotting vegetation and goodness knew what else.

'I read to Papa and we go for walks in the park on a Sunday afternoon if he is not too tired.'

'He is your constant companion?'

'Yes. He needs me.'

'But you leave him to go to work.'

'He is used to that and our housekeeper keeps an eye on him for me. When I am late she cooks him supper.' House-keeper was an euphemism; Mrs Beales, their landlady, lived on the ground floor and did as little as possible for them and then only if she was paid.

'Will he be concerned that you are so late home tonight?'

'He knows I sometimes work late to finish a particular task.'

'My goodness, how conscientious you are! No wonder my father sings your praises.'

'Does he?'

'Oh, yes. I have heard him using you as an example to the others.'

'Oh. I wish he would not. I do not like to be singled out.'

He laughed. 'Too late, you have been. Stephen thinks you are a paragon of virtue and industry and Great-Grandmama has a mischievous gleam in her eye whenever your name is mentioned. She is up to something, I know it.'

'I cannot think what it could be.'

Neither could he. He did not think it was simply concern that Stephen should not make a mistake in marrying her. 'Now we are over the bridge, which direction shall I take?'

'You can let me down here. I am not far from home and can walk the rest.'

'Certainly not. I am going to take you to your door. What do you think my father would say if I admitted to him I had left you short of your destination?' He looked about him at the people in the street. Working men and women trudging home, seamen, dockers, costermongers with their empty carts, a brewer's dray with its heavy horses, a stray dog worrying something it had found in the gutter. It was not the place to leave a young lady on her own and it was obvious that if she was not a lady in the accepted sense, she had been brought up genteelly. She had said she did not want to stand out, but she did. She was well spoken, educated and neatly if not fashionably dressed, so why was she living in an area that was only one degree above a slum? 'Come, direct me.'

Short of jumping out of a moving vehicle she could do nothing and reluctantly directed him to turn left into the next street, which had a row of tenements on one side and warehouses fronting the river on the other. A hundred yards farther down she asked him to stop. 'This will do, thank you.'

He looked up at the row of tenements. 'Which one?'

'It is round the corner, but the way is narrow and it is difficult to turn a vehicle there.'

'Very well.' He drew to a stop and jumped out to hand her down.

She bade him goodnight and turned swiftly to cross the road, hoping he would not follow. A speeding hackney pulled out to overtake the stationary tilbury just as she emerged from behind it, almost under the horse's hooves. Richard, in one quick stride, grabbed her and pulled her to safety, while the cab driver shook his fist but did not stop.

'You little fool!' Richard exclaimed, pulling her against his broad chest. She was shaking like an aspen, unsure whether it was because of the close call she had had or the fact that he still held her in his arms. 'Is my company so disagreeable you must run away from it?'

'No, of course not.' She leaned into him, shutting her eyes, saw again the bulk of the horse rearing over her, heard again the yell of the cab driver and the frightened neighing of the horse and shuddered at what might have happened. 'I did not see the cab. He was driving much too fast.'

'Indeed he was. Are you hurt?' He held her away from him to look down on her. Her bonnet and the silly cap she wore under it had come off, revealing a head of shining red-gold hair that reminded him of someone else with tresses like that, but he could not think who it might be. Surely if he had met her before he would have remembered the occasion? She was too beautiful to forget.

'No, just a little shaken.' She pulled herself away. 'Thank you, I can manage now.'

'I do not know why you are so determined I should not see you home. Is your father an ogre? Will he suppose I have designs on your person?'

'He is not an ogre. He is kind and loving. As for having designs…' She turned to look directly into his face. 'Have you?'

He was taken aback by her forthrightness and then laughed. 'Certainly not. Let us go to him. I shall explain why I felt it necessary to escort you home. And how right I was, considering you nearly got yourself killed.'

She gave a huge sigh of resignation and led the way down the side street. Here the tenements were huddled together, grimy and dilapidated, built years before to house the dockers and those working on the river and in the warehouses. Oh, how she wished she could be going home to the villa in Islington, which had been their home four years before. It had not been grand, not up to the standard of the Harecrofts' residence in Grosvenor Square, which she had taken a look at out of curiosity when she first joined the company, but even so it had been solid and well maintained and her mother had made it comfortable and welcoming. She would not have been ashamed to take him there. And this was what she had come down to: two rooms in a slum, which all the cleaning in the world could not improve.

Two ragged urchins, a girl of about seven and a boy a little younger, stood on the pavement and watched them approach.

Suddenly they smiled and two grimy hands were out-stretched, palms uppermost. 'Who are they?' he asked.

'I do not know, but they often appear as I am coming home. I usually give them a penny each. I think they spend it on bread.'

She went to open her purse, but he put his hand over hers to stop her, then delved into his pocket and produced a sixpence. 'Here,' he said, offering it to the girl. 'Go and buy a meat pie and potatoes for your suppers.'

The waif broke into a wide smile, grabbed the coin in one hand and the boy with the other and they scuttled off up the street.

'Poor little devils,' he said, as they resumed walking. 'Where do they live?'

'I have no idea, but they seem to have adopted me.'

'No doubt because you give them money.'

'Perhaps, but it is little enough. The government should do something for the poor and I do not mean build more unions where they can be conveniently forgotten. They are no better than prisons and most people would rather beg and steal than enter one.'

He agreed wholeheartedly but, until something was done officially, it was up to individuals to make their plight known. He had no voice except through his writing. He did not see himself as a novelist, like Charles Dickens, who was also con-cerned with highlighting poverty, but he could write books and pamphlets pointing out the facts. And the facts made hor-rifying reading. It was a pity too few people troubled them-selves with them. Something else had to be done to make the government pay attention. His visits to the Commons to listen to debates had made him realise that although most of its members paid lip service to the need for action, few were prepared to do it. It was one of the reasons he wanted to join them. 'You evidently feel strongly on the subject,' he said.

'I have seen what poverty can do.' She opened the door of one of the houses, slightly better than the rest for the curtains were relatively clean, the step scrubbed and the door knocker polished. He followed her inside, as she knew he would. 'I live on the first floor,' she said, turning to thank him again and hoping he would take it as a dismissal, although the damage was already done.

'There you are!' A woman came out from the back regions of the hallway. She was very fat, wore a black skirt, pink blouse and an apron that had seen better days. Her greying hair was pulled back so tightly into a bun at the back of her head it seemed to stretch the skin on her face, making her dark eyes look narrow. 'About time, too. I never did undertake to be his warder, you know. I can't keep him in if he is determined to go out.'

'Oh, dear, I am sorry, Mrs Beales. Has he not come back?'

'No, you know he won't shift until they throw him out. I gave him a luvverly plate of stew for his dinner, luvverly it were, and he just looked at it and grunted that he needed food, not pigswill, and slammed outa the house. If you think I'm goin' to put up with that sort of treatment, miss, you can think again. I c'n find plenty of tenants who'd be more appreciative.'

'I am sorry, Mrs Beales. He can be a little difficult about his food sometimes.'

'Don't I know it! You shouldn' be so late home. You know it sets him off.'

'I'm afraid I had to work late.'

'Hmm.' The comment was one of derisory disbelief.

'Thank you, Mrs Beales,' she said levelly, aware that the woman was looking Richard up and down, summing him up and probably coming to quite the wrong conclusion. 'I'll go and look for him.'

'Do you know where he has gone?' Richard asked the woman. 'I came especially to see him.'

She grunted. 'I wouldn't put money on you gettin' much sense outa him tonight.'

'I think I know where he is,' Diana said, giving up all hope of keeping the truth from him or the rest of his family. He was looking at her with an expression she could not quite fathom. Was it curiosity or disgust or compassion? Those blue eyes gave nothing away, but he could not have failed to understand what Mrs Beales had been hinting. She wished the ground would open and swallow her.

'Lead the way,' he commanded, as Mrs Beales plodded back to her own quarters.

'This need not concern you, Mr Harecroft. Please tell Mr Harecroft senior I shall be at work as usual tomorrow.'

'I will do no such thing. Take me to your father.'

'Why?'

'Why?' he repeated impatiently. 'Do you think I am slow-witted? It is as plain as day what is wrong with him and I doubt if you are strong enough to get him home alone.'

'It is not like that. He is not well.'

'Your loyalty is commendable, Miss Bywater. Now let us go and find him.' His apparent abruptness marked a deep concern. How did someone as young and beautiful as she was come to such a pass? Long before he went into the army, he had become aware of the deep chasm between rich and poor, a chasm that the rich for the most part ignored, salving their consciences with donations to charity. The poor had always been part of the population, but in this young lady's case, he was sure it was of recent duration. That she had managed to hide it so successfully said a great deal for her pride and de-termination. Was that the sort of thing his great-grandmother wanted him to find out?

Without answering him, she turned and went out again. Neither spoke as she walked swiftly down the street, holding her grey working skirt out of the mire, with him in attendance. Why had Papa slipped back, after being good for so long? And tonight of all nights.

They could hear the sound of raucous singing long before they reached the door of The Dog and Duck. She hesitated with her hand on the latch, but it wasn't as if it were the first time she had been obliged to enter that establishment, so she took a deep breath and pushed the door open.

'Stay here,' Richard said, putting a hand on her arm to detain her. 'I'll fetch him out.'

'He won't go with a stranger.' It was said half-heartedly. Now her horrible secret was out, the invitation to Borstead Hall would be withdrawn, there would be no marriage to Stephen, probably no job either. She was not so concerned about the invitation or Stephen's half-hearted proposal, but the job was important. And she had a dreadful feeling one depended on the other.

The tavern was crowded with working men, some of whom were singing lustily. James Bywater was sitting in a corner between two scruffy individuals apparently deep in conversation. His suit of clothes had once been smart and his cravat had been clean that morning, but was clean no longer. On the table at his side was a tricorne hat that he had once worn when commanding his ship. Diana hurried over to him. *Oh, let him be sensible*, she prayed. *Make him come home quietly.*

The trouble was that, even sober, he was difficult to handle, rather like a truculent child determined to have his own way. And yet, like a child, he was warm and loving and he never meant to hurt her. For her dead mother's sake she persevered with her effort to help him to help himself.

From his corner seat he saw her and waved his full glass at her, slopping the contents over his fingers. The strong weatherbeaten seaman was gone and in his place was a shabby middle-aged man with an empty sleeve and brown stains on his cravat. His dog, Toby, sat patiently at his feet, waiting to lead him home because that was what had frequently happened in the past. 'Diana, what are you doing here?' She was thankful his speech was not too slurred.

'Looking for you, Papa. I was hoping you would be at home. I have brought someone to meet you.'

He looked past her to where Richard stood. 'Your young man?'

She felt the colour flood her face. Just lately he had been talking to her about making a good marriage, telling her to encourage her employer's son, as if that would solve all their problems. 'You would be well set up there,' he had said. 'No more scrimping and trying to make ends meet and we could leave this sordid place.'

'No, Papa, this is Mr Richard Harecroft.'

James shrugged as if it was all one to him. 'Join me in a drink, young feller.'

'Thank you. I'll have a pot of ale.'

Diana gasped. She had been relying on Richard's help to extricate her father, and here he was encouraging him. 'Papa—' she began.

'Sit down.' Richard spoke quietly, but it was a command and she found herself obeying, even as she opened her mouth to protest that she did not frequent taverns and had only ever stayed long enough to haul her father out and that had not happened for nearly a year. 'Say nothing,' he murmured. 'He has a full glass and he will not come away until it is empty, so be patient a minute.'

That was all very well, she thought as Richard beckoned

a waiter. Papa would not want to leave even when his glass was empty; they would still have a fight on their hands. It was nerve-racking and exhausting and all she wanted was to go home and hide and never have to face the world again.

'You work at the shop with your father?' James asked. The two men who had been with him had disappeared at a nod from Richard and the three of them were alone at the table.

'No, trade is not for me. I am a writer.'

'Writer, eh? What sort of writing?'

'Papa, you should not quiz Mr Harecroft,' Diana said.

'Oh, I do not mind it,' Richard said. 'I only wish more people were interested. I write about the common soldier and the trouble he faces finding employment when his services are no longer required.'

'Not only soldiers,' James said meaningfully. 'Sailors too.'

'True, but I know very little about the navy. You could perhaps enlighten me, tell me about the men and their children. Particularly the children.'

'Like children, do you?'

'Yes.'

'But you have none of your own.'

'I am unmarried.' He began to wonder who was quizzing whom, but he was also aware that he was playing right into his great-grandmother's hands.

'Time enough to remedy that.'

James finished his drink, but before he could suggest ordering another, Richard drained his tankard and stood up. 'Time to go home.'

'Later, let us have one for the road first.'

'Papa.' Diana stood up and bent to take his arm, but he pulled himself roughly from her grasp.

'Do not rush me, girl. You know I hate to be rushed.'

'Papa, please come home.'

Richard turned to Diana. 'You take his arm and I'll take the other side and off we go. Do not give him a chance to struggle.'

It worked like a charm. Diana held firmly on to his one arm and Richard put his hand on his shoulder on the other side and more or less propelled him out to the street. Diana marvelled at his sheer strength and command of the situation. When anything like that had happened before, she had had to plead with her father, but because her strength did not match his, even when he was drunk, she had not been able to drag him away before he wanted to come. He was always sorry afterwards and begged her forgiveness, promising not to let it happen again. And for nearly a year he had kept that promise. Until tonight.

With Toby trotting behind, he walked fairly steadily between them; though he did not appear to need their support, neither released him. He was not as bad as Diana had thought at first, hardly more than slightly tipsy. At any rate the two men were chatting quite amiably. She began to revise her opinion of Richard. Although he was firm, he did not appear to condemn, he simply accepted the situation, almost as if he were used to it. She could not imagine Mr Harecroft senior or Stephen imbibing too much or even condoning it in others, but Richard had been in the army and no doubt that accounted for it.

'How long were you in the army?' the older man asked the younger.

'Six years, most of it in the colonies.'

'I am a naval man myself, man and boy, never knew any other kind of life—' He stopped suddenly and buckled between them, and taken by surprise, neither could hold him. He sank to the ground at their feet.

'Papa!' Diana cried, bending over him. 'Do get up, please.'

Richard gently pushed her to one side and crouched beside

the unconscious man, bending his head to listen to his chest and then leaning back to look at his contorted face. Diana stood looking down at him with her hand to her mouth while the dog whined round them in agitation.

'Stay with him, while I fetch the tilbury,' Richard said, straightening up. 'He is not drunk, he has had a seizure. We must take him to hospital.' They had attracted a small crowd. He turned to them. 'There is nothing to see, my friends. The gentleman is ill. Give him air, if you please.' He ushered them away and then sprinted up the street, leaving Diana to kneel beside her father and lift his head on to her lap. She was angry with herself for the unkind thoughts she had been having about him and wished he could hear her apologising.

Richard returned with the gig very quickly and, hardly appearing to exert himself, lifted the unconscious man into it and propped him in the corner, then helped Diana up beside him. There was now no room for a driver, and so he led the horse, breaking into a run as they reached the end of the street. Diana, cradling her father, called out to him. 'Where are you taking us?'

He called back over his shoulder. 'St Thomas's. It is the nearest. We must not waste time.'

He did not want to take them there, but he could see no alternative. Hospitals catered for the poor whose purses and living conditions precluded them from being treated at home. People who could afford to pay for their treatment expected nurses and doctors to visit them, not the other way about. If that were not possible, there were private nursing homes. He would have had no hesitation in paying for the captain's treatment, but realised that would not be appropriate, and in any case speed was important.

He turned back to look at Miss Bywater. She was very pale, but appeared calm. He was full of admiration for her courage.

To live as she did, looking after a difficult parent in conditions only one step above squalor, and yet put in a day's work at Harecroft's showed a strength of character that was at odds with her femininity. He wondered how much Stephen had told her about himself. Or how much Stephen really knew about her. He had a feeling the party at Borstead Hall would bring everything to a head. Would she come? She had declined the invitation even before this had happened. But Great-Grandmama was a strong character and if she wanted the young lady there, she would find a way of bringing it about.

He pulled up outside the hospital and lifted the older man down and carried him into the building, leaving Diana to follow. In no time, because the Harecroft name was known and they had given generous donations to the hospital in the past and because Richard promised more, Mr Bywater was put into a small room on his own and a nurse was delegated to his care.

The next few hours were a nightmare to Diana. She moved like an automaton, sitting when told to, drinking endless cups of tea that Richard sent out for, unaware of anything except her concern for her father and her own feelings of guilt. She had misjudged Papa and if Richard had not been there, she might have been slower to realise that his condition was caused by illness and not drink. Telling herself that on past performance she could be forgiven for it did not make her feel any better, nor the fact that it was Mr Richard Harecroft, of all people, who was on hand to help her.

At dawn she was still sitting on a bench outside the room where her father lay fighting for his life. Richard had left to take Toby back to Mrs Beales and then he was going home himself. 'I will tell my father what has happened,' he had said before leaving. 'You will not be expected to go to work today.' She wondered what else he would tell his father and the rest of the family. She was thankful that it was Saturday and there was all the next day before she need worry about her job.

If her father lived, she would devote herself to him and try even harder to help him overcome his problem and she would put all ideas of marrying Stephen out of her mind. In any case, as soon as he knew her circumstances, Stephen would make excuses not to take her out again and the subject of marriage between them would be tacitly dropped. It was not that she minded about that. She was not in love with him and had only been considering it because her father had told her not to dismiss the idea out of hand. But Stephen's strange way of proposing had made her wonder if he too might be having pressure put to bear on him. Though why? She was no catch. She had no dowry, no fortune and no more than average good looks.

Thinking about that set her thinking about Lady Harecroft's party. In normal circumstances she might have been thrilled to be asked, would have anticipated it with pleasure, but the circumstances were far from normal. What was going on in that old lady's head? She did not appear demented, but perhaps she was, perhaps she was mistaking her for someone else, someone far more suitable as a bride for her great-grandson. And from those thoughts it was a simple step to thinking about the other great-grandson.

Mr Richard Harecroft had shown himself to be masterful and completely in charge of the situation. He had not turned a hair at having to go into that low tavern, nor shown any kind of disgust, either at their dismal lodgings or the state of her father. And he had known at once that Papa was ill. He had saved both her life and her father's in the space of a couple of hours, and he had paid for the private room. She owed him more than she could ever repay.

She looked up and jumped to her feet as a nurse approached her. 'How is he?'

'He is a fighter, I will give you that. We think he will pull through.'

Diana let out a long breath of relief and scrubbed at her eyes with an already sodden handkerchief. 'Thank God. Can I see him?'

'Yes, you can go in and see him for a few minutes, then I suggest you go home and rest. The worst is over and now only time will tell how far he will recover.'

'What do you mean, how far?'

'He will need careful nursing and a great deal of help and patience. He will have to learn to manage his disability…'

'You mean the loss of his arm. He manages that very well.'

'No, I mean the paralysis of his left side and not being able to speak properly. We do not know how permanent that is. He might recover some speech and movement in time. It is in God's hands. We have done all we can.' She pushed open the door of the sickroom. 'Captain Bywater, here is your daughter, but she must not stay too long and tire you.' She turned to Diana, who had followed her. 'Take his hand and squeeze it now and again,' she murmured. 'You never know, you may arouse a response.'

Diana moved towards the bed. Her father's normally weatherbeaten face looked grey and still had that contorted look, which had so frightened her. She sat in a chair beside the bed and took his hand. 'Papa, it's me, Diana.' He turned to stare at her, but she was not sure if he had taken in what she said.

His lips moved slightly, trying to frame a word, but he gave up and she realised he could not speak and that made her want to cry again. 'Do not try to talk,' she said, determined not to let him see her tears. 'Just squeeze my hand.' But he did not; his own hand lay limply in hers.

'Mr Harecroft took Toby home,' she said, making herself sound cheerful. 'He said he would make sure Mrs Beales looked after him. You remember Mr Harecroft? He came home with me last night. I do not know what I would have done without him. I will go home when I leave here and see how he is.' She forced a laugh. 'Toby, I mean, not Mr Harecroft. I expect Mr Harecroft has gone back to Harecroft House and I did not have a chance to thank him properly.' She prattled on. He neither moved nor spoke and only his eyes seemed to have any life as they searched her face.

The nurse came in. 'Time to go, Miss Bywater. Your father needs to rest and so do you.'

Diana bent over to kiss her father's forehead. 'I must go now, Papa, but I will come back soon.'

He moved his lips and she heard him utter the word, 'Kate'. It was her mother's name and she turned away blinded by tears.

In the corridor the nurse asked, 'Did he say something?'

'Only "Kate". He thinks I am my mother.'

'Do not let it worry you. Saying anything at all is a good sign. Now off you go. He is in good hands.'

'I know and I cannot begin to thank you.'

'You do not have to. It is our job.'

It was more than just a job, Diana thought as she made her way out of the hospital, it took courage and dedication, both of which would be required of her in the next few days and weeks. Or perhaps it would be months and years. How was she ever going to manage?

'Miss Bywater!'

She looked up and was surprised to see Richard Harecroft striding towards her. And suddenly she felt more cheerful, simply because he was there. 'How is he?' he asked.

'Comfortable. He is being well looked after and I have been sent away to rest.'

'Quite right, too. I have brought the gig to take you home. Stephen would have come, but he has gone to work, so I have come in his stead.' He took her elbow to usher her towards the patient pony. 'I know, you are going to say you can easily walk…'

'No.' She managed a smile. 'I am glad you came, I wanted to thank you for what you did for my father last night. And for me.'

'I did nothing.' His tone was brusque, dismissing her gratitude.

'All the same I am grateful, and I am sure Papa will be too, when he understands what happened.'

He helped her into the gig, climbed in beside her and set the pony off at a trot. She was silent, too tired to make conversation, until they came out of the end of the street and turned towards the river. 'Mr Harecroft,' she said, sitting forward in dismay, 'this is not the way. You have taken a wrong turn.'

'I do not think so. Great-Grandmama instructed me to take you home and that is what I am doing, taking you to Harecroft House.'

'Your home! Oh, no. I cannot go.'

'Why not?'

'I am unkempt, my father is in hospital and I must be on hand to visit him; besides, you could not have told her ladyship the whole sorry story.'

He knew what she meant. 'No, that is between you and me and no one else's business unless you choose to tell them.'

'Oh.' She paused to reflect; she could not keep her job and look after her father at the same time, and yet she needed to earn if they were to live. It was a problem that would have to be faced, but at the moment she was too exhausted to think about it. 'Would that not be dishonest?'

'I do not see why. Your father is ill and he is not going to be in a position to go wandering off on his own for a little while, is he? Why stir up more problems for yourself?' He turned to look at her. She was very pale; there were dark circles under her troubled blue-grey eyes and her hands were shaking in her lap. He put one hand over hers. 'Our secret, eh?' Even as he spoke, he wondered what he would say to the dowager if she asked him what he had discovered? What had Great-Grandmother seen in her that had made her so anxious to probe? The whole business was on the way to distracting him from his main purpose, being elected to Parliament and having his book published. He thought becoming an MP ought to come first, but he had heard nothing from Peel or Chadwick.

'Thank you.' She looked down at his strong brown hand covering hers and it felt so comforting and so right, she did not withdraw it as she ought to have done, but a minute later he was obliged to put both hands on the reins to steer the pony to a stop in order to pay the toll over Waterloo Bridge and the moment of intimacy was gone. 'But I still do not think you should take me to Harecroft House. I am an employee, it is not fitting…'

'That makes no difference as far as the old lady is concerned. When she says do something, we all jump to obey.' His voice softened. 'Do not be alarmed. She will not eat you. You will be given a room where you can rest and refresh yourself and later someone will take you to visit your papa. It is better than going back to those dismal rooms and the uncouth Mrs Beales, is it not? You could never rest in the daytime there.'

'Yes, but…'

'I suggest you accept, it will be easier in the long run.'

'Thank you.' She leaned back and shut her eyes and let him carry her forward, though she could not help feeling she was being manipulated, losing control. Accustomed to directing her own life, of looking after her mother before she died and her father since then, she was not sure she liked it. But she was too tired to argue, much too tired...

Chapter Three

Harecroft House was an imposing residence, four storeys high with a porticoed porch to its front door reached by a short flight of steps. Richard pulled up outside, jumped down and handed Diana down. By the time they were walking up the steps, the door had been opened by a footman.

'Tell young Johnny to take the tilbury round to the mews, will you, Braithwaite,' Richard said, ushering Diana into the marble-tiled hall. Then, to Diana, 'Come, I expect Mama is in the drawing room.'

He took her arm and guided her up a magnificent cast-iron staircase, turned along a short corridor, and ushered her ahead of him into a large room whose windows looked out on to the square. The dowager and a younger woman were sitting on sofas, one on either side of the hearth. The younger woman's erect posture was due, Diana surmised, to stiff corseting that diminished her waist and emphasised her bosom, now clad in forest-green taffeta. 'Here she is,' Richard said. 'Mama, may I present Miss Diana Bywater?'

Diana, still feeling bewildered, bowed her head. 'Mrs Harecroft.'

'Miss Bywater, you are welcome.' It was said with rigid correctness and made Diana wonder if she really did welcome her. She turned to the old lady, who was smiling like a child who had got her own way. 'Lady Harecroft.'

'Sit down by me,' the dowager said, patting the seat beside her. 'I was very sorry to hear of your father's illness. Richard tells me he has had a seizure. How is he?'

'They think he will pull through, but it is too soon to talk of a full recovery.'

'Oh, dear, I am very sorry to hear that, very sorry indeed. I hope he has been made comfortable?'

'Yes, thanks to Mr Richard Harecroft. I do not know what I would have done without him.'

'I did nothing,' he said. 'It was fortuitous I was there.'

'Why *were* you there?' his mother demanded.

'Father asked me to escort Miss Bywater home last evening. She had been working late and Stephen had already left or he would have taken her.'

'I told them it was not necessary.' Diana felt she had to explain. Already she had a feeling that Mrs Harecroft disapproved of her and, remembering Richard's expression when he had come upon her and his father in the office, she certainly did not want her to think there was anything untoward going on. 'But in the event I was very glad Mr Harecroft was there.' She paused. 'I did not expect to be brought here today and would not, for the world, intrude—'

'Stephen wished it,' Mrs Harecroft said. 'And it is time we met, I think.'

'Yes, ma'am.'

'Miss Bywater is worn out, Mama,' Richard said. 'She has been sitting up with her father all night. Can you not leave the questions until later, when she has rested?'

'I ought to go to work,' Diana said.

'Certainly not!' the dowager put in. 'Time enough for that on Monday. Richard, ring the bell for Mathilde.' She turned to Diana as Richard obeyed. 'Mathilde is my maid. She will show you to your room and look after you. Poor thing, you look done in. Have you had any breakfast?'

'No, but I am not at all hungry.'

'I will have something sent up to you,' Mrs Harecroft said as a maid entered the room and bobbed to Lady Harecroft.

She was of middle years, very thin and upright. 'My lady, you rang?'

'Yes. This is Miss Bywater. She has had a very trying night and needs to sleep. I believe a room has been prepared for her.'

After expressing her gratitude, Diana was conducted up another flight of stairs and along a corridor to a bedroom. 'Here you are, miss.' The maid pushed open the door to a large well-furnished room. It had a Turkey carpet on the floor and heavy silk curtains. Diana recognised the material from the stock at the shop. 'This room is next to her ladyship's. Where is your baggage?'

'I do not have any. I have not come to stay beyond a few hours. I shall just remove my outer garments and lay on the bed a little while. Wake me at noon, will you please?'

'Very well, miss.' The expression on the woman's face would have made Diana smile had she not been too tired and worried to do so. The maid was obviously not used to such strange behaviour. Guests sleeping in the middle of the day and turning their noses up at a stay at Harecroft House was probably unheard of!

After the maid had gone, Diana took off her dress and sank on to the bed. She was almost too tired to sleep and there was so much going round and round in her head that it felt woolly. What was she doing here? Had she become so weak willed that she could not say no and mean it? It was Mr Richard Harecroft's doing. He had as good as abducted her, taking the place of Stephen, so he said. As for their father, why did he favour one over the other? Was Richard really a black sheep? What had he done? What had *she* done to merit the attention she was receiving?

There was a knock at the door and a maid entered with a tray of food which she put on the table near the window. 'Do you need anything else, miss?'

'No, thank you.'

'The mistress says to sleep as long as you like. Mr Harecroft and Mr Stephen will not be back before three.'

It was a clear instruction to stay out of the way until the rest of the family arrived home and Diana managed a brief smile before sitting at the table to eat the scrambled eggs and bacon, the bread and butter that had been provided along with a pot of coffee. She had not had such a luxurious breakfast for years. It made her realise how much her life had changed since her mother died. And it was all here for her, if she accepted Stephen.

The food eaten, or as much of it as she could manage, she returned to the bed and flung herself across it. To her own surprise, she slept.

Diana did not wake until a maid brought hot water and told her Mr Harecroft and Mr Stephen had returned home and it was time to dress for dinner, which would be taken at five o'clock, in deference to the dowager who hated eating late in the evening. Diana sprang up in dismay; she had asked to be woken at noon, fully intending to return to St Thomas's hospital to see her father and then go home without troubling the Harecroft family again. She was overset with guilt; poor Papa would think she had deserted him.

It took only a few minutes to wash, put on her dress again

and scrape her hair back, then she ventured downstairs, carrying her cape and bonnet. She stopped outside the drawing-room door, knowing she must express her gratitude before leaving and trying to frame the words that would convey her appreciation without bowing and scraping. After all, she had her pride, it was only ill fortune that made it necessary for her to work.

'You could have gone yourself.' It was Richard's voice coming from beyond the door. 'Papa would not have prevented you.'

'Unlike you, I choose to work. I cannot take time off when the fancy takes me.' This was Stephen.

'Fancy, eh? Is that what she is?'

'No. I am seriously inclined to marry her.'

'You cannot mean it.'

'Why not? I have much to offer…'

'Oh, indeed you have, brother. Have you told her exactly what it is you are offering her? Apart from your name and a stake in the Harecroft business, I mean.'

'Is that not enough?'

'It might be for some. I do not know the lady well enough to judge, but if you want my advice—'

'I do not. Just because you helped me out of a hole does not give you the right to tell me what to do.'

'Of course not. I leave that to Papa. Was it his idea?'

'Not at all. I am perfectly capable of making up my own mind. And it has nothing to do with you.'

'I spoke with no other motive than brotherly affection, but if you disdain my advice…'

'You would not take it upon yourself…'

'Me? Good Lord, no! I will say nothing, I promise you, but you have a moral obligation to do so.'

'You are a fine one to talk of moral obligation, Richard.'

Diana had no doubt they were talking about her, though she was puzzled, she could not stay there eavesdropping. She crept halfway back up the stairs and then turned and came down again, clattering her shoes on the marble of the floor, before entering the room.

They both turned towards her. 'Good evening, gentlemen.' She took a certain pride in knowing her voice was light and even.

'Hallo, Diana,' Stephen said. It was only the second time he had used her Christian name, no doubt to impress his brother. 'Are you rested now?'

'Yes, thank you.'

'I was sorry to hear about your papa. I hope he is being looked after.'

'Yes. I must go and see how he is.'

'Of course. After dinner, I will take you.'

'I had not planned to stay here that long. And there really is no need to inconvenience yourself or your family.'

'It is no inconvenience. Work is done for the day and we are dining early on account of Great-Grandmama. I will have the tilbury brought round at six-thirty.'

'Miss Bywater is about to say she can easily walk,' Richard said, giving her a sardonic smile that annoyed her. 'It is her panacea for everything. You will have to persuade her that you desire her company above everything.'

Stephen glared at his brother. Richard turned away as a bell sounded somewhere in the house. 'The dinner bell. I am going to fetch Great-Grandmama down.'

He left the room and Diana turned to go too, only to find her way blocked by Mr John Harecroft and his wife, who had just entered. 'There you are, Miss Bywater,' he said, cheerfully. 'How is your father today?'

'When I left him this morning, he had rallied, but I am anxious to return to see how he is.'

'I am sure you are. Stephen will take you after dinner. Ah, here is Richard and my grandmother. We can go in now.'

Diana had caught a glimpse of Richard and the old lady through the open door. He had carried her down the stairs as if she were a child and was setting her on her feet, ready to escort her into the dining room. Mr and Mrs Harecroft followed and Diana found herself walking beside Stephen.

Still in the clothes she had been wearing the day before and in which she had spent the long worrying night, she felt dishevelled and untidy and could not bring herself to take part in the conversation with any animation. Mr Harecroft, busy talking about something that had happened in the shop that morning, did not seem to notice or if he did, hid it very well. Stephen was not so good at hiding the fact that he would rather have introduced her to the household in different circumstances when she was suitably attired. Richard was silent except for such comments as politeness demanded. The air was charged with tension and Diana was glad when the meal came to an end and Stephen told her the tilbury was at the door.

'We missed you at work today,' he said as they set off.

'Yes, I am sorry about that. I will endeavour to make up for lost time when I come back. If I come back.'

'Whatever do you mean? Of course you will come back.'

'I may have to spend more time with my father. I am told he will need nursing.'

'Then a nurse will be found for him.'

'Mr Harecroft, you cannot think my wages will stretch to a nurse?'

'No, of course not. It will be my privilege to provide the necessary.'

'I cannot expect you to do that. I would never be able to repay you.'

'Nonsense! Have you so soon forgotten that I asked you to marry me? When that comes about, your father's well-being will be one of my chief concerns. After your own happiness, that is.'

'Mr Harecroft, I have not agreed…'

'I know, but I can be patient. I said so, did I not? And do you think you could call me Stephen? At least when we are away from the shop. It would not be appropriate there.'

'That would imply I had accepted you.'

'But you are going to, aren't you?'

'I do not know. I cannot think of anything but my father at the moment.'

'Of course. I understand. St Thomas's, isn't it?'

'Yes.'

'Why choose that hospital?'

'It is the nearest to my home and Mr Harecroft said there was not a moment to lose.'

'Good in a crisis, is my brother Richard.'

She was not sure if it was said with irony or not, but decided to take his words at face value. 'Yes, he was. I could not have managed without him.'

'I did not know you were still at work when I left last evening or I would have been the one to take you home. In future when you work late, let me know and I will wait for you.'

'Thank you, but I do not want to be treated any differently from the other clerks.'

'They are men. And I am not going to marry them.' It was meant to raise a laugh and she dutifully obliged.

He paid the toll and took them over the river and they were soon at St Thomas's. He helped her down and accompanied her into the hospital, following her as she made her way to her father's room. He was awake and had a little more colour than when she had last seen him.

'Papa, how are you today?' She bent over to kiss his cheek,

noting with relief that his face had lost some of the contortion that had accompanied the seizure. 'I am sorry I did not come back sooner, but I overslept.'

His smile was a little lopsided and he did not speak, but it seemed he had understood her.

'Papa, I have brought Mr Stephen Harecroft to see you.' She turned and indicated Stephen, who was standing behind her. He came forward and held out his hand but the patient could not take it. Instead of reaching for it, Stephen dropped his own hand back to his side, while Diana sat on a chair by the bed and told him everything that had happened since she left him.

'Everyone has been so kind,' she said.

He struggled to speak, but his words seemed to be a muddle of incoherent sounds and his frustration was evident. 'Hush,' she said. 'Do not distress yourself. You are being well looked after here and as soon as you are well enough I shall take you home and look after you myself.' He tried to speak again and this time she understood the word 'Toby'. 'Mr Harecroft took Toby home last night, Papa. Mrs Beales is looking after him.' This was followed by more mumbling on his part.

'Oh, dear,' she said, addressing Stephen. 'He is worried about his dog. Mrs Beales, our housekeeper, is not always kind to him.' She turned back to her father. 'I shall go home as soon as I leave here. Do not worry about him.'

She chatted to him a little longer while Stephen stood at the foot of the bed looking uncomfortable, when the nurse came to tell her that it was time to go, he seemed relieved.

'What a dreadful place!' he said as they made their way back to the gig. 'The smell!'

'I do not suppose they can help that and they are doing their best for my father.'

'Could your papa not be nursed at home?'

'He will be as soon as he is well enough to be moved.'

They had reached the gig. 'Thank you for bringing me, I am most grateful.'

'I am glad I did. I had no idea your father was in such straits. We must have him moved to a private hospital and employ some decent nurses. I am appalled that Richard took him there.'

'Your brother did what was best at the time and I cannot afford private nursing, Mr Harecroft.'

'Stephen,' he corrected her. 'I thought we agreed on that. And your father's well-being is my concern. I told you that before.'

'I have not yet agreed to marry you and until I do—'

'Oh, Diana, do not be so stubborn. You know it will be best for everyone concerned.'

'You mean my job at Harecroft's is dependent on my saying yes?'

'I did not say that, did I?' He stood by the trap and held out his hand. 'Now, you go and direct me to your house.'

He might not have said so, but the implication was there. She gave a huge sigh. He was like his brother in one thing: he would not take no for an answer. What did it matter anyway? It was too late for secrets; if he wanted to marry her, he ought to know the background from which she came. If it was going to put him off, the sooner the better. She took his hand and allowed him to help her up.

He did not trouble to hide his distaste when they drew up on the corner of her street and she suggested walking the rest of the way, and he frowned in annoyance when the two urchins appeared as if from nowhere and grinned at Stephen with hands outstretched.

'Your brother gave them money to buy a dinner,' she said. 'No doubt they think you will do the same.'

'Giving to beggars only encourages them and the fact that they are here again proves it.'

'They are half-starved and it is not their fault.'

'People should not have children if they cannot feed and clothe them adequately.'

'That is a rather harsh judgement, sir.'

He did not comment, but looked about him at the row of dingy tenements, the soot-begrimed walls, the dusty windows, some of which were broken, the filthy steps. 'I had no idea you lived like this. I am surprised at your father. You told me he was a sea captain…'

'So he was, but he has been unable to work for some time. As soon as I have saved a little more, we shall move to somewhere better.'

'Whatever my father will say about it, I cannot imagine.'

She did not reply but entered her house, where she was greeted by Toby rushing forward and jumping up at her, barking in delight. 'Hello, old fellow. Pleased to see me, are you? Well I am home now.'

The door to the back regions opened and Mrs Beales came out. 'There you are. That dog was whining all night, no one got a wink of sleep.' She looked Stephen up and down. 'Another man, miss? How many more? You ain't no better than you should be for all your haughty ways.'

'Mrs Beales, that is unfair. This is my employer and the brother of the man who helped my father when he had his seizure.'

'For goodness' sake, Diana, do not try to justify yourself to her. She is disgusting.' Stephen's lip curled.

'I'll have you know I keep a respectable house,' the woman told him angrily. 'And I do not allow gentleman callers for my single ladies. I only let the other one in when he said he had come to see the captain.'

'Mrs Beales, please. Mr Harecroft is leaving. He has only escorted me from the hospital.'

'Fine story!'

'I have heard enough,' Stephen said. 'Diana, collect your belongings. You are leaving here now. At once.'

'Don't be silly. I have nowhere to go and I cannot pack everything up just like that.'

'Yes, you can!' This from Mrs Beales. 'I've had enough of your coming in at all hours. Working late, my eye!'

'Mrs Beales!' she cried in dismay, expecting Stephen to turn on his heel and leave her to her fate. She turned on him angrily. 'Now, see what you have done. You have made me homeless. And where am I going to find somewhere else at this time of night? Mrs Beales, you will allow me to stay tonight, won't you?'

'No,' Stephen said. 'You are coming home with me.' He grabbed her arm and turned towards the door.

'I can't go now. Our belongings…'

'We will send for them later. I am not prepared to stay another minute in this place, nor yet allow you to.'

'Good riddance!' Mrs Beales put in. 'And take that hound with you.'

Before Diana could say another word, she was on the pavement outside the house and the door had been firmly shut. 'Mr Harecroft. Stephen. Let me go, will you? You are hurting my arm.'

He released her. 'I am sorry. But I had no idea how you lived. You kept it very quiet, didn't you?' It was said with a flash of anger.

'Perhaps because I knew what your reaction might be. We had no choice, it was the best we could afford and now I haven't even got that.'

'You can stay at Harecroft House.'

'I cannot do that, it would be an imposition.'

'Nonsense. It will be an opportunity to get to know each other properly and it will help you to decide to accept me.'

'Why do you want to marry me?'

They had reached the gig and he turned to face her. 'Why does anyone marry? To live together, to make a home and a family…'

'No, I meant…why *me*?'

'Because you are exactly the wife I have been looking for, someone I would be proud to have on my arm, to entertain my guests, be a mother to my children, someone to work beside me like Great-Grandmother did for Great-Grandfather, patient, efficient, not giddy or given to the vapours. Does that answer you?' He held out his hand to help her up. 'Come, there will be time to talk about our future when you have settled in at Harecroft House.'

He had not mentioned love, she noticed, and he had reeled off the list of her attributes as if he had learned them by rote. 'Supposing I do not want to come.'

'Oh, do be sensible, Diana. Where else can you go at this time of night?'

'Mrs Beales might change her mind…'

'You know she will not. And in any case, I am not letting my future wife live in a place like that. It is a slum.'

'I have no nightgown and toiletries or a change of linen….'

'None of which matters. Mama will find something for you until your own things can be fetched.'

'Stephen, you are bullying me.'

'I am sorry for that, my dear, it was not intended, but we could have stood arguing with that dreadful woman all night if I had not done something. Now, please get in the tilbury.'

The dog, who had been trotting beside her, jumped up into the gig and seemed to make up her mind for her. 'What about Toby?'

'He can go to the stables. The grooms will look after him.'

She knew she had no choice; it was too late to go searching for a bed and, being a woman on her own, no good-class establishment would entertain her. 'Very well, just for tonight.' She stepped up into the gig and he seated himself beside her and they set off. Neither spoke.

She was too worried and angry with him to make conversation. He had manoeuvred her into a corner. Why did a man so disgusted with the way she lived want to marry her? Unless he, too, was being manipulated. But why? What did she have to offer that dozens of others in more advantageous circumstances did not? She had been worried about losing her job when the Harecrofts found out about her father and where she lived; she had not dreamt she would be prised out of her home and carried off, because that was what it amounted to.

'Why?' she demanded suddenly. 'Why, when you discovered where I lived, did you not turn your back on me?'

'I am not fickle, Diana. I do not like your circumstances, but that does not mean I feel any differently about you. You are still you, still the person I have come to know and regard with great affection. And I would be less than a gentleman if I did not try to do something to improve your situation. Please give me a chance to do so.'

It was not a declaration of love, but perhaps he found it difficult to express his true feelings. She had known him long enough to know he was not the effusive kind. He had always been quiet and stiffly correct; it was his way. She ought not to yearn for anything else. But, oh, how she longed to be enfolded in someone's arms, to be comforted and told that she need no longer worry about anything, that she was loved. If she married Stephen, the responsibility of looking after her father would be lifted from her shoulders and perhaps love would come. At the moment, with Papa in hospital fighting for his life, no home to take him to when he recovered sufficiently to be discharged and Toby trying to lick the skin off her face, she could not think clearly.

The first person they saw when they entered the house was Richard. He had apparently just come in because he was handing his top hat to a footman. 'Miss Bywater, you are back again.'

'Yes, your brother insisted.' There was no doubt he had the power to make her heart turn somersaults; it was beating like a steam hammer in her breast. Did he know the effect he had? She suspected he did, because he was very self-assured and at ease with himself.

'It is not like him to be so decisive. What happened? How is your father?'

'Papa is comfortable and I think improving. He is trying to speak, but it is a great effort. He was worried about Toby.'

'You told him I had taken him home?'

'Yes, of course, and I thank you.'

'What has happened to the dog?'

'We brought him with us,' Stephen put in. 'He will be looked after in the stables. I could not leave Diana at that place. I was appalled by the squalor. Heaven knows what pestilential miasmas are drifting in the air. I wonder Diana has not succumbed long before now.'

'It is not as bad as that,' Diana put in. 'It is in a poor district, but I have always kept our apartment clean and tidy and Papa was looked after when I was at work. Now I have been made homeless and must look for new lodgings.'

'Why?' Richard asked. 'Did Mrs Beales throw you out?'

'Not until after Mr Harecroft insulted her.'

'She insulted you.' This from Stephen. 'I was not going to stand by and allow the lady I mean to marry being spoken to in that fashion. I won't tell you what she said, Richard, but it was insupportable.'

'Oh, I see, so you fetched Miss Bywater away?'

'What was I supposed to do? Ignore the insult? Diana can stay here. I am going to find Mama and put it to her. She needs a nightgown and whatever else ladies need for a stay.'

'You mean you dragged her away without even allowing her time to pack her night things. No wonder the poor lady looks worried and bewildered.'

'Does she?' Stephen turned to Diana. 'Are you bewildered, my dear?'

'No, furious with the pair of you. I think being high-handed must be a Harecroft trait, for you are both as bad as one another, and I certainly do not want you quarrelling over me. I shall stay here tonight because it is late, but tomorrow I shall begin looking for new lodgings. I must have somewhere for when my father is discharged from hospital. Would you be kind enough to arrange for me to go to my room now? I am tired and need to rest.'

'Of course. Wait here, while I find my mother.'

He set off down the hall, leaving her with Richard. 'Come,' he said, indicating a door to the left of the hall. 'Let us sit in the library and wait for him to come back.' He paused and smiled wryly. 'Only if you wish it, of course.'

She found herself responding, if only a little wearily. 'Thank you.'

He led the way into a book-lined room with a large heavy desk in the middle and two deep armchairs on either side of the fireplace. Above it was a large portrait of some earlier Harecroft in a satin coat, breeches and a bag wig. 'My great-grandfather,' he said, noticing her interest. 'Great-Grand-mama's husband. It was painted soon after he returned from India, I believe. He was a great man of business and ruled his family with a stout rod, no one dare defy him, but he did have his softer side, especially where Great-Grandmama was concerned. Her idolised her. Do sit down.' He indicated one of the chairs and folded himself into the other. 'Tell me about your father. What do the medical staff say about him?'

'His recovery will be slow and he will need a lot of help when he comes home.'

'Except you have no home now. I am sorry for the way that happened, Miss Bywater, but if I can help, do not hesitate to ask me.'

'Thank you.'

'I am also sorry if you found my manner overbearing. I suppose, being in the army, I became used to command and it has become a habit to take charge of things. And especially when a beautiful young lady is involved and needs help.'

'Mr Harecroft, that is outright flummery. I thought you were more honest than that.'

'What is dishonest about telling a lady she is beautiful, if you mean it?' He paused. 'You know, you remind me of someone I have met, but I cannot for the life of me think when or where. Do you think we have met?'

'I think it very unlikely, sir. I am sure I should have remembered.'

He found it difficult to dislike her; she was articulate, intelligent and perceptive. No wonder his father thought she was an asset to the business and would be an asset to Stephen, too. But, remembering his great-grandmother's doubts, he knew he must guard against feeling sorry for her.

Stephen came into the room. 'There you are,' he said to Diana. 'For a minute I thought you had taken flight, until I heard your voice. It is all arranged. Mathilde is sorting out some night attire for you and she will conduct you to the room you occupied this morning. It is yours for as long as you want it.'

She stood up. 'Thank you. I must pay my respects to your

parents and her ladyship and then I should like to go up. It has been a very eventful twenty-four hours.'

'Mother and Father are about to retire and Great-Grand-mama went to her room ages ago. You will see them in the morning. We go to church at ten o'clock.'

'I understand. I will be gone by then.'

'Gone where?' He looked puzzled.

'To see my father, to find new lodgings and arrange for my belongings to be moved.'

He opened his mouth to speak, but Richard silenced him. 'Do not start arguing again, Stephen. You can see Miss Bywater is exhausted.'

'Yes, we will talk in the morning.' He opened the door to Mathilde. 'Ah there you are. Miss Bywater is ready to go up now.' He took Diana's hand and lifted it to his lips. 'Good-night, my dear.'

'Goodnight,' she answered and then to Richard. 'Good-night, sir.'

He stood up and bowed stiffly. 'Your servant.'

Diana followed the maid up to the room she had left only a few hours before, to find the bed had been remade and a cotton nightgown laid across it. 'It is one of Lady Hare-croft's,' Mathilde said.

'Her ladyship is very kind.'

'Do you need help to undress?'

Diana smiled at the question. It was a very long time since she had shared her mother's maid. 'No, thank you. I can manage.'

'Then I will say goodnight.' Then she was gone and Diana was alone. She picked up the nightgown and sat on the bed with it on her lap, almost too weary to undress. It had been the longest twenty-four hours of her life and she knew nothing would ever be the same again. Was that a good thing or a bad thing? If she accepted Stephen, she would become part of this household; almost everything she wanted or needed would be at her fingertips. Her father would be nursed back to health and she would be able to spend more time with him; no one would expect her to go to work, certainly not to sit over ledgers all day. It was very tempting.

Slowly she began unbuttoning her dress. Having nothing else with her, she would have to put it on again tomorrow. She was beginning to feel very dowdy. She slipped the nightgown over her head and crept between the sheets. She did not expect to sleep, but after a short prayer, which mainly consisted of asking for her father to be restored to health and for guidance in what to do, she drifted off to sleep. But it was not Stephen who filled her dreams, but someone bigger and broader and altogether more striking.

She was woken by a maid with her breakfast on a tray. She put it down to draw the curtain and the room was flooded with sunshine. Diana ate a little, then washed and dressed and went down to find everyone gathered in the drawing room, waiting for the carriage to be brought round to convey them to church. Mrs Harecroft was dressed in a light blue taffeta gown, severely plain but exquisitely cut. It had a cowl collar and lace-edged sleeves. Her bonnet was ruched in matching lace. Mr Harecroft and Stephen were both in black frockcoats and grey trousers. Richard was in dove grey. Lady Harecroft was not present.

Diana, in her working dress, felt much too dishevelled to be seen in public in their company, and was relieved when Mrs Harecroft said, 'I am sure you are anxious to fetch your things, Miss Bywater, so we will excuse you from attending church.'

'Thank you.'

'How much do you have to bring?' Mr Harecroft asked. 'Is there anything heavy or bulky?'

'No, sir, only our clothes and books and a few pictures and household items. I intend to find alternative accommodation and will have everything conveyed there as soon as possible.'

'I understood from Stephen you had accepted our hospitality, Miss Bywater, at least so long as your father is in hospital. There is no need to go searching for accommodation.'

'Mr Harecroft, I cannot presume on your generosity…'

'Think nothing of it. You are one of us, or soon will be. And until that time, it will be delightful, not to say convenient, to have you here. You will be able to travel to work with us and there will always be someone to take you to visit your father.'

'Please say you agree,' Stephen said.

She capitulated. It was so much easier than arguing and in the back of her mind was the possibility of losing her job if she was obstinate about it. 'Very well, just until my father is discharged from hospital.'

'You will need a conveyance,' Mr Harecroft senior said. 'Richard, do you know if Grandmother is using her carriage today? We shall need ours.'

'I will go and ask her.'

'Well, hurry up,' Mrs Harecroft said, drawing on her gloves. 'I heard our carriage arriving.'

'No, do not trouble yourself,' Diana said quickly. 'I can hire a cab. I have very little to bring.'

'Are you sure?' Stephen asked her, picking up his hat and gloves to follow his parents to the door. 'I would come with you, but I cannot guarantee to keep my temper with that dreadful woman.'

'Then, Mama, if you will excuse me from church attendance, I shall accompany Miss Bywater,' Richard said. He turned to Diana. 'If you are agreeable, of course.'

How did he know she was dreading having to face Mrs

Beales again? The woman had a caustic tongue and was just as likely to throw her things out in the street as allow her inside to pack them and remove them carefully. 'Thank you,' she said quietly.

Mr and Mrs Harecroft and Stephen trooped out and she and Richard were left alone. 'Come up and talk to Great-Grandmama while I make the arrangements,' he said. 'She likes to stay in her room until noon these days, but I know she will be pleased to see you.'

She followed him upstairs and stood outside while he knocked on the old lady's door. Mathilde answered it. 'Tell Lady Harecroft I have a visitor for her,' he said.

'Have you brought Miss Bywater?' a voice called from inside the room.

'Yes, Great-Grandmama. Everyone else has gone to church.'

'Then do not stand dithering outside, bring her in.'

Richard took her elbow to lead her into the room. The old lady was dressed in a black silk peignoir with a matching lace cap on top of her white hair. She was sitting in a chair by the window with a book on her lap and a large magnifying glass in one hand. She put it down and closed her book as Diana moved forward and bobbed a curtsy. 'My lady.'

'Miss Bywater has agreed to stay with us until her papa comes out of hospital,' Richard said.

'Good. Sit down on that stool where I can see you, child. Goodness, you are still in working clothes.'

'Yes, I am going to my lodgings to fetch my belongings, my lady, then I shall make myself more presentable.'

'I wonder if we might borrow your carriage, Great-Grandmama,' Richard put in. 'Mama and Papa have gone to church in theirs.'

'Of course you can, you do not need to ask. Where is Stephen?'

'Gone to church with them.'

'Really?' She sounded surprised.

'He cannot get on with my landlady, my lady,' Diana said, feeling she ought to defend the young man. 'She is very out-spoken. They had an altercation.'

'I am surprised at that. Stephen is usually so mild-mannered.'

'He was defending me.'

'Ah, then it is understandable. Go on, Richard, what are you waiting for? Order out the carriage.'

He disappeared and the old lady settled down for a chat. 'Now, my dear, tell me how your papa is.'

Diana repeated what she had told everyone else, wondering as she did so, if Richard had said anything at all about her father's drinking habits. 'I am very glad Mr Harecroft was on hand to help me,' she said.

'Mr Harecroft.' The old lady chuckled. 'There are three of them and so that we know one from the other, they are known as Mr John, Mr Richard and Mr Stephen by servants and employees.'

'Then I referred to Mr Richard. He escorted me home and was present when my father had his seizure. I am very grateful. Mr Stephen took me to see my father last night and that was when he spoke to my landlady…'

The old lady smiled. 'And now you feel as though you are being buffeted in a violent storm.'

'Something like that. Everyone is so forceful. At any other time I would have been able to withstand it, but with my father lying helpless and Mr John Harecroft being my employer, I feel powerless. I am sorry if that sounds ungracious.'

'No, I can understand that.' She paused. 'Tell me about yourself. For instance, where were you born, where were you educated?'

'I was born in Portsmouth, my lady, and educated by my parents. Because we were always on the move, I had no formal schooling.'

'Your parents appear to have made a very good fist of it. It suggests to me that they were well educated themselves.'

'I have always assumed so, I do not really know.'

'Have you never been curious about that, about their history? Do you not sometimes wonder who they were, the families they came from?'

'I always understood they had no immediate family. Papa always said we were his family, Mama and I, and he did not want anyone else. She and Papa were devoted, which is why her death hit him so hard.'

'It must have been a sad time for you, too.'

'It was, my lady. But we have managed, Papa and I, until his seizure, that is. What I cannot understand is why everyone is so anxious to help me.'

'Because you are you, child.'

And on that enigmatic note the conversation was ended by the return of Richard, who said the carriage was at the door.

'Off you go, then,' her ladyship said. 'I shall see you both at luncheon.'

Once again Diana found herself alone in Richard's company. The more she knew of him, the more she appreciated his qualities, especially his understanding and his way of handling tricky situations. It was difficult to believe that he was supposed to be a black sheep. And what had her ladyship meant by saying you are you? Of course she was, but there was more to it than that. She followed Richard downstairs and out to the carriage, determined to find out what Lady Harecroft meant.

Chapter Four

'Mr Harecroft,' she began when they were seated in the luxurious carriage and being conveyed to St Thomas's hospital. 'You said you thought we had met before.'

'So I did. Have you remembered the occasion?'

'No, I am sure we have not. But do you think Lady Harecroft thinks that too and she is muddling me up with someone else?'

'Great-Grandmama is rarely muddled, Miss Bywater. Her faculties are as sharp as ever they were. I should bear that in mind if you should ever think of deceiving her.'

'But you were the one who said there was no need to tell anyone. Between you and me and no one else's business, you said.'

'I did not mean that.'

'Then what did you mean?'

'I meant taking advantage of an old lady's generosity.'

'Coming to Harecroft House was none of my doing, Mr Harecroft, you know that. I expected my services to be dispensed with when my circumstances became known, but that seems not to be the case. Even though Mr Stephen was appalled, he has not withdrawn his proposal. And surely it is up to him and his parents to question my motives, not you.'

'*Touché*, Miss Bywater. But perhaps the onlooker sees more of the game.'

'I am not playing games, Mr Harecroft.'

It was said sharply, to put him down. He was not used to that. 'Neither am I.'

'If your brother wishes to marry me, I cannot see it has anything to do with you. You would not like him to interfere in your life, would you?'

He acknowledged the truth of that with a wry smile. 'No, but then he would not dare.'

He was insufferably arrogant at times, she decided, even as she acknowledged the debt she owed him. She supposed it was inherent in his nature, or perhaps the result of his military career, to take charge, and she had been glad of that when her father was taken ill, but she had expressed her gratitude more than once and she did not see why she should allow him to question her motives. She had done nothing to deserve it.

He turned to look at her. She was looking straight ahead, but he could tell by the heightened colour in her cheeks and the set of her jaw that he had made her uncomfortable, but his moment of triumph was quickly dashed by an incongruous wish to protect her. 'If Stephen loves you…'

'If,' she repeated. 'Have you any reason to believe that he does not?'

'One must suppose he does or he would not have asked you to marry him.' He paused and turned to look closely at her. 'I assume he has asked?'

'Oh, yes.'

'And?'

'I have not given him an answer.'

'Then I should be very, very sure before you say yes, Miss Bywater. Marriage is for life and you cannot change your mind once committed.'

'Why should I change my mind?'

'I was speaking hypothetically.'

'Oh, I see.' She was reminded of the conversation she had overheard between the brothers. Richard had been urging Stephen to tell her something. She could not ask him what he meant without revealing that she had been eavesdropping. She was curious. Perhaps in the next few days while she was staying at Harecroft House, she might discover what it was. And she might also find out why Lady Harecroft had taken her under her wing and why Mr Richard Harecroft was so protective of the old lady. Did he suppose she was a fortune hunter? Such an idea had never entered her head. All she wanted was a job that paid a decent wage and a comfortable home. Was that asking too much?

She was still musing on this as they crossed the bridge and arrived outside the hospital. He jumped down, threw a few coppers to an urchin to mind the pony and turned to hand her down and escort her to the ward.

James was sitting up in bed, staring into space. He saw Diana and managed to lift his right hand and she was thankful that his seizure had not struck him on that side. 'Papa, how are you?' She bent to kiss his cheek. His answer was a mumble. 'And here is Mr Richard Harecroft to see you.' He looked past her to see Richard behind her and his face contorted in a semblance of a smile and his eyes lit up with pleasure.

Richard leaned forward to take his hand. 'Glad to see you are improving, Captain.'

More mumbling before they understood anything of what he was saying, but Richard seemed to guess what he meant before she did. He was worried about her being on her own and about Toby, whom he missed.

'I am not on my own, Papa. Mr Harecroft senior has invited me to stay at Harecroft House while you are here. And Toby is there, too. Everyone has been very kind. You are not to worry about a thing.'

They spent a little more time with him and then were told he needed to rest and they left him, looking brighter than he had when they arrived. 'I shall come tomorrow evening,' Diana told him. 'After work. It is Monday tomorrow and we are very busy.'

'You did not tell him about leaving Mrs Beales,' Richard said as they made their way back to the carriage.

'No, there is no sense in worrying him unnecessarily. By the time he is ready to leave, I shall have found us somewhere else to live.'

'You are determined on that, then.'

'Yes, I am. You must allow me a little pride, Mr Harecroft. I have been independent all my life. I cannot change what I am.'

'I would not change a hair of your head,' he said, directing the coachman and getting into the carriage beside her. 'You are admirable as you are.'

'Mr Harecroft, you are flirting with me. Please refrain.'

The words had slipped from his tongue without conscious thought; he had certainly not said them in order to flirt with her, though when he came to consider the matter he realised he might enjoy doing so, seeing how far he could go before raising her ire. Not far, it seemed. 'Nothing was further from my mind,' he said. 'I leave that to my brother.'

'He is a gentleman.'

'Meaning I am not.'

'I did not say that. You are confusing me. You have been

kind to me and I am grateful, but please do not take gratitude for anything else.'

'Then I won't,' he said curtly, as the carriage stopped. Her
coolness was inexplicable, considering she was being offered
a way out of her dilemma over her father. Surely any woman
in her situation would jump at the chance to marry into money?
She was either very foolish or very clever. Although she had
denied it, he could not rid himself of the notion he had seen
her somewhere before and it worried at his brain like canker.
Where? When? How? And why did he want to remember?

He jumped down, banged on the door and, in the face of
his obvious authority, Mrs Beales let them in to pack Diana's
belongings into a trunk, two portmanteaux, a wooden box and
two hat boxes. When everything had been stowed either in the
boot or strapped to the roof, he handed Mrs Beales several
guineas for her trouble and escorted Diana out.

'You are not sorry to leave, are you?' he asked as they set
off again, to the cheers of a small group of onlookers who had
been drawn by curiosity over how one of Mrs Beales's tenants
should have such high-and-mighty connections. Some had
even climbed on the step of the coach to peer inside.

'No, except we had trouble enough finding lodgings we
could afford when we went there. I am apprehensive about
obtaining anything as good for the rent we were paying,
bearing in mind that, with the coronation on Thursday, every
bed in London must be taken.'

'Not all of them. There are spare beds in Harecroft House.'

'I know.'

'Then why not avail yourself of one of them?'

'And if I do, will you tell me again I am taking advantage?
It is not my fault I am homeless.'

He found himself increasingly intrigued by her. She
wavered between stiff reserve and a determination to stand

on her dignity to a willingness to trade repartee, to make the apt rejoinder. It was not the attitude of an employee whose job depended on being subservient. Was she manipulating his brother or the other way about? Was her father cunning enough to fake his illness to help his daughter? His collapse in the street had been very sudden and his evasiveness about his family was strange. Was Mrs Beales part of the plot to make them homeless and reliant on Stephen? Were they trying to hoodwink a wealthy old lady? Did they realise she was not easily deceived? The questions plagued him. Having refused to do as his great-grandmother asked, he was beginning to wonder if he ought, after all, to humour her. If he could discover something about Miss Bywater that would put his brother off marrying her, then he would.

'No,' he conceded. 'But it is surely foolish to turn down an offer of help. I have seen what you have had to cope with and I am full of admiration for your courage. It cannot have been easy with your father the way he is.'

'He cannot seem to help it. It is like an illness, and, because I love him dearly, I do my best for him. He has no one else but me.'

'I understand. I have seen people like it in the army, too sensitive, too imaginative to make good soldiers and because they are forced into a situation they cannot handle, they drink.'

'You do not condemn?'

'No. I always think: there, but for the grace of God, go I.'

'It is one of the worries I have about accepting Stephen,' she said, wondering if he had meant he was sensitive or that he had been tempted by the demon drink. He did not give that impression. 'I would have to tell him and yet I do not want to. It seems disloyal to Papa. But I cannot let him find out as you did.' Her father's drinking habits might very well put

Stephen off, but as he had promised her he would keep her secret, that way was not open to him.

'The captain is ill, Miss Bywater. Circumstances have changed. He may have changed. My advice is to wait and see.'

'Yes, perhaps you are right.'

They fell into silence. Diana could not make him out. One minute he was sceptical and disparaging, almost threatening, the next compassionate and understanding, able to see inside her and divine how she felt without her having to say anything. He could make light of a problem and yet in the space of a second turn to being sombre. He was an enigma and she wondered what had made him that way.

They arrived back at Harecroft House and Diana barely had time to stow her belongings away in her room, with the help of two of the footmen, before the rest of the family returned from church. Hastily she washed and found a dress in cerise-and-cream striped cotton, which was cool and neat and a striking contrast to the serviceable working dress she had been wearing. She put up her hair and went downstairs, feeling more confident.

The family had gathered in the drawing room except Richard and the dowager, but they arrived almost as soon as she had greeted everyone and answered their queries about the progress of her father, and then they all went into luncheon.

'You had no trouble with Mrs Beales?' Stephen asked her, when the servants had left after serving them. 'You have all your belongings safe and sound?'

'Yes, thank you. Your brother was a great help.'

'Then I owe you,' he said, addressing Richard.

'Forget it.'

'I am glad you are clear of that place,' Stephen went on, speaking to Diana. 'I would have been worried to death if you had stayed there a moment longer. You could have been killed in your bed, especially when your father is not there.'

'I never felt at risk,' she said.

'What about those little beggars? They presumably have parents somewhere who might use your trusting nature to rob you—'

'You cannot know they have parents,' Richard put in. 'They could be orphans.'

'Then I would expect them to be in an orphanage or the union, not roaming the street.'

'Oh, how little you know about how the poor live,' Richard said. 'Perhaps you should live among them for a spell, it might open your eyes.'

'Really, Richard,' his mother said. 'How can you say such a thing? I beg you to desist. I, for one, do not want to hear about it.'

Dutifully he fell silent. If he was going to do anything for the poor, it would have to be done alone, for none of his family would support him. They considered him eccentric, if not worse. They paid their taxes and gave to selected charities, always distinguishing the deserving poor from the undeserving, and their consciences did not trouble them. If he had toed the line as a child, if he had only associated with children of whom his parents approved and not run around with the village boys and seen how they lived, if he had not played truant from his boarding school to roam the Berkshire countryside, if he had not gone into the army and shared the lives of his men, talked to them about their homes and families, then he might have had the same attitude.

While he mused, the conversation had moved on to general

topics, mostly about the Harecroft business, things happening on the estate at Borstead Hall and the coronation.

Talking of the coronation reminded Diana of Stephen's invitation to the ball, which, in her concern for her father and everything else, she had forgotten about. Was he still expecting her to go? But she had nothing to wear; buying ball gowns was very low on her list of priorities. It would have been easier to decline the invitation when she was living with Mrs Beales, but as part of the Harecroft household, how could she refuse to go? She had one or two of her mother's dresses carefully folded among her baggage and one in particular she thought she might alter. In a diaphanous pale green gauze over a paler silk, the skirt was very full and heavily embroidered with swathes of flowers in pink and blue and a delicate yellow, which her mama had worked herself. It was the gown she had taken to show Madame Francoise as an example of her work and which had resulted in her being employed doing the intricate work on that lady's creations. Although of necessity some of her mother's things had had to be sold, Diana could not bear to part with all of them and that gown in particular.

'Shall we take a stroll in the park this afternoon, Diana?' Stephen asked, as the pudding, a light lemony concoction, was served.

She forced herself out of her contemplation to pay attention. 'Yes, that would be very nice. Perhaps we can take Toby with us. He would like a run in the park.'

There was only a moment's hesitation before he said, 'Of course.'

'Shall we all go?' John suggested. 'It is a lovely day, too nice to stay indoors. You do not mind, Grandmama, do you?'

'No,' the old lady said. 'You know I always take a nap in the afternoons. I shall see you all at dinner.'

* * *

Diana enjoyed the walk. Stephen was at his charming best and Mrs Harecroft unbent sufficiently to talk to her. Richard let Toby off his lead and sent him scampering after a ball, throwing it again when he retrieved it. It was the most relaxed she had seen him.

'Mr Richard is not at all like Mr Stephen, is he?' Diana ventured, as Stephen went ahead to speak to his father, who was inclined to stride out and not stroll as the ladies were doing.

'No, he never was. He was always out on the estate, helping with the horses, riding, full of restless energy. When he left school, he was expected to go into the shop, but he hated it and in the end he chose to go into the army. For Stephen, of course, the shop is his life. He loves the cut and thrust of business. I am glad of that. Richard will inherit the title and the estate eventually, but second sons need something to occupy them and I could not bear it if Stephen went into the army. It seems to change people.' She did not elaborate on that, but turned to look at Diana. 'Stephen tells me he has proposed.'

'Yes. I have not yet given him an answer.'

'Take your time, Miss Bywater. It does not do to rush into these things.'

'No, I told him that.' She took a deep breath before going on. 'I should like to know what you think.'

'About you as a wife for Stephen?'

'Yes.'

'If Stephen has chosen you, then I will be happy to welcome you into the family as a daughter-in-law.'

'Thank you.'

'I am told my husband's grandmother has invited you to her party.'

'Yes, but I cannot leave my father.'

'You are a dutiful daughter, Miss Bywater, and that inclines me to believe you will also be a dutiful wife.'

'Thank you.'

Stephen slowed to allow them to come up with him just as a breathless Richard returned, the dog scampering at his heels. Diana smiled. 'You have made a conquest, Mr Richard,' she said. 'Toby does not take to everyone.'

'No, he does not,' Stephen put in. 'He nipped my hand when I gave him over to the groom the other evening.'

'I expect he was confused by his new surroundings and missing Papa,' she told him, bending to pat the dog's head and fasten his lead, ready to return to the street and back to Harecroft House, where the evening would be spent quietly reading.

The next morning, Diana set off with Mr Harecroft and Stephen to go to work. She came home with them and then Stephen took her to see her father after dinner. He was improving slowly, and though he found speaking a trial and his words were still slurred, she was beginning to understand what he was saying. 'I am sorry I let you down,' he told her as soon as he felt confident enough to talk. 'I was thinking of your mama all day. It was our wedding anniversary. She was an angel…' Tears came to his eyes.

'Yes, Papa, I know, but do not distress yourself over it.' She wanted to stop him before Stephen realised what he meant.

'Can't stand that Beales woman,' he went on. 'Gave me some damned awful stew. Couldn't eat it…'

'You are not going back there, Captain,' Stephen put in. 'Indeed, I cannot imagine anything worse to put a man off recovering his health than the prospect of that place. It will be my privilege to find you somewhere more wholesome.'

'Thank you. And you will look after my girl?'

'Of course.'

'Good.' He lay back and closed his eyes as if that was all he wanted to hear.

'It is late,' Diana whispered, wishing her father had not intimated that she meant to accept Stephen's proposal and he approved. 'I think he has tired himself out with the effort of talking. Shall we go and allow him to sleep?'

Stephen was doing his best, she conceded, and if he helped her to look after Papa, then it was a point in his favour, but she still could not rid herself of a niggling doubt, a doubt his brother had put there. She could not help wondering what it was that Richard had been urging Stephen to tell her. Was there some dark secret, the telling of which might make her think differently about him? Stephen was so stiffly correct, she could not imagine him doing anything he should not. And he deferred to his father in everything. Richard, with his background, was the more likely to have a secret past. Why was he so distrustful of her? Did he truly think she would take advantage of a situation that was none of her making?

Why did she keep thinking of him? Why, when she was busy at work, did a picture of the older brother come to her from nowhere, larger than life, his blue eyes boring into hers, almost reading her thoughts, making her tremble. Stephen never had that effect on her. But it was Stephen who wanted to marry her, not Richard. It was Stephen who had promised to look after her father, Stephen who had asked her to stay at Harecroft House and go to the ball with him, not Richard. Perhaps when Richard and his great-grandmother returned to Borstead Hall after the coronation, she would settle down and stop making comparisons.

She retired to her room on their return in order to work on the alterations to her mother's ballgown. The skirt she would leave as it was, except for shortening it because she was not as tall as her mother had been. In order not to spoil the embroidery, she was going to lift it from the waist. The bodice was pleated and had a boat-shaped neck and very voluminous sleeves, which were no longer fashionable, she meant to replace them with little puffed sleeves and use some of the excess material to fill in the neckline, which she felt was too low for a single young woman.

Each evening on returning from the hospital, she worked on it. In a way she was glad of the excuse to keep to herself. Whatever Stephen said and the half-hearted acceptance of Mrs Harecroft, she still looked upon herself as an employee until such time as she decided to accept Stephen's proposal, or turn it down. And then she risked losing her job. Better to keep out of the way.

One evening Lady Harecroft wandered into her room to talk to her and admired the gown. 'Your mother had an exceptional talent,' she said on being told who had done the embroidery. 'Where did she learn her skills?'

'I do not know—I think she was largely self-taught.'

'I think you will look very beautiful in it.'

'Thank you.'

'You will wear it for my party, won't you?'

'My lady, I am flattered to be asked, but I do not see how I can possibly come. My father…'

'We will contrive something, my dear.'

'He does not like being pushed into things, my lady. He is used to command. It comes hard being told what he may and may not do.'

'I understand. I promise you, no one is going to push him into anything. Now I am off to my bed. Do not stay up too long, straining your eyes on that sewing.'

Diana went to open the door for her and found herself face to face with Richard and the object of his scrutiny. Try as she might to keep to herself, she seemed to encounter him at every turn. He would look at her searchingly, taking in every line of her face, as if trying to commit it to memory. 'Miss Bywater.' Even her name coming from his lips had a different resonance than when others spoke it.

'Richard,' her ladyship said. 'Come with me, I want to talk to you.'

Richard looked at Diana, a half-smile on his lips, and shrugged his shoulders at her, as if he would have liked to stay, but duty called him away. 'I am coming,' he said. 'Good-night, Miss Bywater.'

She bade him goodnight and retreated into her room, shut the door and leaned heavily against it. Her life was spiralling out of control.

'Richard, tell me how Mr Bywater really is,' Lady Harecroft said as soon as they arrived back in her room. 'Is he a man with whom you can converse easily?'

'Conversation is a little one-sided,' he said. 'But I can understand him most of the time. I gather he is improving day by day. And before you ask, it has not been possible to talk to him without Miss Bywater being present. And I still strongly disapprove. And suggesting Miss Bywater should bring him to your party was not a good idea. He is not ready for social intercourse yet.' It was as near as he could go to telling her the truth without betraying Miss Bywater's confidence. He was torn between the two—one trying to keep her shame from becoming common knowledge and the other determined to use her position to winkle out something she only hinted at. For someone used to being in control, it was an uncomfortable feeling.

'Then perhaps he will consent to going into a private nursing home? There is a very good one not three miles from Borstead Hall.'

'Miss Bywater says not.'

'Yes, but has he been asked? I am sure if the idea is put to him, he will not wish to deprive his daughter of a little break from routine.'

'No,' he said firmly, anticipating her next demand.

She chuckled. 'Do not tell me you are not curious, because I will not believe it. You are usually out and about, pursuing your own affairs, but suddenly you decide to dine at home and join in family evenings and walks in the park, not to mention escorting Miss Bywater when Stephen should be doing it. I wonder at him allowing it.'

'Perhaps he is not as committed as he pretends.'

'Or perhaps he trusts you.'

'I wish he did. He might listen—' He stopped suddenly. He did not want to be quizzed on that subject.

She laughed. 'So, you have tried to warn him off, have you?'

'I simply suggested he should think carefully.'

'And what did he say?'

'Told me to mind my own business.'

She laughed. 'Oh, off with you. I am going to my bed.'

He kissed her and left her to the ministrations of Mathilde. He loved his great-grandmother devotedly and he wanted to please her. And there was Stephen to consider. Would having both Miss Bywater and her father down to Borstead make that any easier?

Mr Harecroft, knowing he would get no work out of anyone on the day of Queen Victoria's coronation and there were unlikely to be any customers, bowed to the inevitable and shut the shop, so that the staff could enjoy watching the procession and taking part in the festivities. The day began very early with guns firing in Hyde Park, bands playing and the rumble of every conceivable form of transport taking their passengers to their chosen viewing places. Soldiers were out early, marching to their positions. Every imaginable view-point along the route was soon taken; windows, balconies, walls and parapets, even some roofs were soon crammed with noisy people, high and low, all mixing together. The Harecroft household was up at dawn, the servants excitedly completing their chores in record time in order to rush off and view the procession.

Lady Harecroft, being a peeress in her own right, had been invited to the Abbey and would be conveyed there by coach at eight o'clock. Lord and Lady Harecroft had declined the invitation; he had too much to do to waste time sitting for hours in a draughty church, dressed up like a peacock, he had told his mother. Mr and Mrs John Harecroft, with Richard, Stephen and Diana, elected to walk to Piccadilly, where a friend of the family had invited them to view the procession from their balcony.

The crush in the streets was so great they began to doubt the wisdom of going on foot. They were forced out into the road with Mrs Harecroft clinging to her husband's arm, and Stephen and Richard following with Diana firmly wedged between them. Each, in his own way, was determined to look after her. She felt she ought to be flattered, but the doubts remained. There was solid dependable Stephen who wanted to marry her, and the strong, masterful, so-called black sheep, who did not. She was not being asked to choose one or the other, so why did she keep comparing them? Why did she shiver at Richard's touch? He had his hand under her right elbow and she could feel its strength and warmth. Stephen had tucked her other hand under his arm, possessively, protectively; she could feel it there, firm and comfortable but it did not ignite anything in her, no fire, no passion. She was ashamed of herself for her thoughts and determinedly shook them from her.

They reached the house on the corner of Piccadilly and St James's Street and were admitted by a footman and conducted up to the first-floor drawing room that overlooked the route of the procession where their host and his wife waited for them. They were offered refreshments and then went out on to the balcony where there were chairs placed for the ladies to sit while waiting for the procession to pass. They had a long wait, but there was so much to see as the crowds gathered, and so much to comment on, that the time passed quickly. The sound of cheering at a little after ten told them the procession was on its way. They stood up and craned their necks to catch a first glimpse of the state coach, accompanied by outriders of the Household Cavalry.

Pulled by eight matched greys, it drew gasps of admiration as it came into sight, gleaming gold in the sunshine. Every bit of its elaborate decoration symbolised something: there were four large Tritons at each corner, the roof was supported by eight palm trees, laden with symbols. The roof was topped by a crown held by three boys holding the Sceptre, the Sword of State and the Ensigns of Knighthood, and the panels were painted with allegorical pictures. Inside sat the diminutive and very young Queen wearing a robe of crimson velvet trimmed with ermine and gold lace and a circlet of gold and diamonds on her head. The nearer she came, the louder were the cheers and the more frantically the crowds waved their little Union flags.

The coach passed very slowly, but was soon lost to sight, with a deep sigh they turned back indoors to enjoy a light repast until the newly crowned Queen returned. The newspapers and the commemorative booklets that had been printed by the thousand told them what would be happening inside the Abbey and they talked a little about that as they ate. 'I hope it is not all too much for Grandmother,' Mr Harecroft said. 'She would go, though I advised her against it.'

'Great-Grandmama always does what she wants,' Richard said. 'She is always telling me she is old enough to do as she pleases.'

'Yes, I know. It is the same with this party of hers. I have tried to dissuade her but to no avail. I wish you would talk to her, Richard.'

'I have no influence with her, Father. Besides, I do not think it will hurt her. She is not going to do any of the preparations. It is all being organised by Great-Aunt Alicia. All she has to do is appear.'

'Aunt Alicia is no longer young herself.'

Richard laughed. 'Do not let her hear you say that. You will risk a set-down if you do.'

'What is she planning, do you know?'

'Perhaps she hopes to announce our engagement,' Stephen said, smiling at Diana and making her squirm.

'Unlikely, brother. I doubt even she would presume to anticipate Miss Bywater's decision.' His conversation with the captain the day before had been enlightening but it had not answered his doubts about her. Naturally the captain was full of praise for his daughter, saying he knew how hard she worked and how he had let her down and he would be glad to see her settled with a good husband, which indicated he was in favour of the match with Stephen, but he had learned nothing of the real Diana. Fortune-hunter or the genuine article? Would she come to the party or stick by her refusal? If she did not come, then he would consider the dowager's questions answered. She would remain simply Miss Diana

Bywater, clerk, and he would probably never see her again. He wondered why that mattered if it meant his brother was free of her.

The sound of guns being fired in the Park signalled the moment when the crown was placed on the Queen's head and they all trooped back on to the balcony, though it would be some time before the great golden coach came back into sight. The people in the street were cheering and shouting and waving banners with added frenzy. It was half past four when the coach returned and this time the Queen was wearing the great crown on her head, the Orb in her left hand and Sceptre in her right. She looked weighed down with it all, but smiled to left and right as the coach went by. 'She is the same age as me and she rules an empire,' Diana murmured. 'Do you think that now there is a woman on the throne it will make any difference to ordinary lives?'

'She will be guided by her ministers,' Mr Harecroft said. 'Men of wisdom and experience. I doubt much will change.'

'I heard she can be wilful,' their host told them. 'She has banished her mother from her bedchamber and insists on seeing her ministers alone.'

'Good for her,' Richard said. 'Perhaps she will be more inclined to address some of the evils we face and do something about poverty and lack of education for the poorer children.'

'I do not know what you expect her to do,' his father said. 'The poor are always with us. It is a fact of life. And education only makes the masses discontented.'

'I do not agree. If everyone was educated even to a minimal degree and had a vote, they could have a say in how the country is run.'

'That's Chartist rubbish. I do not want to hear any more of it, Richard.'

Diana wanted very much to join the debate, but decided to keep silent. Arguing on the side of the poor would not endear her to her employer, but she admired Richard for his stance. She had witnessed his concern when he had given the two urchins money for food. But charity was not enough. Richard had once said, 'There but for the Grace of God go I' and the same could be said of her. She had been desperate when she walked into Harecroft's Emporium that day a year ago and she would be eternally grateful to Mr Harecroft and more especially to the dowager Lady Harecroft for giving her employment. She dare not do anything to risk that. Would its continuance depend on the answer she gave Stephen? She had a strong feeling it would. She would have to think long and hard before making up her mind.

When the last of the carriages had passed, they thanked their host and made their way down into the street where the crowds showed no sign of dispersing. They were still noisily cheering. It was quite a struggle to make their way through them. Diana had her bonnet knocked off and someone trod on the hem of her skirt and tore it, but she dare not stop and try to do anything about it for fear of being bowled over. Somehow Stephen became separated from her and it was Richard who took her arm and guided her through the throng.

'Oh, dear,' she said. 'I did not know crowds could be so frightening. I feel as if I am going to be trampled underfoot.'

'No, I have firm hold of you,' he said, tucking her hand under his arm and holding it with his other hand. 'I will not let you go.'

She looked sharply at him, but his expression was bland and she decided his words had no hidden meaning.

* * *

They had only been at home a few minutes and hardly had time to wash and change for dinner, when Lady Harecroft returned. She was very tired and disinclined to talk and said she was going straight up to bed and would tell them all about it the next day.

'I knew it would be too much for you,' John said.

'At least I did not fall down like poor old Lord Rollo when he tottered up the steps to pay homage to the Queen. He is well named—he rolled all the way down them.'

'I hope he was not hurt,' Diana said.

'He said not. The Queen rose to help him herself, but he got up and made his obeisance without further mishap. Now, I am off to bed. Are you going to watch the fireworks?'

'I am not venturing out again tonight,' Mrs Harecroft said. 'I shall watch from the upstairs windows.'

'Neither am I,' Stephen added. He had been knocked over in the mêlée and had grazed his hands. 'I am sorry if you had hoped to go out, Diana.'

'No, I would not dream of it,' she said. 'I think the crush will be too great and we can see as much as we want to from the windows.'

'And tomorrow is a working day,' John added, proving that the business was never far from his mind, even in the midst of national rejoicing.

'And tomorrow evening there is the Coronation Ball at Almack's,' Mrs Harecroft put in. 'Stephen tells me you have consented to be one of our party, Miss Bywater.'

'If that is agreeable to you, ma'am.'

'Certainly it is. Do you have something suitable to wear?'

'Yes, thank you,' she said, wondering if, had she said no, they would have rushed round to find her something or decided not to take her. 'It is something of my mother's I have altered.'

Mrs Harecroft gave an almost imperceptible grunt, but did not comment.

They ate the cold collation Cook had prepared and afterwards they trooped upstairs to Mrs Harecroft's boudoir, whose windows faced towards Green Park where the fireworks were going to be set off. They could not see the park because of the buildings in the way, but they had a good view of the sky above it, which was lit by brilliant colours and patterns. It was two o'clock in the morning when they made their way to their beds.

It was hard to settle down to work the next day, but Diana was determined not to give Mr Harecroft any cause for dissatisfaction and so she put her head down and got on with it. In the middle of the day, she went down to join Stephen in the staff dining room to eat the packed lunch the Harecroft House cook prepared for them each day. 'I expect Lady Harecroft is on her way back to Borstead Hall by now,' she said, though it was Richard and not her ladyship she was thinking of.

'No, she over-tired herself yesterday and is going to rest today. Richard will take her tomorrow.'

'Oh.' Why did her spirits suddenly rise at the thought that he had not gone from her life? If she were sensible, she would wish him gone. He made her uncomfortable with his steady gaze as if he could read her thoughts. Oh, she hoped he could not; it would be too mortifying for him to know the effect he had on her. But perhaps he did know. Perhaps it was something he practised on every woman who came into his orbit. His character was so contradictory; he was compassionate, a champion of the poor, and yet cynical and disparaging, especially to his brother and quite often to her. He helped her, protected her, at the same time as he distrusted her. He did not want her to marry Stephen. He had not said so in as many words, but he had implied it. Was he simply trying to protect his brother—what did he suppose she was after? The Harecroft money? But if she were as coldly calculating as that, would she not have chosen to ensnare Richard, who was after all his father's heir? The idea of anyone being able to ensnare that gentleman was almost laughable. She gave up asking questions she could not answer, to pay attention to what Stephen was saying.

'Father has said we may leave work early to visit your papa, then we will have plenty of time to prepare for the ball. I am really looking forward to dancing with you. Do you know all the time we have known each other, we have not danced together?'

'The opportunity has not arisen.'

'We will make up for it tonight.'

She smiled, but did not answer, and a minute later they rose to go back to work.

At four o'clock he came to her room. 'Put that ledger away,' he said. 'Father has said we may go. I have had the gig brought round. It will have us at St Thomas's in no time.'

Her father was looking very much better: his mouth was lop-sided, but nothing like as bad as it had been and he was almost coherent. 'You are early,' he said, looking past her at Stephen. 'Good afternoon, young sir.'

'Good afternoon, Captain. We are early because we are going to a ball tonight.'

'Lucky you.'

'Yes, I believe I am.'

'Going to a party too, I hear.'

'Who told you that?' Diana demanded. She had been careful not to mention it to him. It might make him miserable if he thought he was depriving her of enjoyment.

'Captain Richard Harecroft.' He looked at Stephen. 'Your brother, I believe.'

'Yes.'

'Came to see me. Said he hoped I would allow it.'

'It was not his place to do so,' Stephen said, a statement with which Diana totally concurred. 'I was going to speak to you about it myself.'

'He saved you the bother.'

'I cannot think why he would,' Diana said. 'He knows, as everyone knows, I have declined to go.'

'Why?' her father asked. 'It will do you good to enjoy yourself for a change.'

'I cannot and will not leave you.'

'Do not worry about me. I have been offered a place in a private nursing home. Clean and wholesome, not like this place.'

'By Mr Richard?'

'He was the emissary for his great-grandmother. She sounds a redoubtable old lady.'

'She is,' Stephen said. 'And she is very fond of your daughter.'

'Papa, do you mean you have agreed?'

He looked at her and smiled his crooked smile. 'Wouldn't you? I have been promised attentive nurses, good food, fresh country air, walks in the garden and Toby for company.'

'Where? How will I be able to visit you?'

'I am told it is near Borstead Hall.'

Stephen laughed and turned to Diana. 'You must remind me to thank Great-Grandmama. You will have to come now.'

Diana managed to keep her temper long enough to kiss her father goodbye.

Diana returned to Harecroft House and, seeing Richard taking his ease in the drawing room reading a pamphlet, she exploded. 'You had to take it out of my hands, didn't you? You had to go behind my back and wriggle your way into my father's good books, making promises…'

He had risen when she entered and now put up his hand. 'Hold your horses! What have I done?'

'You went to see my father without me. You did not even say you were going. How dare you! How dare you assume I would agree to go to that silly party, simply because you had removed all obstacles.' She was furious, even more so when she noticed Stephen grinning as if he enjoyed seeing his brother put down.

'I have not removed all obstacles, Miss Bywater. The biggest one remains.'

She had opened her mouth to carry on in like vein, but stopped. 'What is that?'

'Why, you. No one can make you go if you do not want to. And it is all one to me what you do.'

'Then why did you do it?'

'Great-Grandmama asked me to.' He was having trouble keeping a straight face. Angry she was magnificent; her expressive blue-grey eyes flashed like polished steel. Either she was genuinely aggrieved or she was a consummate actress.

'And that makes it right, does it?'

'Naturally, it does. She is even more terrifying than you are when she is thwarted.'

'Oh, Diana, do calm down,' Stephen said. 'You want to come, you know you do, and if your father is agreeable, what harm has Richard done?'

'Are you blind or stupid? Papa has had his head filled with promises of goodness knows what and now nothing will satisfy him but he must go.'

'Can you blame him? That place he is in is the most unwholesome, disgusting place I have ever entered that does not call itself a pigsty.'

'But have you thought what will happen after the party is over? Where will he go? I cannot afford the luxury of a private nursing home.' And then she burst into tears.

The brothers looked at each other in consternation. 'Diana, why are you crying? It is nothing to weep over,' Stephen said, raising his hand to touch her arm.

She shrugged him off. 'Let me alone.' And with that she ran from the room.

'Are you going after her?' Richard asked. His first reaction on seeing her tears was to rush to her and take her in his arms to comfort her, if Stephen had not been there, he might very well have done so, which would have been a grave mistake.

'Do you think I should?'

'It is up to you.'

'I think I will leave her to compose herself. When she is calm, I will talk to her. What I cannot understand is why Great-Grandmama asked you to see the old man.'

'I suppose she thought you were too busy. You had better ask her.'

'Maybe I will. Are we eating before we go to Almack's? The food there is nothing to boast about and is served so late, I shall faint from hunger before we get to it.'

'Oh, we cannot have you fainting, poor Miss Bywater has had enough to contend with today without standing over your inert body. I believe we are to have dinner at six, which will give everyone ample time to dress afterwards.'

Diana, who had gone to her room and flung herself on the bed, could not bring herself to go down to dinner. She was so angry she was sure she would not be able to keep her temper and her eyes were so red they would all know she had been crying. How could she have let herself down so badly, letting them see her in tears? She looked at the lovely gown, hanging on the wardrobe door. She had spent hours altering it and was very pleased with the result. Now she would not wear it. It wasn't fair, it really was not.

There was a light tap at the door and before she could tidy herself or splash her face, the door opened and Lady Hare-croft entered. 'Oh, my dear child, what is the matter?'

Diana straightened her back and lifted her chin. 'My lady, you may rule your family, but I am not one of them and I do not think it was fair of Mr Richard to go behind my back to my father. He might have known that Papa would be tempted by the offer of good food and country air. It was not well done, not well done at all.'

The old lady smiled a little; this young woman was not overawed and spoke her mind. She admired her for it, though it was no more than she expected. She sat beside her and took her hand. 'Do not be angry with Richard, my dear. I asked him to go.'

'So that you could manipulate me into going to your party. I do not know why it is so important that I should be there. I have not accepted Mr Stephen's offer of marriage. I am not even sure he meant it.'

'Why do you say that?'

'Oh, I don't know. It was the way he said it, I suppose. He talked about my job and how we could work together, implying my job depended on my saying yes.' And tears began to well up again. Angrily she scrubbed at them with a sodden handkerchief. 'And now I have no home, thanks to him.'

'He was perhaps a little clumsy.' The old lady offered her a clean handkerchief from her own pocket. 'But I am sure he was sincere. And I am sure something can be done to find respectable accommodation for you and your father when he has recovered.' She watched as Diana pulled herself together. 'Now, we are not going to talk about your job or whether you are going to accept Stephen or not. I am going to tell you why I asked Richard to speak to your papa.'

'Why did you?'

'I am a very old lady and I have taken it into my head to have a birthday party.' She held up her hand as Diana opened her mouth to speak. 'My daughter, Alicia, has said she will arrange it, but I am afraid it will be too much for her without assistance and it came to my mind that you could be a great help to her. My grandson tells me you are very practical and good at organising and so I want you to come down to Borstead Hall for the week before the party.'

'A week! But what about my work at Harecroft's?'

'John is prepared to let you go.'

'That does not excuse going to my father behind my back. I had decided not to go and so I told him nothing of the party.'

'I guessed that was the case and I thought any father who loved his daughter would not want her to make such a sacrifice for him. And I was right. He wants you to go.' She patted Diana's hand. 'Do not be angry with me. I need you. Please say you will come.'

Diana thought about her father in that poky room in the hospital with nothing but four dingy walls to look at and only a busy doctor and a nurse to talk to until she arrived and then her visits did not last long. And he missed Toby and Toby missed him. Country air, if only for a week, would help him to get better. She gave the old lady a watery smile. 'Very well, but I come as an employee to help make your party a success.'

The old lady clapped her hands like a child being given a

treat. 'Oh, that is wonderful. Now, no more moping. I shall have a tray of something sent up to you and then Mathilde will come to help you dress for the ball. Go and enjoy yourself.'

Chapter Five

By the time Mathilde had bathed her eyes with lavender water, helped her to wash and dress and done wonderful things with her hair, Diana was feeling more cheerful and was looking forward to the ball. There was nothing she could do about lodgings or her job until she returned from Borstead Hall and she had to admit that country air would help her father to recover and perhaps later he might even be able to find some light work for himself. She should be grateful, not angry. All the same, she did not intend to forgive Richard and Stephen too readily.

She clasped her mother's necklace at her throat and, picking up her fan and reticule, made her way downstairs. She was halfway down when she realised Richard was at the foot of the stairs looking up at her. His expression was one of open admiration as he bowed to her.

'The chrysalis has turned into the most dazzling butterfly,' he said, unable to take his eyes off her. He had known she was beautiful, but in that soft green gown with its delicate embroidering, she was truly lovely and a match for any society beauty.

'If you think flattery is going to turn me up sweet, you are mistaken, sir,' she said. 'I am still displeased with you.'

She reached the ground floor and he took her gloved hand and raised the back of it to his lips. 'I am truly penitent.' The trouble was that the laughter in his eyes belied his words.

'Where is Stephen?' she asked to remind herself, and him too, who was really her escort.

'Not down yet. He always takes longer to dress than I do. Allow me to escort you into the drawing room.' He offered his arm, but she pointedly ignored it and walked a little apart from him. It was easier to maintain her stance if she did not touch him, not even to lay her fingers on his sleeve. The sleeve belonged to a black grosgrain dinner suit, which fitted him so well she knew it must have been fashioned by one of the capital's premier tailors. With it he wore a white brocade waistcoat and a white cravat carefully, but not flamboyantly, tied. His hair, almost the same colour as her own, was carefully brushed and curled about his ears and into his neck. She had an almost overwhelming urge to touch it and clenched her fists firmly by her side lest she do it without thinking.

They did not speak as they entered the drawing room. No one was there. She was standing beside him near the hearth when Stephen joined them. He was dressed almost identically to his brother, the only difference being that he wore a purple cravat and had slicked down his hair instead of letting it curl. He stopped when he saw Diana. 'My dear, you look beautiful in that dress. It is most becoming. Do you not agree, Richard?'

'Indeed I do. Quite a transformation. You are a lucky dog, Stephen. That is, if you can persuade her to forgive you, because she has certainly not forgiven me.'

'Forgive me for what?'

'Stop it, both of you,' she said. 'I do not like conversations being carried on about me as if I were not in the room.' She paused to gather herself. 'Nor do I like them going on behind my back either.'

'Oh, I see,' Stephen said. 'It is Richard you are angry with.'

'And you,' she said. 'Now let us say no more about it or we shall be out of sorts with each other the whole way through the ball.'

Stephen smiled. 'Of course. I am really looking forward to this evening, so we will not mar it by quarrelling.'

Mr and Mrs Harecroft came into the room and added their compliments on Diana's appearance before they made their way out to the carriage.

The Almack's ballroom had been decorated with bunting and Union flags and its many pillars swathed in greenery and flowers. A large picture of the Queen draped in red velvet stood on an easel on the platform next to the musicians. The room was crowded and noisy and the Harecrofts were soon greeting friends and acquaintances and introducing Diana as a friend of the family. Diana noticed she was attracting some strange looks and wondered why. Could it be her dress? Was it too splendid for someone in her position? She tried to hide herself behind Mrs Harecroft, but Stephen winkled her out.

'Dance with me, Diana,' he said, holding out his hand to her.

She allowed him to take her onto the floor. He danced well, if a little stiffly, but she had made up her mind to enjoy herself and so she relaxed and answered him cheerfully when he repeated how well she looked and he had been quite right in saying he would be proud to have her on his arm as his wife. 'Do not assume I am going to accept you,' she said, making herself sound light and teasing. 'You must suffer a little longer.'

'But you have forgiven me for taking you away from Mrs Beales?'

'Not altogether. When I have found somewhere else to live, I might.'

'But, Diana…'

'We will not talk about it tonight.'

'Very well.' He stopped speaking as they executed some steps that took them away from each other. When they met again, he said, 'Great-Grandmama has said you have agreed to go to Borstead Hall for the whole week before the party.'

'Yes. I am going to help your great-aunt with the arrangements.'

He grinned. 'I knew you would agree in the end.'

'I was not given much choice.'

'Oh, dear, I thought we were not going to talk about that. You are breaking your own rules.'

'I will not say another word on the subject.'

'I shall miss you at work.'

'Are you not going down too?'

'No, I cannot leave the business for a whole week. I shall come down with my father on the Friday evening before the party.'

'Oh, I see.'

They danced on in silence while she contemplated the prospect of being at Borstead Hall without him.

'They look very well together, do they not?' Mrs Harecroft said to her husband. They were sitting side by side where they could survey the dance floor. Richard was standing behind her chair.

'Yes, they do,' John said. 'I hope this visit to Borstead Hall will do the trick.'

'What trick?' Richard asked. Though he spoke to his mother, he did not take his eyes off the couple as they danced, apparently in animated conversation.

'Why, the engagement, of course,' his father said. 'It is time Stephen settled down with a wife and Miss Bywater will undoubtedly be an asset. I thought so before, when she proved she had a good grasp of the business, but tonight she has shown that she can display well too. Out of her working garb she is lovely. Everyone will envy him.'

'But you know so little about her,' Richard said.

'I think I know enough. Besides, a week at Borstead will soon tell us whether she will fit into the family.'

'And if she does not?'

'Then, of course, we shall have to dispense with her services. And I should be sorry to have to do that.'

'It is time you settled down too, Richard,' his mother put in, while he digested his father's words. 'You are your father's heir and ought to make a good marriage, someone with some lineage. I could introduce you to one or two suitable young ladies…'

'No, thank you, Mama. When the time comes, I shall choose my own wife.'

'Before you do, you must rid yourself of your disreputable friends,' she added. 'They give quite the wrong impression. Any well-bred young lady seeing them will undoubtedly be put off.'

'Not if she loves me.'

'Pah!' his father said, to which his son had no answer.

The dance concluded and Stephen and Diana rejoined them. Diana had a little more colour in her cheeks than she had of late, and her eyes sparkled. Richard found himself admiring her all over again. At first it had been her courage in adversity, her pride in her job and her loyalty to her father that had attracted him, but tonight it was her beauty, her slim figure, her animation, the graceful way she moved. Could someone so lovely hide a cunning mind? And if she was as straightforward as she seemed and there was no guile in her, she was in for a dreadful shock.

He smiled and held out his hand to her as the musicians began to play a waltz. 'My turn, Miss Bywater.'

She took his hand and he led her on to the floor. She was immediately transported into another world, a world where there was no sickness, no poverty, no homelessness, no anger. It was a world of music and dreams, sunshine and sweet-smelling flowers. There were no yesterdays, no tomorrows, only the present and that was magical. There was no need for words. Words would spoil it, because words between her and Mr Richard Harecroft were nearly always either acrimonious or mocking and she did not want to break the spell. It was only when the dance ended and she was once again sitting beside Mrs Harecroft that she realised how foolish she was being. There was nothing between her and Richard and never could be. It was time to be sensible. She gave Stephen one of her most winning smiles as he asked for the next dance.

After that she danced with other young gentlemen to whom she had been introduced, and once with Mr John Harecroft, who took the opportunity to tell her how well she looked and how he was happy for her to go to Borstead Hall for a week to help his Aunt Alicia with the party.

'I have agreed to go on that understanding,' she said. 'I am an employee.'

'Of course. No doubt my aunt will keep you busy, but a word of advice. Avoid the dower house.'

'Why?'

'My son's friends are a strange crowd, hanging on to his coat tails like leeches. I am hopeful they will tire of that and leave him in peace, but until they do, we give the dower house a wide berth.'

'Lady Harecroft seems not to mind.'

'My grandmother is very old, Miss Bywater and her judgement is sometimes at fault, especially where Richard is concerned. Now, I think I have said enough.'

He had said enough to whet her curiosity, not enough to

convince her of anything except that he did not approve of his elder son. It seemed such a pity. Was it that which had made Richard such a strange mixture of caring and uncaring?

They went into supper and afterwards Diana danced again with Stephen and then again with Richard. She was tempted to ask him what his father had meant about the dower house, but decided it would only widen the rift between father and son and desisted.

Long before the ball ended in the early hours of the morning, she was exhausted. It was not only the dancing, but the worry over her father, the lack of sleep, and the constant pressure being put on her by the Harecroft family, that contributed to it.

'You poor thing,' Richard murmured as they danced a minuet. Stephen was dancing with the daughter of one of his mother's friends. 'You are done in, aren't you?'

'Yes, it has been a long day.'

'You are not going to work tomorrow, are you?'

'Of course. It is Saturday, but I leave off at two.'

'And then you will hurry to St Thomas's.'

'Yes.'

'I would take you, but my great-grandmother wants me to take her back to Borstead Hall tomorrow.'

'So Stephen said.'

'I shall see you when you come down.'

'Perhaps. I expect to be kept busy, and if you live at the dower house…'

He laughed. 'I have no doubt you have been told about my disreputable friends.'

'Are they disreputable?'

'Certainly not. They are simply trying to make an honest living.'

'As everyone must.'

'True. Each in his own way. My friends are artists.'

'And you write.'

'I try, but I cannot say I earn a living at it. I do have money of my own. One day, perhaps, I will make my mark.'

'You encourage each other perhaps?'

'Yes, we do.'

'Is that why you live at the dower house, because they encourage you to be yourself?'

'You may be right,' he said, noting again how perceptive she was. He needed to be careful what he said; she seemed able to divine his meaning from a very few words. 'But I am not there all the time. Great-Grandmama likes me to dine with the family, so I expect to see you then.'

'I am not sure I shall be dining with the family.'

'Of course you will. Where else would you dine? I shall look forward to it.' He surprised himself because he found he meant it. And therein lay danger. Perhaps a week away from her might settle him, might curb his temptation to tell her everything when he had promised Stephen he would not. It was difficult being the custodian of other people's secrets. He had plenty to keep him occupied. There was his campaign over poverty and child labour, which he shared with Edwin Chadwick and Ashley Cooper, as well as arranging a venue to exhibit his boarders' works of art and trying to find a publisher for his book, not to mention his hopes of finding a seat in the House of Commons. So far nothing had come his way.

No one in the family knew what he was doing and he remained, as far as they were concerned, the black sheep, someone who would not toe the line, someone who entertained people of whom his parents disapproved, the outcast. He had not minded that, had taken a certain perverse pride in letting them think the worst of him, while Stephen enjoyed their favours and could, in their eyes, do no wrong. But matters were changing and Stephen must be made to see where his best interests lay. He had said as much to him and been told to mind his own business. But someone was going to be hurt. And badly.

'I have never known you so silent,' Diana said. 'What are you thinking of?'

He could not tell her. Instead he said, 'About how much I am enjoying dancing with this newly emerged butterfly.'

'Was I such an ugly caterpillar before?'

'No, far from it, but a butterfly is a delicate creature; one must not hold it too tightly for fear of damaging it. One must let it fly free. Are you a butterfly, Miss Bywater, flitting from flower to flower, sipping the nectar and moving on? Or are you constant?'

She smiled. 'You are talking in riddles.'

'That's better,' he said, 'you know, you are even more beautiful when you smile.'

'Am I?' She had never thought of herself as beautiful and the compliment took her by surprise.

'Yes. Surely Stephen has told you that over and over again.'

'I cannot say that he has.'

'Then he is an insensitive oaf.'

'No, he is not, it's just that he is not like you…' Her voice faltered and faded away. She should not be talking about Stephen to him; it sounded disloyal and comparisons were unfair.

If his questions had been meant to discover more about her, whether she loved Stephen enough to stay with him for better or worse, they achieved nothing. She was clever enough not to be drawn into an argument.

'No,' he said. 'But we are alike in one thing—we can appreciate a beautiful woman when we see one.'

There was no answer to that and they finished the dance in silence and he returned her to his mother.

Soon after that, the evening was brought to an end and they returned to Harecroft House. All the way home Diana wondered what he had meant about the butterfly flitting and being constant. Did he mean she was given to whims and fancies and was unreliable? Did he think that she would not be a faithful wife to Stephen if she married him? But what grounds had he for thinking that? She was still musing on it when she bade them all goodnight and went to her room. By the time she was ready for bed, she had decided to have it out with him and demand to know what he meant.

She was not afforded the opportunity. He did not appear before she and Stephen left for work the next morning and when they returned in the afternoon he and his great-grand-mother had gone.

Her life fell back into routine of work, visiting her father and returning to Harecroft House to sleep. Without the old lady and Richard, some of the life seemed to have gone out of the place; the sun seemed not to reach the corners of the rooms and Mrs Harecroft rarely smiled. She found herself be-ginning to look forward to going to Borstead Hall and began altering more of her mother's dresses. Mr Harecroft, guessing she might need to do some shopping, had given her an advance on her wages that enabled her to buy two gowns in a small shop in a side street—one a forest green jaconet and the other a printed cotton in yellow-and-white stripes—which together with the dresses of her mother's she had altered would be sufficient for her needs, considering she was going down there to work, not to enjoy herself, and most of the time she would be in her grey working dresses.

Her father was to be conveyed to Borstead Nursing Home in an ambulance accompanied by a nurse. Diana had wondered if she might go with him, but Mr Harecroft said Lady Harecroft would send her own carriage to fetch her. 'The ambulance will travel too slowly,' he had said. 'You will go more quickly by chaise on Saturday afternoon and that way will not miss a morning's work. It is all arranged, you do not have to do anything except pack your belongings.' He had paused and smiled. 'And her ladyship bade me to tell you to be sure to take that lovely green gown.'

And so the two weeks passed and she found herself on the Friday evening visiting her father in St Thomas's for the last time. He had made great strides, though he was still weak, he could, with a little help, stand out of bed and take a few steps using a walking stick. And his speech had improved immeasurably. She took him some toiletries, a new nightshirt, a dressing gown and a selection of his day clothes in case he felt up to dressing.

'No escort today?' he queried.

'No. Are you sure you want to go?'

'Of course I am sure. It will do us both good. And you will meet your future family.'

'Papa, I have not accepted Stephen yet.'

'Family is important,' he went on as if she had not spoken. 'Marry that young man and you will have a ready-made family, which I never did. Nor did your mama. We only ever had each other and you, when you came along. Our world consisted of three people. I thought that was enough, but I was wrong. Better to have a family to rally round in times of trouble. If we had had a bigger family, we might not have sunk so low and you might not have been burdened with caring for me.'

'I do not begrudge what I do, Papa. It is little enough in all conscience.'

'So you say, but it has been on my mind lately that if I died, you would have no one, no one at all.'

'That is not going to happen for a long time yet,' she said briskly. 'You are becoming stronger every day. Now I must go. The next time I see you will be in Borstead.'

She kissed him and went back to Harecroft House to start packing her own things. In spite of her determination to treat it as part of her work, she began to look forward with pleasure to a week away from the capital, especially knowing her father was being looked after.

At dinner that night, Stephen was full of how she would love Borstead Hall and the things they might do together after he had joined her the following weekend. Mr Harecroft talked about the business and asked her to be sure not to allow Lady Harecroft to overtire herself, though how she could make the old lady stop doing whatever it was she wanted to do, she did not know. Mrs Harecroft found it necessary to speak to her of etiquette and what she should and should not wear and how to greet the guests when they arrived which she did not need telling. By the time she went to bed, her head was reeling.

Returning from work with Mr Harecroft and Stephen the following afternoon, she was surprised to find Richard had come with her ladyship's carriage. 'Come to escort you,' he said. 'Can't have you going all that way alone.'

'That is very kind of you, but I could have managed.'

'Oh, I do not doubt it, but I had an errand I wanted to do in town, so it fitted in very well. If you are ready, we can set out after luncheon. The journey takes about three hours, so we should arrive in time for dinner.'

If she had been considered of equal rank she would have

had a maid to accompany her, but as she was a lowly employee, no one seemed to bother that she would be unchaperoned. She thanked him again, unsure whether the prospect of spending several hours in his company was something to look forward to with pleasure or trepidation.

'The weather is fine and we should make good time,' Richard remarked, as they set off just after three o'clock. 'Are you a good traveller? Oh, but of course you are, you have travelled the world.'

'I would not go so far as to say that, Mr Harecroft. I have been to India and the East Indies and once to the West Indies when Papa's ships were stationed at foreign ports. He did not like to leave Mama and me behind. He and Mama were devoted to each other, which was why my mother's death hit him so hard. As did the loss of his arm. I do not know if the navy would have forced him to retire or not—after all, Nelson managed to command a fleet with only one arm—but Mama was afraid it would weaken him and in a rough sea he might be thrown about and be unable to hold on and might even be swept overboard, so he gave in to her pleading and left the service.'

'And could not settle.'

'No, and he could not find work for his particular skills. With his disability, it was doubly difficult and I am afraid he lost heart, especially when Mama died.'

'It is understandable, but perhaps matters will improve from now on.'

'If I accept Stephen, you mean.'

'Not necessarily. You would be unwise to allow that to influence your decision.'

'My father's welfare is very important to me.'

'Naturally it is, but I am sure he would not expect you to make such a sacrifice if it was not something you wanted yourself.'

'Why would it be a sacrifice? And what makes you think I do not want it?'

'You told me you had doubts.'

'Surely that is natural? It is a big step to take.'

'My point exactly, Miss Bywater.'

'You do not think I should marry Stephen, do you?'

'I never said that.'

'No, but I feel it. You think I am after a home for myself and my father and the life of idleness that marrying into the Harecroft family will give me.'

'Not at all,' he said promptly, though it was exactly what he had been thinking. 'But I wonder if you know what you would be taking on.'

'What would I be taking on?'

He shrugged. 'The Harecrofts are not an easy family to live with,' he answered warily. 'My father is only interested in the business and Stephen is going a long way to match him, except—' He stopped suddenly, realising he was straying into dangerous waters.

'Except what?'

He laughed. 'Don't take any notice of me, Miss Bywater. It is only sour grapes on my part.'

And because he said it himself, she was suddenly sure it was nothing of the kind. What was he warning her against? One thing she determined on—she would make no decisions until she knew. The trouble was that everyone was making assumptions, from Lady Harecroft and Mr John Harecroft, to Stephen and even Richard himself. She could not help thinking of him as Richard now and must guard her tongue in case it slipped out.

'Are you perhaps a little jealous of your brother, Mr Harecroft?'

'Jealous? In what way jealous?'

'Because your father seems to favour him.'

'I do not mind that, Miss Bywater, it has been the same all my life. I have come to accept that, if I do not conform, then I must pay the price for my stubbornness.'

'Is it entirely because you did not want to work in the business?'

He knew she was probing, but strangely he did not mind. 'Oh, it started long before that. Even as a boy I was different. I was always playing in the dirt. I associated with the village boys, ran wild in the countryside and came home scratched, bruised and dirty. I was the despair of our governess.'

'Surely all small boys do that?'

'Not Stephen, he was far too particular. Even as a small child, he used to like to go to work with our father and right from the start was interested in the business. I loathed it. I wanted to be out in the fields and the woods with my dog. That was before my great-grandfather died and we, as a family, still lived at Borstead Hall. My grandfather, who was running Harecroft's business at the time, lived at the London house. Father used to live with him during the week and come home to Borstead Hall at weekends.'

'That's why Toby has taken to you so well,' she said. 'He knows a kindred spirit.' The dog, stretched on the opposite seat, cocked an ear at the sound of his name, but, perceiving all was well, put his head down and shut his eyes again. 'What was he called? Was it a he?'

'Yes. I called him Pal. He was my pal.'

She sensed there was more to be told. 'What happened to him?'

'Unfortunately he had to be put down for worrying sheep.'

'That must have been a sad day for you.'

'Yes.' He stopped suddenly. Even after so many years, thinking of that dog made him bitterly angry all over again.

He had been seven years old when a local farmer had come to his father to complain the dog had been worrying sheep and demanded he be put down. Richard had hotly denied the dog had been anywhere near the sheep, but his father would not listen and, without asking for any sort of proof for the accusation, had ordered Pal to be shot. Richard had stormed and yelled and physically tried to prevent the gamekeeper from firing his shotgun and had to be restrained. As soon as he was freed, he had run and wrapped his arms about his bloodied pet until he was prised away and sent to his room where he wept for hours. His mother dare not defy his father and go to him, so it was his great-grandmother who comforted him. When he eventually faced his father again, he told him venomously that he would never forgive him for it.

'It is a fact of life that when dogs worry sheep, they are shot,' his father had told him coldly. 'The sooner you learn that the better. You are too soft for you own good. Perhaps at school you will learn to harden your heart.' And so to boarding school he was sent, leaving his brother to continue enjoying his father's favours. It was at school, a place he hated fervently for its cruelty, that he learned to hide his feelings under a veneer of urbanity. He had been doing it so long now, it had become a habit, part of the man he had become.

He had been silent so long Diana turned to glance at him. He seemed to be looking at her, but she soon realised he was not with her in spirit at all—his eyes had a faraway look and there was something disturbing in their blue depths. She wondered whether to speak or to remain silent when they drew up for their first change of horses and he left the coach to supervise the operation.

'Tell me about Borstead Hall,' she said when he returned and they were on their way again. 'Is it very big?'

'It is a fair size,' he said, mentally picturing the mansion. 'It was built on the foundations of an old priory and some of the stone was used in its early construction, though so much has been added to it since then, it is hard to find them. There are four large reception rooms, one of them big enough for a ballroom, a library and study, a smaller sitting room, as well as the usual offices, kitchens, dairy, butler's pantry, cellars. I don't know how many bedrooms there are, upwards of a dozen, I should think, not counting the servant's quarters in the attic. Oh, and two bathrooms.'

'Bathrooms!'

'Yes, my grandfather had them installed after he inherited the title from my great-grandfather. Besides the house, which is surrounded by its own gardens and park, there are outbuildings, a coach house and domestic stables and a ruined chapel where the nuns once worshipped. The stables where my grandfather breeds race horses are a little way from the main house and they are of more recent construction.'

'And the countryside?'

'Farmland and heath, most of it. Borstead is the nearest village. It is ten miles from Ascot. It has the usual amenities: a church, a few shops, a blacksmith, a saddler and two inns. And the Borstead stud, of course. When you have settled in and met the family, I shall be pleased to show you round.'

'Thank you. If I am not kept too busy, I should like that.'

'Too busy! I doubt that very much. Great-Aunt Alicia is very capable.'

'Then why am I being asked to help?' she asked. 'Lady Harecroft said I was needed.'

'Oh, then you must be and I am mistaken.' His reply was so swift she began to wonder.

'Who else will be at the party?'

'My grandparents and my parents, of course, Uncle Henry

and his son and daughter, the local doctor, family lawyer, various family friends. I am only guessing, of course, the old lady is keeping the arrangements close to her chest. I imagine you will soon know more about them than I will.'

'I am very nervous.'

'Why? There is nothing to be nervous about. You could quell every one of us with a look, if you chose.'

'Now you are being silly.'

He looked sharply at her, unused to being declared silly, but decided not to comment and they rode in silence until they stopped again to change the horses. Having been arranged in advance, the new ones were ready for them and they were soon on their way again. London had been left a long way behind and they were in rolling countryside, where cereal crops were ripening in the fields and cows inhabited the meadows. The hedgerows were scattered with elder flowers, brambles, not yet in fruit, and wild roses, interspersed with honeysuckle. Their conversation became desultory. She leaned back against the padded back of the seat and shut her eyes. So much had happened in the last two or three weeks, what with the coronation and the ball and visits to her father on top of living in strange surroundings, that she was worn out with it all. And there was more to come…

The next thing she knew she was being shaken gently awake. 'Miss Bywater, time for some refreshment.'

She sat up with a start and tried to straighten her hat. The swaying movement of the coach had stopped. 'Where are we?'

'A little over halfway. Shall we leave the coach and go into the inn for some refreshment? They are expecting us.'

With his hand under her elbow, he escorted her into the inn where they were served tea and bread and butter and cake. 'To tide us over until supper time,' he said.

'There is enough here for a regiment.'

'Not quite. What we do not eat, I am sure Toby will.'

'You seem to have thought of everything,' she said, seating herself next to the teapot. 'Are you always so well organised?'

'Put it down to my time in the army,' he said. 'Supply lines are often very long and without careful organisation the troops would go hungry. Your father would understand that. A ship must be provisioned.'

'Yes, I know.' She poured tea for them both. 'I often helped check the supplies coming on board. It was one of the ways my father educated me. I checked their use so that we knew how long they lasted and when we must think of provisioning again.'

'That is why you understand Harecroft's so well.'

'Oh, I have much yet to learn.'

'But you are determined to learn it for my brother's sake, is that not so?'

'And for my own. I take a pride in my work.'

'Well said, Miss Bywater.'

'Did you never try to work alongside your father at Harecroft's?'

'Oh, yes, I tried. When I left school, I spent two years learning the ropes, but I hated every minute.'

'Why? Did you think being in trade was too demeaning for a gentleman?'

'Not at all,' he said sharply. 'Each to his own bent. The Harecrofts have always been divided on the issue. Those who favour the business are called "Trading Harecrofts" and they enjoy the cut and thrust of buying and selling. The others occupy themselves in other ways, as I wanted to do.'

'What did your father say when you said you wanted to leave?'

'In a way I think he was relieved. My approach to business was unconventional.'

'How so?'

'I sometimes allowed discounts on goods without consulting him and that did not please him.'

'I should think not. It is not the way to run a successful business.'

'No, it is all about profit.' He sounded disapproving.

'Without it, you would not have had the advantages you have had: a good home, good food, an education.'

'Oh dear, you sound just like my father.'

She smiled. 'I am sorry, I have no right to lecture you. But why did you decide to give discounts?'

'I only did it if I thought it was deserved. The last time was when a friend came in to buy mourning for his wife, who had just lost her mother. He wanted her to be suitably attired and I knew he could not afford it, so I let him have a length of the best black silk at cost. It did not go down well with my father.' It was said lightly, but she knew him well enough by now to realise the quarrel over it had been a bitter one.

'I do not think you would make a good businessman, Mr Harecroft.'

'No,' he admitted. 'Fortunately my brother was leaving school at that time and was able to step into my shoes. I could not expect my father to support me in idleness and so I joined the army.'

'But you did not stay in the army. Did you not like the life?'

'I liked it well enough. I liked the comradeship, the changing scene, the feeling I was doing something useful, but I never meant it to be my life's work, and when I received a legacy from my maternal grandmother, I bought my way out.'

'So, what is your life's work?'

'Now, there's a question,' he said. 'I am not sure I know

the answer, except that I should like to help the underdog, those too poor to help themselves, like those two urchins who lived near you in Southwark.'

'But there are hundreds and thousands like them. You cannot help them all.'

'I can try to influence those who can.'

'Politics?'

'Why not? Have you anything against politicians?'

'Nothing at all, if they are working for the common good. Do you mean to stand for Parliament?'

'If I can find a seat.'

'Your father can surely have nothing against that?'

'I have not told him. After all, nothing might come of it and I fear we would be on opposing sides.' He paused, embarrassed by the turn the conversation was taking. 'Do you not think we could dispense with the formal address and call each other by our given names?'

'I am an employee, Mr Bywater, you may call me what you will, but it would not be fitting for me to address you by your Christian name.'

He had set out intending to find out more about her, to try to trip her up, make her reveal her true self; instead, she had turned the tables on him and he had told her things he had never told anyone else. He must guard against falling for her charm. 'The trouble is that I cannot think of you in those terms,' he said. 'And if you accept my brother…'

'You do not want me to, do you?'

He shrugged.

'Whether I do or not will not affect my position while I am at Borstead Hall. I am only going for a week, after all.'

'And then you intend to return to London and look for new lodgings.'

'I must.'

He did not answer that. They finished their meal and returned to the coach and were soon on their way again. They continued to talk about her travels and his time in the army and gradually she felt the tension easing from her shoulders. The journey had enabled her to understand him better and why there was a clash of wills with his father, but what he had told her certainly did not justify him being called a black sheep. In her experience Mr John Harecroft was not an unjust man, so there must be something else.

At Ascot they made a final stop for the Harecrofts' own horses, left there on the outward journey that morning, to be harnessed to the carriage for the last leg.

It was early evening when they turned into the gates of Borstead Hall. Diana sat forward as the house came into view at the end of the carriage drive. It stood on a slight hill, surrounded by immaculate gardens and an extensive park. Its stone façade seemed to reflect the warmth of the sun and its rows of windows gleamed like dozens of mirrors. One side was covered in purple wisteria in full bloom. They drew up at a huge oak door, which was certainly older than the rest of the house. Almost before the carriage stopped, Richard was out and handing her down. 'Here we are at last.'

She was standing on the gravel feeling rather lost, when the door was thrown open by a plump, younger version of Lady Harecroft. 'Here is Great Aunt Alicia to greet us,' he said.

Miss Harecroft was in her late forties, not much older than her nephew, John Harecroft. She had a pale complexion, clear blue eyes and light brown hair just beginning to go grey, though it hinted at the red-gold of the rest of the Harecrofts. Smiling, she came down the steps to greet them. 'Aunt, this is Miss Bywater,' Richard said and to Diana, 'My Great-Aunt Alicia.'

'Not so much of the great,' she said, teasing him. 'You are very welcome, Miss Bywater. I have heard so much about you, I feel I know you already. May I call you Diana?'

'Please do.'

'Come along in. Richard will arrange for someone to fetch in the baggage.' She stooped to make a fuss of Toby, who had jumped down from the carriage and was wagging his tail ecstatically. 'Who is this?'

'Toby,' Diana said. 'I hope you do not mind me bringing him. He is my father's dog.'

'Not at all. Richard will see that he is looked after. I'll show you to your room. You are just in time for supper. That is, if you are not too tired after your journey.'

'Miss Bywater thinks because she is an employee she will be eating with the servants,' Richard put in.

'Good gracious, no, you are a guest, Diana. You will dine with the family. Richard, I hope you will stay.'

'Wild horses would not keep me away.' He was smiling at Diana as he spoke and she realised he had reverted to his teasing mockery and she would be wise to forget his confidences in the carriage coming down. That had been another, more vulnerable side to the man, which he would not like mentioned again.

He ushered Toby back into the carriage, climbed in himself and it was taken round the side of the house and out of sight.

'Now,' Alicia said, leading the way. 'Let us go straight up to your room. There will be time enough for a tour of the house tomorrow.'

Diana found herself in a wide hall, furnished with small tables on which stood vases of flowers, a long case clock and half a dozen velvet-padded chairs. To the right were several doors and to the left a curving staircase whose walls were lined with paintings. They crossed the hall and went up the stairs, their footsteps silent on the thick red carpet, and along the corridor. Alicia opened the door of a bedroom and ushered Diana in. 'I hope you will be comfortable here. I will have hot water sent up to you. If there is anything else you need, just ring the bell.'

Diana looked about her. The room was on the corner of the house which was covered in the ancient wisteria. It had windows on two sides, one of which looked out over the front drive. From the other Diana glimpsed a terrace and a lawn with colourful flower beds and beyond it the park with walks and trees. She noticed two men walking in the park. 'Richard's friends,' Alicia said, following her gaze. 'They live in the dower house on the other side of the grounds.'

So these were the so-called disreputable friends! They looked perfectly normal to Diana.

'My mother should be living there,' her guide went on. 'But my brother, Lord Harecroft, will not let her live there with only servants for company.' She chuckled suddenly, a sound that reminded Diana of Richard. 'He thinks she would get into mischief.'

Diana turned back from the window. 'Do you know if my father has arrived?'

'Oh, how remiss of me. You must be concerned about him. Yes, a message arrived about an hour ago that he had arrived and been made comfortable. I am told he is very tired, but otherwise well. You will no doubt want to see him as soon as possible but I should leave him to sleep tonight. Now, I will leave you to wash and change. Come down to the drawing room when you are ready.'

After she had left, Diana sank on to the bed with a head that was reeling with the sights and sounds she had experienced, and her whole body felt as if she was still swaying in the coach. For two pins she would have dropped back on the bed and gone to sleep, but she could not do that if she was expected to put in an appearance at supper. When her water came she washed and changed into one of her mother's altered gowns, a rose-coloured silk trimmed with cream embroidery and matching lace and had just finished brushing and arranging her hair when she was startled by a knock on the door and Mathilde entered and said her ladyship wished to see her in her boudoir.

Lady Harecroft was dressed to go down to supper in a gown of purple silk, a black widow's cap on her white hair. There were diamonds at her throat and on her fingers. She looked Diana up and down. 'Charming,' her ladyship said, appraising her. 'Do you not think so, Richard?'

Diana had not noticed Richard in the shadow by the window, but now he came forward with a smile. He was dressed for dinner in a black evening suit, white waistcoat and mulberry-coloured cummerbund. 'Yes, indeed. Miss Bywater has excellent taste,' he said, the intensity in his blue eyes causing Diana to glance away, hoping she was not blushing.

'Did you have a good journey?' the old lady asked her. 'Did Richard look after you?'

'Yes, thank you, my lady. The journey was very comfortable and Mr Harecroft arranged everything beautifully.'

'Good. Do you like your room?'

'Yes, very much. I can see some of the gardens and grounds and the woods from the windows.'

'We will explore tomorrow,' Richard said.

'Tomorrow I shall have to learn my duties and also I want to go and see my father.'

'As she is so fond of telling us, she is an employee,' Richard said, addressing the dowager. 'And is determined we shall not forget it.'

'Fustian! There will be time for everything.'

The sound of a gong in the distance alerted them to the fact that supper would soon be served. Richard picked the old lady up with easy grace and carried her from the room, followed by Diana. 'I could walk,' the old lady said, laughing. 'But I like to keep my grandchildren and great-grandchildren on their toes.'

At the bottom of the stairs, he set her down and offered his arms, one to the old lady and one to Diana, and thus they entered the drawing room. Everyone had already assembled and so their entrance was dramatic. Diana stood erect and proud in the doorway, her mother's gown shimmering about her feet, her red-gold hair piled into a becoming coronet with a few wayward curls about her ears. It was a moment before anyone spoke. 'Richard, do the honours,' the dowager commanded.

He led Diana forward to a couple who could only have been the master and mistress of Borstead Hall, Lord and Lady Harecroft. 'Grandfather, Grandmother,' he said. 'May I present Miss Diana Bywater?'

'How d'e do,' Lord Harecroft said, smiling as she bobbed a curtsy. He was white-haired, his face lined, but his carriage was upright and his way of speaking clipped as if he had other things on his mind than making polite conversation.

'Miss Bywater, you are welcome,' the younger Lady Harecroft said, coming forward to take both Diana's hands and look at her with arms extended. She was dark and petite and dressed in lemon yellow trimmed with green. 'How pretty you are. No wonder Stephen sings your praises. I am sorry he is not with us, but my son keeps his nose to the grindstone, though I imagine you know all about that, working as you do in the business.' She gave an embarrassed little laugh. Ladies who worked were a complete mystery to her.

'You have already met my Great-Aunt Alicia,' Richard said, moving on.

'Yes, indeed. Good evening, Miss Harecroft.'

The butler came to announce supper was ready and they all moved off in file to the dining room. 'Miss Bywater, sit here, beside me,' the younger Lady Harecroft said. 'Then you can tell us all about yourself. I believe your father was a sea captain, but what about your mother—did she come from a good family?'

'I have always thought so, but she never told me she did. She was always very genteel and ladylike and knew how to conduct herself in every kind of situation. She and Papa were devoted, which is why her death hit him so hard. You see, he had no family. He does not talk about his childhood very much, but he told me he did not remember his parents and was brought up in an orphanage.' She paused as she saw the dowager's eyes widen in surprise. It stiffened her spine; she was not going to be cowed. 'If you are looking for a pedigree, my lady, I am afraid I must disappoint you.'

'Do not be so prickly,' Richard said. He, too, had seen the effect Diana's words had had on the dowager. But surely, if the girl was up to no good, she would have invented a background that would satisfy the family? He was leaning more and more to the conclusion that she was genuinely who she said she was and it would all end in tears.

She turned sharply towards him. 'I am simply stating facts. I have nothing to hide.' And then blushed furiously, thinking about her father's affliction, which she was most definitely trying to hide. As far as she knew, only Richard was cognisant of that and, for all his haughty ways, she trusted him. She turned back to Miss Harecroft. 'I will tell you anything you want to know about my own childhood, but cannot enlighten you about my father's or my mother's, simply because I know so little.'

There was silence after this and then the conversation

picked up again when Richard, to change the subject, asked his grandfather about the chances of North Wind, a horse belonging to the dowager, winning at Ascot races later in the week.

'Good, I think,' his lordship said. 'Depends on the ground.'

They talked a little about the horse and after that the conversation ranged from the coronation and the Queen's rift with her mother, to the likely yield of corn in the coming harvest and the tension was eased. Diana, who was sitting opposite Richard, was acutely aware of him. Whenever she looked up from her plate she found him looking at her, a quizzical look on his face.

When the meal was finished, the ladies retired to the withdrawing room to take tea, but were soon joined by the gentlemen. After a few moments' polite conversation, Richard carried the dowager back to her room and then returned to bid them all goodnight. Diana assumed he was going home to the dower house. She was left with Lord and Lady Harecroft and Miss Harecroft, who talked about the old lady's party and how the arrangements were coming along. 'I sincerely hope she does not overtax her strength with it,' Lady Harecroft said. 'But there is no gainsaying her.'

'Oh, Mama is tough as an old boot,' Alicia said. 'But she is up to something, I know she is, but whenever I ask, she simply taps the side of her nose and says, "Wait and see."'

'Then that is what we must do,' William said, getting to his feet. 'I have work to do in the library, so I will leave you ladies to your gossip. Goodnight, Miss Bywater.'

'Goodnight, my lord.'

After he had left, the conversation became desultory and it was not long before the ladies also said goodnight and Diana made her way to her room.

Lying in the huge canopied bed, with the curtains drawn back so that she could see the star-filled sky, she mused on her day. Richard had been a thoughtful and courteous companion, not talking too much or too little, but she had learned enough about him to feel sympathy for the small boy he had been and the reserved adult he had become. Beneath his sombre exterior beat a heart full of compassion. Why did his father not understand that? Why did he assume that the exterior was all there was to his elder son? How close was Richard to Stephen? She realised with a start she had hardly given Stephen a thought all day. Soon she would have to give him an answer. What was she to do?

Chapter Six

'You'll soon get used to everyone,' Alicia said, after they had been to early morning service with Lord and Lady Harecroft and she was conducting Diana round the house. The dowager had not attended church and neither had Richard or his friends.

The servants occupied the back of the house, working in the kitchens and usual domestic offices. There was a strict hierarchy among them, from Mr Catchpole the butler, Mrs Shaw the housekeeper, Mrs Evans the cook, two footmen, chambermaids, parlour maids, kitchen maids, a tiny skivvy called Milly and an even smaller backhouse boy who cleaned the boots and shoes and ran errands. Diana wondered where she fitted in. She could not imagine why they needed her.

'The servants have their allotted tasks in the running of the house,' Alicia said when Diana voiced her doubts. 'The help I need from you is with the organisation, making suggestions and reminding me if I have forgotten anything. The invitations have all gone out and almost every one has been accepted.' She gave a light laugh. 'Being entertained at Borstead Hall is considered a rare treat.'

'I am sure it is,' Diana murmured, still bemused by the situation in which she found herself.

'There will be two parties,' Alicia went on. 'One for the staff, tenants and villagers to be held in the barn of the Home Farm and the other for family and close friends which will naturally take place here in the Hall.'

'Won't the servants be needed to help in the house?'

'They will for the preparations, but the hired staff will take over from them when everything is ready. I have made a start on the menus and arranged for musicians to play for dancing, but the details have yet to be decided upon. Then there are flowers to be arranged, extra chairs and tables to be brought in, temporary servants to hire and bedrooms to be readied for those of the family staying the weekend, so you see how invaluable your help will be. You and I will meet each morning to decide on what is to be done that day. I do not expect it to be too onerous, so you will have plenty of time to explore and visit your father. Now I will take you to see my mother. She is anxious to see you again and satisfy herself that you are being looked after.'

The old lady was sitting in the window of her boudoir dressed in a dark blue silk peignoir. Her white hair was piled up on top of her head on which was perched a tiny black cap. She beckoned Diana towards her and indicated a chair placed facing her. 'Sit there, child, where I can see you. Did you sleep well?'

'Yes, very well, thank you.'

'What do you think of Borstead Hall?'

'It is a lovely house.'

'So it is. My husband's grandfather had it built at the beginning of the last century, when he was given a baronetcy for some favour he had done the crown. My husband came to it through an uncle. But enough of that. Let us talk of the party. John and Stephen will come down on Friday and the rest of the family on Saturday morning. Other guests, some ninety in all, will arrive after dinner. There will be dancing in the ballroom and supper in the large dining room and cards in one of the drawing rooms for those who do not dance. And we shall round it all off with fireworks. I am sure you will enjoy it.'

'I came here to work,' Diana reminded her. Even though it was a Sunday, she had put on one of her grey business dresses in order to let everyone know she had no pretensions about what her role was to be.

'Oh, I know that. How else could I get you here when you were so determined to decline the invitation?' It was said with a smile bordering on mischievous.

'You are expecting me to accept Stephen…'

'That is up to you. I will bring no pressure to bear.'

It was all very well for the old lady to say that, but the very fact that she had been persuaded to come was pressure of a kind and she was still mystified. She would have liked to ask questions, but did not think her curiosity would be satisfied; the old lady liked her mysteries.

'How is your father?' her ladyship asked, 'Did he have a comfortable journey?'

'I believe so, my lady, but I have yet to visit him. If you would allow me a little time…'

'Goodness, child, take all the time you want. Go and see him now and convey my best wishes for his speedy recovery. I shall hope to meet him soon.'

'Thank you, my lady.'

Diana rose and left her to find her way to the stables to fetch Toby and ask directions to the nursing home.

* * *

The sun was shining from a cloudless sky, the air was redolent with the scent of cut hay and hawthorn blossom. Toby scampered ahead of her, sniffing in the hedgerows, dashing backwards and forwards, enjoying the change from urban streets and grimy pavement. Diana followed a path through the wood which she had been told would lead her to the village.

She had not seen Richard since the previous evening and was curious about the occupants of the dower house. She could not go calling, it would not be polite without an invitation—besides, Mr John had warned against going—but if she should see anyone in passing, surely she could pass the time of day? Particularly if it were Richard. She realised quite suddenly that she was looking forward to seeing him again.

She left the trees and joined a carriageway and there was the dower house, a sturdy square brick-built building with neat gardens laid out with lawns and flower beds. At first she saw no one, then she heard a child's squeal of happy laughter and a little boy ran round from the side of the house, chased by a young woman who was also laughing. She scooped him up in her arms. 'Dick, you little terror. I'll teach you to tease the cat,' and she pretended to spank his bottom, which only made him laugh the more.

Diana was transfixed. The woman was lovely, dark-haired, dark-eyed, with an enviable figure, but it was not the woman who grabbed her attention, but the boy. About two years old, he had soft red-gold hair and bright blue eyes and features so like Richard's, she was in no doubt in her mind he was Richard's son and the woman was the child's mother. That was what Stephen had been trying to tell her about his brother being a black sheep and why Mr John had warned her to stay clear of the dower house. It must have been hard to know one's son and heir was living with his mistress only a mile away. Richard was obviously not ashamed of his affair or he would not have installed the woman in his home, so close to his family.

He ought to have told her when they were chatting so amiably in the carriage about his friends, then perhaps she would not have been so shocked. And she was shocked, shaken to the core. She thought she was getting to know him, that they might be establishing a rapport, but now she realised she did not know him at all. Disappointed and disillusioned, she hurried away and found the road to the village.

The nursing home was easy to find. It had been converted from a substantial villa and stood facing the village green with its pump, ancient stocks and a bench where an old man sat enjoying the sun. The house had a small well-kept garden and a neat signboard announcing it to be 'The Borstead Convalescent Home for Recovering Gentlefolk'. Diana made her way up the drive and rang the bell.

She was admitted by a servant who fetched the matron, a formidable lady of large proportions and from whose ample waist dangled a huge bunch of keys. On learning Diana had come from Borstead Hall, she was all sunny smiles, though she refused to entertain Toby in the house and he was left tied up outside. 'Mr Bywater has settled down well,' she said as she conducted Diana to a ground-floor room that overlooked the back garden. It was a spacious room with light furniture and bright curtains, which matched the coverlet on the bed. This was unoccupied. The patient was dressed and sitting in a chair looking out of the window at some squabbling starlings.

'Papa,' Diana said, going forward to drop a kiss on his forehead as the matron withdrew. 'How are you?'

'Grand,' he said. 'A few weeks here and I shall be as good as new.'

'Oh.' She pulled a chair forward to sit beside him. A few weeks, he had said. What had he been told about the length of his stay? Once the week was over, she could not afford to keep him here. She had no idea what it was costing, but, looking around her at what could only be described as luxurious surroundings, she realised it must be very expensive. And what could she offer as an alternative? Another place like St Thomas's, which was all very well for someone who was acutely ill, but not conducive to real recovery? Or cheap lodgings with someone coming in to look after him while she went to work? He would start drinking again and they would be back to where they were before she walked into the Harecroft Emporium on that momentous day just over a year before. She could not let that happen. Did it mean she was destined to marry Stephen? Could they have a happy life together?

'That young fellow of yours has done me proud,' her father went on. 'You've done well for yourself there, my girl.'

'Papa, I have not accepted Stephen yet.'

'What are you waiting for?'

'He said he would not ask me again until her ladyship's party, to give me time to think about it.'

'And have you?'

'Yes, but I am not sure…'

'Not sure? He's rich and generous, and thinks highly of you—what more do you want? You tell him yes and be quick about it before someone else snaps him up.'

'But, Papa, is that reason enough to marry? Should there not be something more? Love, for instance, and a meeting of minds.'

'That will come in time, as you get to know him better.' He paused. 'What is the house like? And the family? Can you deal well with them?'

'I have not yet met all the family, only the men who work

at the shop, besides Mr Richard, Lady Harecroft, of course, and Miss Alicia Harecroft, who is the one arranging the party. She is very agreeable. I am sure I shall get on with her.' She stopped speaking, wondering whether to go on; he had obviously been thinking of the future but his thoughts ran along different lines from her own. 'Papa, we must think what we are to do after this week is over. I only came to help with the party.'

'Play your cards right and you need never leave. I've done all I can to help you. That other one, the one you call Mr Richard, asked a great many searching questions about me and you and your mama when he came to see me.'

'He had no business to do so. I was very angry.'

'Why? He was only trying to find out if you would make a suitable bride for his brother. Families are like that; they look after each other. It is why I want you to have a family around you. I was careful what I said and he seemed satisfied, so you can accept Stephen without feeling you are too far beneath him.'

'I certainly don't feel that,' she snapped.

'No, of course not, but others might think it.'

She had no opportunity to argue with him because Matron returned and said the patient ought to rest. Diana stood up. 'I will come again soon.'

'And bring me a drink,' he said. 'A man may die of thirst here.'

'You are served tea and chocolate and cordial,' Matron said, her hackles rising. 'How can you be thirsty?'

'A bottle of cognac to have after my dinner would not go amiss.'

'That would not be conducive to your recovery.' It was Matron who spoke, but she was only voicing what Diana was thinking. It was to Richard's credit he had never breathed a word of her father's drinking to anyone else; they would not have been invited to Borstead if he had. He had intimated to her that the stroke and his incapacity might have cured Papa, but this morning had told her that was a vain hope. Papa was longing for cognac. She hoped the matron would not give it to him.

She bent to kiss him, whispering close to his ear, 'Be good, Papa, please.'

He gave a lop-sided grimace. 'I do not have much choice, stuck here, do I?'

She thanked the matron and left, only to find Richard squatting beside Toby, who was wagging his tail in raptures and trying to lick his face. Dogs did not worry themselves about morals and ethics, they could display their pleasure without inhibitions.

'How is your father?' Richard asked, standing up to face her.

She did not know why she should be so upset and angry. What Richard Harecroft did was none of her business and yet she felt hurt by it, which was very silly of her considering the child had been born long before she met any of the Hare-crofts. Why did she feel so injured? A month ago she would have shrugged it off as nothing to do with her and nothing had changed. She shook herself, making herself answer what was, after all, only a polite enquiry. 'He has settled in well.'

'Good. The country air will do him good.' Toby was jumping up at him and he fondled the dog's ear. 'Shall we take him for a run? I could show you the rest of the village.' He did not wait for a reply, but began untying Toby's lead from the gate post. The dog was off like a shot, nose to the ground, sniffing along the hedgerow.

'There are usually rabbits in that bank,' Richard said. 'I remember Pal searching them out.'

He was his usual urbane self and had no idea of the turmoil in her breast. How could he embarrass his family and lecture his brother about what he should do, even try to advise her, when his own life was so blatantly immoral? No wonder his father disparaged him. She forced herself to speak coolly; it was the only way she could maintain her composure. 'Did he catch many?'

'No, very few. He was not an aggressive dog.'

'And yet you said he worried sheep.'

'I was not the one to say that, the farmer was. I knew the dog was innocent, but he had to pay for another dog's crime.'

'How sad.'

'Yes. It happens. To humans as well sometimes.' He stopped speaking and then abruptly changed the subject. 'That is the village church, but I expect you have already seen that.'

'Yes, I accompanied your grandparents and great-aunt to morning service. The church is a large one for the size of the village, is it not?'

'I believe at the time it was built the population was larger. Since then many have decamped into the capital to find work. The big house on the hill is the doctor's and down Green Lane you will find Berry Farm, the only one of any size in Borstead, apart from Home Farm. The remainder are small holdings and peasant cottages.'

'They all look very clean and neat. Are they part of the estate?'

'Yes, the whole village is, including the Borstead Arms and the Traveller's Rest.'

'Quite an inheritance.'

'Yes, and a responsibility too. It is one my grandfather does not shirk.' He stopped to greet a man walking towards them with a scythe over his shoulder and was answered with a deferential tug of a forelock. 'That's not to say there is no discontent. Times are hard for agriculture. It is fortunate that my grandfather has large breeding stables a few miles away that subsidise the farming and help to pay the labourers' wages. I will show you those another time when we do not have Toby with us.'

'Thank you. You have been most kind.'

'How did you find my great-aunt?'

'I like her. I am sure we shall deal well together. We talked about the party and what I am expected to do. I think you were right when you said she would have everything organised. I am sure I am not truly needed.'

'Oh, you are needed,' he said. 'Great-Grandmama needs you and so does Stephen. At any rate he thinks he does.'

'You doubt it?'

He shrugged. 'Time will tell. My great-grandmother's party is on Saturday. I have a feeling that will be a kind of turning point.'

She felt that too. 'Yes. My work here will be done and I must decide on my future.'

'Something of the sort.' He paused to throw a stick for Toby to fetch. 'But if you have any doubts about marrying Stephen, then I urge you to think carefully.'

Had he met her and offered to show her round in order to lecture her? 'What do you think I have been doing? And what business is it of yours?'

'Contrary to everyone's belief, I am very fond of my brother. I should hate him to make a mistake.'

'Oh, and there was me thinking you were concerned for me.'

'That, too,' he said, wondering what had put her into such a temper. 'I should be very unhappy to see you unhappy.'

'Flirting again, Mr Harecroft? I think perhaps you are a past master at it. Did you learn the art in the army? I believe the uniform attracts a certain kind of woman.'

Surprised by her almost venomous tone, he turned to look at her. She was pale and her grey eyes had changed from smoky to steely. He wondered what he had done to bring that on. 'What do you mean by that?'

'I think you might have told me.' She hadn't meant to say anything, but it was so large in her mind she could not help it. 'Yesterday we spent three hours in a carriage talking about all manner of things, and yet you did not see fit to tell me you had a…a mistress.'

'Mistress?' he echoed.

'Yes, and a son. I saw them this morning. No wonder your father says your friends are disreputable and you are a black sheep.'

He opened his mouth and shut it again. If she thought that of him, what did it matter? Everyone else, except Great-Grand-mama, thought the worst of him, so why should she be any different? He was used to it. And he was not the only one to have secrets. She did too and he wasn't thinking of her father's drinking. He didn't know why he felt so angry, so disap-pointed.

They had been walking back towards the estate in silence when he suddenly said, 'Come with me. I should like you to meet my friends.' He laughed harshly. 'My disreputable friends.'

'You said they were not.'

'Nor are they. I was quoting my father. But if you doubt it, come and meet them.'

'I do not have the time. Miss Harecroft might be needing me.'

'Nonsense, she does not expect you to work on a Sunday.'

He took her hand and almost hauled her along. Even in her anger she could feel herself responding to his touch and hated herself for her weakness. 'Let me go.'

He stopped and turned to face her, his anger matching hers. 'What are you afraid of? Do you think they will corrupt you?'

'No, of course not.'

'Then come and meet them. They do not have horns and a tail, they will not eat you. And you might learn something to help you make up your mind.'

In spite of Mr John's advice to avoid the dower house, in spite of her disappointment in him, she was curious. 'Very well.'

Without speaking again, he led the way back to the dower house, opened the gate and ushered her along the path to the door. The first person they met in the hall was the little boy who ran to Richard and was hoisted onto his shoulder. 'This is Dick,' Richard told Diana.

'He is like you.'

'So they tell me.' It was said laconically, knowing he was reinforcing her belief. 'But all I see is the Carson hair and eyes, inherited from Great-Grandmother's side of the family. We were all the same in childhood, even Grandfather, who is white-haired now, and Papa, whose hair is flecked with grey.'

They made their way into the drawing room where the young woman Diana had seen earlier was busy sewing. 'Miss Bywater, allow me to introduce Miss Lucy Standish. You may have heard of her; as Lucinda Standish, she is an actress of some repute. This little rogue is her son and quite a handful.' He lifted the child from his shoulder and set him on his feet, while Diana acknowledged the introduction to Lucy with a smile she hoped was warm and did not betray her inner turmoil.

Perhaps he was truly in love with the woman, but why hadn't he married her? She did not think he would be put off by his father's disapproval. He was strong enough to stand up to him. Could it be because she was an actress and marriage to such a one would not sit well with those he wanted to sponsor his political career? Was he cruelly ambitious? If that were the case, she felt sorry for the young woman.

She turned as Richard introduced the two other occupants of the room. They were both young, both dark-haired, but there the similarity ended. 'This is Mr Joseph Harris.' He indicated a solidly build man in a wrinkled suit of clothes and paint in his fingernails. 'And this is Mr Frederick Somers.' Mr Somers was thin as a rake, though his clothes were neat and clean, they were also well worn. 'They are artists and very good they are too. Gentlemen, Miss Diana Bywater, a guest at Borstead Hall.'

They greeted her politely and she bade them good afternoon, noting that Richard had not explained who she was or her role at the big house. 'I am down from London to help with her ladyship's party,' she said, remedying the omission. 'Normally I work at the Harecroft Emporium.'

'A clerk, no less,' Richard added. 'It seems my father is a convert to female emancipation.'

'How interesting,' Lucy said. 'Do you enjoy your work?'

'Very much.' Diana looked about her. The room was well proportioned, though furnished with a mixture of old and new with little thought to colour and style, and it was very untidy. Books, magazines, Dick's toys, empty cups and half-finished drawings were scattered about, some portraying Lucy. 'You certainly have a talented group of friends, Mr Harecroft,' she said. 'Where did you meet them?'

'Joe was commissioned by the army to illustrate the life of the regiment and the conflicts in which it had taken part. All finished now, of course. Freddie was a fellow officer.'

'And Miss Standish is your model.' She was addressing the young men, not Richard. She could not meet his eye.

Freddie laughed. 'Yes. We do not have to pay her.'

Lucy rescued Dick from a pot of paint left carelessly in the hearth and, despite his protests, picked him up and carried him off to have his hands washed before he spread paint everywhere. 'You shan't go on the picnic if you do not behave,' Lucy scolded, but her tone was not severe. The men laughed and Diana found herself smiling. It was not the child's fault that his parents were not married.

'We are going on a picnic this afternoon,' Freddie told Diana. 'Do join us. Lucy has packed a hamper big enough for an army.'

'Yes, do come,' Joe added his weight. 'We plan to go to Borstead Heath and watch the horses on the gallops. Dick loves the horses.'

'I must go back to the house,' she said, noting that Richard had not added his voice to theirs. 'Lady Harecroft will be wondering what has become of me.'

'Surely not,' Freddie put in. 'It is Sunday, you may do as you please.'

'But I should be intruding—'

'Nonsense! You will be company for Lucy—she is always complaining that she is outnumbered. Isn't that so, Lucy?' Lucy had returned at that moment, leading Dick by the hand. The child had been washed and had his curls brushed.

'Isn't what so?'

'You often complain you are outnumbered by men and would be glad of Miss Bywater's company on our little jaunt this afternoon.'

'Of course.'

Was there just a tiny hesitation before her reply, Diana wondered, or did she imagine it? Before she could make any more excuses, Freddie turned to Richard. 'You ask her, Richard, she will listen to you.'

He hesitated. He was not at all sure it was a good idea. He did not want Diana accusing Lucy of immoral behaviour. Poor Lucy had enough to contend with as it was. Until today he had not realised Diana could be quite so condemnatory. Her own background was not an open book and there were skeletons in her cupboard too. He was beginning to wish he had not been so impulsive in bringing her to the house. It was, after all, his sanctuary, a place to be himself. Wasn't that what she had said? How could she be so understanding one minute and so critical the next? On the other hand, if she spent some time with Lucy, might she be made to understand?

'Please come,' he said. 'Both Great-Aunt Alicia and the dowager take a nap in the afternoons. You will hardly be missed.'

'But I cannot go without asking their permission.'

'Then I will come with you to do so while the others finish the preparations.' He turned to his friends. 'We will meet you at the beginning of the path through the wood.'

Diana felt bewildered, as if she was being tossed on the tide, ebbing and flowing and coming ever nearer to dangerous rocks on which she would surely be dashed to pieces. And yet she could not make herself change direction, could not help herself. Richard strode beside her, making no attempt to engage her in conversation. She was glad of that; she doubted if she would have been able to string together a single coherent sentence.

They found Alicia reading to the dowager and both ladies exclaimed with delight that she had been invited to join the picnic and told her to go and enjoy herself. 'But do go and change, my dear,' her ladyship said. 'You must be too hot in that dress. Wear something light and make sure you take a hat.'

While she went to obey, Richard went downstairs to wait for her. He was halfway down the stairs when he happened to look up at one of the pictures that lined the walls. They had been hanging there all his life, almost part of the fabric of the building, and he took them for granted, never giving them a passing glance. Now he stopped in his tracks and gazed at the portrait of his great-grandmother painted in her youth. The clothes were old-fashioned, but she was not wearing a wig as most people sitting for a portrait in those days would have done. Her hair was her own, even though it was puffed out with stuffing and decorated with feathers and a small bird. The afternoon sun, coming through the window on the half-landing, lit it up like a ball of red-gold fire. Her blue eyes looked out from the canvas as if they were watching everyone coming and going on the stairs and a faint smile of amusement lifted the corners of her mouth. She had been a real beauty in her day, but what struck him now, like a hammer blow, was how much Diana resembled her. The hair was exactly the same shade and her features were similar too: oval face, high cheekbones, well-defined brows, though Great-Grandmama's eyes were china blue and Diana's a smoky grey.

Was that why the old lady had so taken to her? She brought back a lost youth and allowed her to indulge in the sort of prank for which she had had a reputation as a young woman. Could some earlier Carson have had a mistress and a child, a child to be farmed out and forgotten by the rest of the family? Was history repeating itself? Was Diana being used? Had his great-grandmother deliberately allowed him to think there was something wrong with her, something unacceptable, when she asked him to make enquiries? Or had he been too ready to jump to that conclusion? From thinking of Diana as the villain, he began to wonder if she might be the victim.

The idea that he might have misjudged her bothered him. He would have to have it out with the old lady.

When Diana joined him in the hall fifteen minutes later, she was wearing a printed cotton dress in yellow-and-white stripes, one of the gowns she had purchased with the advance of her salary, and a plain straw bonnet tied on with a yellow ribbon. In her hand she carried a parasol. He stood back and appraised her from head to toe as if it were the first time he had seen her. It only reinforced his doubts.

'Is something wrong?' she asked.

He shook himself. 'Nothing at all. Are you ready?'

They left the house together, Toby bounding along beside them, and soon caught up with the rest of the party. Once Toby had sniffed all round them and established they were friendly, they set off along a path through the wood, which led to a brook. The water, only a few inches deep, sparkled in the sunlight, dappled by overhanging willows. In places the bank had been eroded by the cattle who grazed the pasture and it was easy to reach the water's edge.

'Want to paddle,' Dick said, pulling on his mother's hand.

'Not today,' she told him. 'We are going to see the horses and have a picnic. There is no time to do both.'

He accepted her explanation and toddled along beside her as they turned along the towpath to a narrow wooden bridge. Toby ran ahead and explored the bank and the next minute had jumped into the water and was swimming strongly to the other side. He greeted them as they crossed the bridge by shaking himself so vigorously he showered the little boy with water, making him giggle.

'He is a happy child,' Diana said, as they walked along the towpath on the other side.

'He has nothing to be unhappy about,' Lucy said, picking

him up to carry him. 'Richard has provided us with a comfortable home in idyllic surroundings; he wants for nothing.'

'That is Richard all over,' Freddie said. 'Always ready and willing to offer a helping hand. I owe him a lot. Without his generosity, I would be destitute.'

'Nonsense!' Richard said. He could see by Diana's expression his friends were reinforcing her poor opinion of him even as they praised him. 'You work for your keep and one day you will be rich and famous and I shall have my reward.'

'Freddie is right,' Joe put in. 'He took me in when I was at my lowest ebb and since then I have begun to paint again. We are trying to put together an exhibition of our work, though we have yet to find a venue. If that is a success and results in sales, we shall feel we have justified his faith in us. And perhaps we can repay him.'

'He helped me, too,' Diana admitted, 'when my father had a seizure. He seemed to know exactly what to do. His brother, Mr Stephen, said he was good in a crisis.'

'Of course, you will know Stephen,' Lucy said. 'Working in the business as you do.'

'Yes. He showed me how to go on when I first went to work at Harecroft's.'

'I have not see him for some time,' Lucy said. 'He is so busy he does not come to Borstead Hall very often.'

'He will be down this weekend for her ladyship's party. Perhaps you will see him then.'

'He will have to come to the dower house. I am not welcome at the Hall.'

'I am sorry to hear that. It is such a pity when parents and grandparents deny themselves the pleasure of the company of their grandchildren and great-grandchildren.' She smiled suddenly. 'In this case, great-great-grandson, unless I am mistaken.'

'No, you are not mistaken,' Lucy admitted. 'But I am an actress and unmarried at that.'

Diana looked at Richard to see how he received this admission, said with a hint of regret. How could Richard live so openly with her and not marry her? The caring and uncaring side of his nature seemed to be inexplicably woven together in his attitude towards Lucy. He was walking a little ahead with Dick astride his shoulders, the picture of a devoted and doting father. 'Perhaps that will soon be remedied,' she said.

'Perhaps.'

There did not seem to be anything else to say on the subject that did not imply a criticism of Richard and they walked on in silence until they came to a meadow where haymaking was in full swing. When the grass was ready and the sun shone, the work had to be done, Sunday or not. Diana could see no signs of dissent as the men scythed the grass in great swathes and the women and children raked it out to dry. 'It looks idyllic,' she said. 'I find it hard to believe these people are discontented.'

'Oh, they are not discontented,' Freddie said. 'Grumbling adds a little spice to dull lives.'

'Rubbish!' Joe said. 'The time will come when Parliament will have to take notice. The labourer should be worthy of his hire. It is the labourer who creates the rich man's wealth and it is only fair he should have a say in how he is governed.'

'You will note from that, Miss Bywater, that Mr Harris is a Chartist,' Richard put in.

'What about you?' she asked. 'Are you also Chartist, Mr Harecroft?'

'I think perhaps I might be.'

This led to a discussion about the problems of agriculture and what should be done to address the evils of poverty in general to which everyone contributed. Freddie said the corn laws ought to be repealed to bring the price of bread down,

Joe maintained that would not be enough and nothing short of revolution would suffice. Richard argued against revolution but did say he thought universal suffrage would be a step in the right direction. Revolution would be unnecessary if every man had a say in how the country was run.

'I agree with Mr Harecroft,' Diana said. Now that the subject was one she was genuinely interested in, she could relax a little. 'But before that can happen, the government must be woken up to what is happening here and now. While there are thousands out of work, their children are slaving away because they cost less in wages. It is a disgrace to any country that calls itself civilised.'

In spite of the shelter of the brim of her hat, Richard noted the change, noted the slight blush that stained her cheeks and her earlier comment that she had seen what poverty could do. She would be a superb helpmate to anyone addressing that problem. He wondered idly if Stephen knew her views. 'I concur wholeheartedly,' he said.

'But you would not subscribe to the notion that women should have the vote?'

'No, I do not think I would go that far,' he said.

'Pity,' she said. 'Women work too, you know.'

He laughed, making Lucy, who had been talking to Dick, look up at them. 'What is so funny?'

'Miss Bywater was reminding me that women work and ought to have a vote.'

'So they do and so they should,' Diana said. 'The idea that women are the chattels of men is fast becoming outdated.'

'But would you not like to be married?' Lucy asked her.

'Yes, but I would still want to be myself, not an echo of my husband.'

'I think your husband might have something to say on the matter,' Freddie said.

'I do not see why,' she countered.

'It is the husband's role to take the lead. It always has been.'

'Oh, so you are going to quote that as justification for putting women down, are you?' Diana enjoyed a good debate, especially if there were no emotion involved. Arguing with Mr Somers was enjoyable, so different from the tense exchanges she had with Richard. 'You are saying that because it was always so is reason enough to maintain the status quo.'

'But it is history that shapes our destiny,' Richard said.

Freddie laughed. 'You mean what we are doing now will determine out future lives? That if we had not decided to come out for a picnic and did something else instead, our whole lives might be different?'

'Possibly.'

'I fail to see how. Whether we walk or ride or take a picnic or eat luncheon at home cannot possibly make one iota of difference. We would still be struggling to make a name for ourselves as artists and you would still be second in line to your grandfather's estate and Lucy would still be a doting mother. And do you think it would make any difference to you, Miss Bywater?'

Diana knew exactly what Richard meant and it did make a difference. Everything she had done since taking that job at Harecroft's had been life-changing. Without that Stephen would not have proposed, she would not have come to Borstead and she would not have met the rest of the Harecroft family, Richard Harecroft's ménage in particular. 'It remains to be seen, considering we cannot see into the future,' she said diplomatically.

'An enigmatic answer if ever I heard one,' Richard said. 'But our children are our future and it is up to those of us who are in a position to do so, to ensure a future for them. It is why I intend to do my small bit and stand for Parliament.'

'Are you, by Jove!' Joe said. 'Good luck to you, but you will have some formidable opposition.'

'I know; whenever I apply for a candidature, I am turned down when my views become known. But I shall persevere.'

'That is not the only obstacle,' Diana said. 'Is it not true that Members of Parliament are expected to be married?'

He looked at her sharply, detecting more in the question than appeared on the surface. 'I believe so. When the time comes, I might think about it.'

Diana looked across at Lucy, but she was stooping beside Dick, pointing out a butterfly, telling him it was called a painted lady. 'I think you are despicable,' she murmured. 'Stephen is twice the man you are.' He did not answer and marched ahead of them, anger in every tense muscle.

While they had been talking they had skirted the meadow where the men were working, crossed a lane and come on to the heath covered in purple heather, butter-yellow broom, and dotted here and there with dainty blue harebells. A cool breeze wafted in their faces as they made their way along a well-worn path and soon came to the wooden rails that delineated the gallops for the Harecroft horses. There was a knoll of higher ground and it was here, beside a stunted hawthorn, they settled for their picnic.

Freddie had been right in saying Lucy had packed ample provisions. They sat down to chicken and ham and meat pies with several kinds of cheese and strawberries doused in thick cream, all to be washed down with lemonade. Diana had no appetite and only nibbled at the food, which almost choked her. When everyone had eaten their fill, the basket was repacked and the conversation dwindled to an occasional comment. Richard fetched out a ball and began tossing it to Dick. Diana leaned back against the trunk of the hawthorn and shut her eyes, but even with her eyes closed she could picture Richard playing with the child and her heart contracted with pain. It was all wrong. Everything was wrong.

She was roused when a thundering reverberated through the ground beneath her and everyone stood up to watch a group of horses galloping towards them on the other side of the rails. Richard produced binoculars and studied them as they came nearer, then held the glasses out to Diana. She took them and put them to her eyes. The horses were magnificent animals, fine limbed, muscular, heads forward as they raced each other.

'Let me see! Let me see!' Dick cried, dancing at her feet and pulling on her skirt.

She picked him up and put the binoculars to his eyes and tried to adjust them for him. His little body was soft and warm and smelled of soap. Diana hugged him to her and her eyes filled with tears. Hurriedly she handed him to Richard. 'Here, you take him. I can't hold him and adjust the glasses at the same time.'

He lifted the boy from her arms, noticing the tears glistening on her lashes and began to wonder if he had been right to introduce her to Lucy and young Dick, but she had to know about them sooner or later. 'Come on, young fellow-m'-lad,' he said jovially, taking the binoculars from Diana. 'You stand on the rails while I show you how to see the horses.' He balanced the boy on the middle rail and held him firmly. But the horses had gone and only their haunches and the backsides of the riders were visible as they galloped away. The boy wailed in disappointment. 'No need to cry,' he said, dropping a kiss on the top of the child's head. 'There will be more and next time we shall be ready for them.'

A second group of horses soon followed the first and this time Dick squealed in delight when he found he could see them through the binoculars. Freddie had a stopwatch with him and he clicked it as the leader went by. 'By God, he's fast,' he said.

'Which one were you timing?' Diana asked, finding it easier to turn and talk to him than watch Richard with the child.

'The white colt. When does he race, Richard?'

'North Wind? On Friday, if the going is good. My grand-father has high hopes of him.'

'Then I must go to the races and put a guinea or two on him.'

'Don't blame me if you lose your money. He has only raced once before and came nowhere.'

'Then the odds will be good.'

'Time to make for home,' Lucy said. 'Dick has had enough excitement for one day.'

They returned the way they had come. At the edge of the park Richard, who was carrying a sleeping Dick, asked Diana if she could find her way from there.

'Oh, yes, easily,' she said. 'Thank you for a pleasant af-ternoon.'

She had spoken formally and he replied in a like vein. 'I am glad to be of service. I shall see you at dinner.'

Diana hurried back to the Hall and let herself into the house through the servants' entrance. The kitchen staff were all busy preparing dinner, Catchpole was polishing glasses in the butler's pantry and the two footmen were going back-wards and forwards to the dining room, laden with cutlery. They ignored her as if she were invisible.

Once in her room, she sat on a chair by the window and let herself slump. She was exhausted, not because of the walk, which had been no more than three miles, but the nervous strain of watching Richard with Lucy and their little son, of making polite conversation when all she could think of was that someone she had looked up to and admired had turned out to have feet of clay. He put his ambition to be a Member of Parliament before the happiness of the mother of his son. No wonder his father and brother had washed their hands of him.

Yet he cared about the poor, she had seen more than one instance of that, and had given his friends a home for which they could not praise him highly enough, even Lucy, who had every reason to feel aggrieved. And he had been so good when her father had his seizure. She could not condemn him utterly. She heard the first dinner gong and rose wearily to change her clothes. She would have to face him again.

The evening meal, although taken at the earlier hour of six o'clock, was a repeat of the previous evening. Diana listened to the conversation and spoke only when addressed. Only Richard realised she was not her usual bright self. He knew why; she had condemned him as a lecher and he, in his madness, had let her do it. He should not have introduced her to Lucy and Dick. He had done it in a fit of anger and that had not had the effect he hoped for. If she were the fortune hunter he had at first supposed her to be, it would not have mattered, she would have had to take her chances; most families had skeletons in their cupboards and, if they were kept discreetly hidden, they could be ignored. He had no business to interfere. But how could he not, when so many people's happiness and reputations were at stake, not least his own?

As soon as the meal was over he carried his great-grandmother back to her room. 'Tell me the real reason you asked me to talk to Mr Bywater,' he asked, when he had settled her in her favourite chair beside the window. 'It wasn't just because Stephen asked her to marry him, was it?'

'No.'

'I wish she had never been brought to Borstead. And I wish my father had not encouraged Stephen to propose to her. You know how he likes to please Papa. And you are equally to blame for inviting her down here.'

'Stephen will come to his senses.'

'He would never be so dishonourable as to retract a proposal.'

'Diana has not yet accepted him.'

'I am afraid she will.'

'You had better do something about it, then.'

'It is not up to me to tell her why she should not. I have hinted but that only annoys her. Is she a fortune hunter, worming her way into the family on the strength of the colour of her hair?'

She smiled. 'Do you think so?'

'I did at first, but now I am not so sure. If she is, she is being very clever about it, but perhaps she is nothing of the sort and you are making mischief.'

'Me?' Her eyes widened. 'Make mischief?'

'Yes. Are you?'

'I promise you I am not. But I do have another errand for you.' She paused. 'Have you ever heard of the Foundling Hospital?'

'Of course. It is one of the organisations I support.'

'Good, then you will have no trouble gaining access to their records.'

'Why?'

'Because Diana herself has given us a clue. You remember at dinner last night she said her father had been brought up in an orphanage?'

'Yes, but there are dozens of orphanages. Why the Foundling Hospital?'

'Because it is known for providing the navy with boys and Mr Bywater told you himself he had been in the navy, man and boy, did he not?'

'And if I discover he is a foundling and has no roots, what then? Will you say his daughter is not a fit person to marry Stephen?'

'It depends,' she said guardedly. 'I am not one to interfere…'

He gave a cracked laugh. 'And that's a whisker. Who was it encouraged me to bring Miss Standish to Borstead? And that has had repercussions I could never have foreseen.'

She looked at him and smiled knowingly. 'It will come right in the end, you'll see. Now, will you do as I ask?'

'I am going to London on Tuesday. I have heard there might be a bye-election in one of the northern seats and I am going to offer myself as a candidate. I could visit the Foundling Hospital then, but I will not do it unless you tell me why it is so important.'

'I will think about it. But not tonight. I am tired and need my sleep and explaining it all is going to take some time.'

Mathilde came in to help her undress and with that he had to be satisfied.

Chapter Seven

Diana could not sleep; her head was whirling, her mind going over the afternoon's events. She relived every moment. She had said some terrible things, made some dreadful accusations, which Richard had not refuted. If he had tried to explain, she might have been able to understand, wanted to understand. Now they were at daggers drawn and it was hurting more than she would ever have believed possible.

She was tempted to make some excuse to leave, but she had promised to stay the week, had been given an advance on her wages on the strength of that. And what about her father? She must consider him. He had only just arrived, how could she uproot him again? And where could they go if she did? They had no home and she would have no employment. The Harecrofts paid her wages; without that, she would be destitute. Leaving abruptly, she decided, was ill mannered and the act of a coward. And there was Stephen. She had not given him a thought all afternoon. He was not his brother's keeper. The situation must be dealt with and the best way to do it was to do the work she had come to do with cool efficiency and stay to the end.

She slept at last.

* * *

Next morning, after her discussion with Lady Harecroft and Alicia about the party, which only required her to confirm what Alicia was planning and to make one or two suggestions of her own, Diana found herself with the rest of the day free. She decided to take a different route to the nursing home, which did not take her past the dower house.

At the back of the Hall between the stables and the kitchen garden, a gate gave on to a path that led across a wide expanse of grass to the wood and the brook. Remembering their walk of the day before, she crossed the bridge and turned in the opposite direction, away from the gallops, a route she surmised would take her to the village. She had not gone far when she heard footsteps behind her. She turned to find Richard gaining on her. Although he was walking, he was dressed in a brown riding coat and tan leather breeches tucked into highly polished riding boots. 'Good morning, Diana,' he said, doffing his hat. 'Where are you off to, today?'

She took a deep breath to calm herself. 'Good morning, Mr Harecroft. I am on my way to see my father.'

'This is not the shortest way.'

'No, but I thought I would have a change and explore a little farther afield.'

'That is best done on horseback. Shall I come with you to visit your father and then we could go riding? Does a sea captain's daughter ride?'

'Oh, yes,' she said before she could stop herself. 'I used to ride when we lived in Calcutta.'

'Then come riding with me.'

He was everywhere and she could not escape him. He seemed to have taken on the role of companion and guide, which surprised her; she would have expected him to spend more time with Lucy and his child. Was he the rake he was reputed to be? His relationship with Lucy was hardly rake-like, but neither was it honourable. Yesterday, he had seemed a caring, almost doting father, today he was the careless bachelor again, assuming she would agree to whatever he asked. 'To go riding you need a mount,' she said.

'Of course. You may ride Aunt Alicia's mare. Since she gave up riding, the animal has grown fat and lazy. I have asked her and she gives her consent. So, what do you say?'

'I have no habit with me.'

'I am sure something can be found for you. The house is full of clothes, something is sure to fit.'

'I would not wish to take up your time when you have other things to do.'

'I have nothing else to do today. Tomorrow might be a different matter, but today I plan to go riding and would be pleased if you would accompany me.' He stopped and regarded her quizzically. 'Am I such an ogre, so steeped in sin, you cannot bear my company?'

'I never said that!'

'As near as, damnit.'

'I spoke hastily. What you do is none of my business.'

'Then make amends. Come riding with me.'

She could not help herself. 'Very well.' She ought to have refused, politely but firmly, instead she had allowed herself to be persuaded. Her weakness worried her, but underlying that was a frisson of excitement, an element of risk, sweet and bitter together, and it set her heart pumping in her throat.

'Good. Now let us go and see your papa.'

James was sitting on a bench in the garden. Seeing him, Toby ran to him in an ecstasy of delight, wagging his tail and barking joyously. James leaned forward and the dog bounded into his arms. 'Have you missed me, old fellow?' he asked.

'I think the answer to that is in the affirmative,' Richard said, smiling and holding out his hand to be shaken. James disentangled his hand from the dog's fur to take it. 'How are you?'

'Getting better every day. Missing my cognac, though. You wouldn't have a flask about you, would you?'

'No, sir, I would not.'

'Pity.'

'Papa, did you walk out here?' Diana asked.

'Yes.' He picked up a walking stick propped against the bench. 'With this to help me.'

'Shall we take a turn about the garden?' Richard suggested.

James used his stick to get to his feet and the three of them began a slow perambulation of the garden, keeping to the paths. 'Everywhere is so dry,' Diana said. 'The flowers are wilting.'

'Not the roses,' James put in. 'They remind me of summer nights when we were out in Calcutta. The Europeans had imported roses to make English gardens and their perfume was overpowering. When I was on shore, your mama and I used to stroll in the gardens after dusk when it was cooler. The smell of roses always brings those times back.'

'Did you not have roses in the gardens of your childhood?' Richard asked, deliberately probing.

'There may have been, I don't remember.'

'What do you remember of your childhood?' Diana asked, wondering why she had never asked him before. Lady Harecroft seemed to think it strange she knew so little. 'You have never said.'

'Loneliness. Surrounded by other boys, all of them boisterous, I was alone. I prefer not to recall that. Later, in the navy, as a very young midshipman, there were no gardens, only the sea and salt spray. That was my life, but it changed when I met your dear mama. She was everything to me.' His voice choked on a sob.

'And Diana?' Richard murmured.

'Diana was, is, part of my wife, the child we made together and I want what is best for her.'

'Naturally, you do.'

'Papa, where did you meet Mama?'

'At a dance in Southampton. It was held at the Assembly Rooms especially to welcome us home when our ship docked. It was in the early years of the war with Napoleon and we were celebrating a successful voyage and a safe return to our homeland. Kate was young and beautiful and always laughing and she danced with me and that was it. I was enslaved. We married when I was promoted that same year and she stuck by me through thick and thin. Even when—' He stopped suddenly; both his listeners knew what he was thinking.

'And she had no family?' Diana queried. 'Parents? Brothers? Sisters?'

'No, I told you that before. We were both orphans, brought up in different institutions. It was that which brought us together, something in common, so I have that at least to thank them for.'

'And your parents? What do you know of them?' Richard prompted.

'Nothing. I have no memory of them. It was the same for Kate.' He paused. 'They could have been angels or villains, we had no way of knowing. Just be thankful, young fellow, that you have a family around you. It is what I most want for Diana. I have been telling her to accept your brother's offer, then she will not be alone when I go.'

'Papa!' Diana protested, the colour flaring in her face.

Richard gave a wry smile. 'No, she will have the whole Harecroft dynasty about her, but there are disadvantages as well as advantages to that. She will have to toe the family line.'

'You did not!' She turned towards him. 'And you seem to have survived.'

'I am strong willed.'

'And so, I promise you, am I.'

He chuckled. 'Good.'

James looked from one to the other and laughed too, but he did not comment and the tour of the garden completed, they returned the invalid to his bench and Richard and Diana took their leave.

Back at Borstead Hall, they left Toby in the care of a stable lad and, while two horses were being saddled for them, went indoors, where Alicia told Diana that two riding habits had been laid out on her bed for her to choose one. 'Thank goodness the fashion for those has changed little since I last went riding,' she said. 'I have had several pairs of boots put out for you too, so you should find something to fit you.'

Twenty minutes later, Diana returned downstairs wearing a dark blue taffeta skirt and a military-style tailored jacket with rows of braiding across the front, which fitted as if they had been made for her. Her outfit was completed with black boots and a tall hat tied under the chin with a wisp of veil. Richard looked her up and down in the intense way he had whenever she changed her clothes. 'You look just like Great-Aunt Alicia when she used to go riding,' he said. 'I remember when I was very little, she would ride like the wind. Even Grandfather's race horses sometimes.'

'I am not that accomplished,' Diana said. 'And I have not ridden for years. A gentle hack will suffice.'

'Then a gentle hack you shall have.'

Their horses had been brought round to the side of the house by a groom who helped Diana to mount Mayfly while Richard flung himself easily into the saddle of Thunderer. They rode across the park, crossed the river bridge and made for the heath. He watched her, noting how well she rode; the old mare responded to her every move. After a few minutes, during which neither spoke, she put her horse to a canter. He followed, keeping half a head behind her. When she decided to gallop, he followed suit, laughing.

'A gentle hack, you said,' he commented when they fell back to a walk.

'I had forgotten how exhilarating it could be.'

'You ride well.'

'Thank you.'

'Would you like to visit my grandfather's stables?'

'Yes, very much.' At the stables there would be other people; she was afraid of being alone with him for any length of time. She certainly did not want to be quizzed, either about Stephen and whether she was going to accept him, or about her father. Today Papa had told her more than he ever had before and it had opened her eyes to his childhood. There was no shame in being brought up in an orphanage, but if he had been taken there because his mother was unmarried, it would make all the difference.

She wondered if that was why she had been brought to Borstead Hall, not to help with the party, but so that her antecedents could be investigated. Were Mr John and Stephen doing that in London even now, as she rode, or was that Richard's task? After all, he had quizzed her and her father. She smiled grimly to herself; perhaps the decision whether to marry Stephen or not would be taken out of her hands. The daughter of a man who did not know who his own parents

were would not be considered an acceptable wife for Stephen.
To people like the Harecrofts, having known roots was of
prime importance. Was that why Richard had not married
Lucy?

'A penny for them,' he asked.

His voice startled her. 'What? Oh, I was miles away.'

'Where? With Stephen at Harecroft's Emporium, wondering if he is thinking of you?' He paused, watching for her
reaction, but when she said nothing, added, 'I do not find that
very flattering.'

'I am sorry. I will try to pay attention in future. What were
you saying?'

'I was asking if you liked to watch horse racing.'

'I did in Calcutta. They had some fine races there. We
have not gone to the races since we returned to England. My
life has been too busy.'

'Of course. We must not forget you work for a living.'
She was aware of the irony in his tone but ignored it.
'Yes, I do.'

'But if you marry Stephen you will not need to.'

'I enjoy my work and Stephen intimated that he would be
happy for me to work alongside him as your great-grandmother did for your great-grandfather.'

'Did he? Then you would make your home in London and
not in Borstead.'

'I suppose so. Does that make a difference?'

'Not at all,' he said.

They rode on in silence, each thinking their own thoughts
while very conscious of the other. Richard had learned more
about James Bywater and decided most of what the man had
said was new to his daughter. If there was a conspiracy for
her to join the family for gain, she was not part of it. She was
truly innocent and he regretted his suspicions, suspicions en-

gendered by his great-grandmother. Did Diana love Stephen? Stephen had always been selfish, even as a child. He had a way of wheedling what he wanted from Papa and Mama, and often did not consider the impact of that on other people. The death of Pal was a case in point. It was Stephen's dog that had worried the sheep. The dogs were brothers and looked alike, but Stephen's way of treating his dog was very different from his own and as a result the dog was disobedient, unmanageable and vicious. There had been no point in bringing that to the notice of his father, who would not have believed him. And so Pal had died and some of Richard, the child, had died with him. If Stephen wanted Diana, he would do his utmost to have her, no matter who else might be hurt. But he could not tell her that, it would be disloyal and, like his father over the dog, she would not believe it.

'Where did you meet Miss Standish?' she asked him suddenly.

'Lucy? In London. At supper after an evening at the theatre with friends. She came into the eating house where we were enjoying pork chops and boiled potatoes, I remember.'

'The friends who are living with you now?'

'Yes, Freddie and Joe.'

'So she came to live with you.'

'Yes. It seemed the easiest solution.' He did not enlarge on that and his answers, though not exactly reluctant, were guarded. She understood that and refrained from asking him why he had not married Lucy. It would make him angry and she hated being the object of his anger.

They were approaching the stables, a series of buildings round an open square. In a paddock nearby horses grazed, among them the white colt. 'Do you think he can win?' she asked.

'It depends on the going. Soft to firm is good, but at the

moment it is too hard. If we do not have rain, I think my grandfather might withdraw him. There is no sense in risking a valuable animal.' They dismounted and walked their horses to the fence round the paddock and stood leaning on the bars watching the horses. A stable hand joined them.

'Afternoon, Mr Harecroft.'

'Good afternoon, Jarman. Will North Wind run?'

'Dunno, 'tis in the lap of the gods. His lordship will make a decision on Friday morning.'

'If he runs, is he worth a wager?'

The man laughed. 'Now, sir, you know 'tis more than my job's worth to venture an opinion on that.'

'Then we shall have to make up our own minds. Is it permissible to show Miss Bywater round the stables?'

'I will ask your grandfather. He is about somewhere. I'll tell him you are here.' And with that he strode off.

'He was being very circumspect,' Diana ventured.

'Yes, if it leaks out that Grandfather has a horse running with more than a good chance of winning, it will shorten the odds and that would not be desirable. Ah, there is Grandfather.'

They led their horses towards the old man, who strode out to greet them and stayed with them while they hitched their own mounts to railings and then showed them round himself. Everywhere was spotless and well ordered and it was apparent to Diana that there was a true rapport between the two men. If Richard did not get on with his father, his grandfather compensated for it. They talked knowledgeably about the horses, while she listened and admired the whole arrangement, from the pristine buildings and shining tackle to the busy stable lads and well-groomed animals. Afterwards they returned to their mounts and rode slowly back to Borstead Hall.

They crossed the little bridge over the brook, but instead

of riding on, he reined in and dismounted. 'There is something else I would like you to see,' he said, turning and holding out his hands to help her down. She put her hands in his and jumped lightly to the ground.

She looked up to thank him and found him gazing down at her with a puzzled expression on his face, as if he could not quite understand how he came to be there. It was gone in an instant and he was smiling, but something hung in the air between them, something almost tangible, a thread, thin as a hair, strong as wire. 'You will have to be very, very quiet.' His voice was so cool, so normal, she was taken aback, though she did not know what she expected. Warmth perhaps, but that was silly, considering she was doing her best not to let him see the unnerving effect he had on her.

He let go of her hands and led her a little way along the bank where he stopped to take off his coat and spread it on the grass. 'Sit down,' he whispered. 'And don't move or say a word.'

Puzzled, but trusting, she obeyed. He sat beside her, close enough for her to feel the warmth of his body, making every nerve in her own tingle. 'Now what?' she asked, whispering herself because he had done so, though she did not know the reason for it.

He put a finger on her lips and the pressure of that finger sent her giddy with desire and she had to take firm hold of herself to stop herself moaning. She wanted him, oh, how she wanted him! It was disgraceful, wanton and impossible.

'We wait,' he murmured.

And so they waited, sitting side by side with the sun beating on their backs and the cool water lapping at their feet, saying nothing. She did not know what she was waiting for—it could have been anything or nothing, significant or insignificant.

And then she saw it, a bright flash of iridescent green and blue, alighting on the overhanging branch of a willow. 'A kingfisher,' she breathed. As she watched, it flew down to the water like a well-aimed dart and then surfaced with a wriggling fish in its beak and flew back to the bush, trailing sparkling droplets of water. 'Oh, it is so beautiful!' She turned towards him, eyes shining. 'Thank you, thank you for showing it to me.'

He was looking at her, not the bird. Something inside him gave a great lurch and a lump came to his throat he could not dislodge. 'Diana.' His voice was a hoarse whisper.

'Hallo, you two, what are you doing there?'

They turned startled eyes on Freddie Somers, who had come upon them so silently they had not heard his tread, or perhaps they were so absorbed in each other, they were oblivious to anything else.

Richard recovered first. 'Bird watching,' he said.

Freddie dropped to the ground beside them. 'And what have you seen?'

'A beautiful kingfisher,' Diana told him. 'It caught a fish.'

'You like the things of nature, Miss Bywater?' he asked, apparently unaware of what he had interrupted and where it might have led if he had not.

Diana was thankful for it, but that was tinged with regret. What might Richard have said if his friend had not come upon them? 'Yes, of course. Do you?'

'Indeed I do. As I walked I saw a kestrel swoop down and fly off with a tiny creature in its beak, a peacock butterfly and a wild orchid in the grass, all in the space of a few yards.'

'How observant you are.'

'An artist needs to be.'

'Do you use living things as subjects?'

'Often. Come and see.' He scrambled to his feet.

'Now?'

'Yes, now. You too, Richard, I have something new to show you.'

They rose and he went ahead, while Richard and Diana led their horses, through a gate in the wall that surrounded the park and down a narrow path to a small chapel. The area around it was overgrown, but well trampled. 'Here is where we work, Joe and I.' He led the way to its blackened oak door and pushed it open.

The inside had been cleared of pews and the area divided into two. There were easels and tables covered with pots of paint and jars of brushes and innumerable canvases stacked against the walls. He moved forward and pulled aside the cloth that draped an easel in the centre of the room and she found herself looking at a portrait of Dick. He had captured the child exactly, his red-gold hair, blue eyes and chubby cheeks. 'It is lovely,' she said. 'Do you not think so, Mr Harecroft?'

'Your best yet,' Richard said, studying it carefully. 'How much more time do you need to finish it?'

'A few days, maybe a little longer. Then we need to catalogue everything before we can go public.'

'You are surely not going to sell it?' Diana said. 'If Dick were mine, I could not bear to part with it.'

'I can always paint another if Lucy wants one, but she already has several.' He began pulling the covers off other pictures: some were of broad sweeping vistas, including one of Borstead Hall, another was of the dower house with the tiny figures of a woman and child standing in the corner of the garden, almost as if they had been put there as an afterthought. Others were portraits, though, not knowing the sitters, she could not tell if they were true likenesses. She guessed they might be if the one he was painting of Dick could be used as a yardstick. One was a muscular figure of a man that made her think of Richard and sent the colour flying to her cheeks. There were horses, dogs, birds at rest and on the wing, little animals like squirrels and beavers, all display-ing the nervous energy of the painter. When they were all un-covered she wandered round the room stopping at each, turning her head this way and that to view them.

'What do you think?' he asked.

'Oh, they are all so well done, they should not be hidden away here.'

'They are not hidden away. We are hoping to hold an ex-hibition when we can find a venue that will do them justice.'

'Then I am sure you will soon be rich and famous.'

He laughed. 'Are you a connoisseur, Miss Bywater?'

'No, but my father taught me to appreciate the finer things in life and that included art. He said it was all part of my edu-cation. He believes in education for women as well as men and always maintains knowledge makes men free.'

'Good for him,' Richard said. 'Your papa and I have much in common.'

She looked sharply at him, noting the humour in his eyes and his half-mocking smile. It was an attitude he seemed to adopt when anyone else was around, as if he were afraid to show the real Richard. And yet if anyone knew the man, it must surely be his close friends. And his mistress. She delib-erately shut her mind off from thinking of Lucy.

'Joe's work is here,' Richard said, indicating some canvases stacked against the wall on the other aside of the chapel. She went to stand beside him as he turned them round one by one. They were very different: street scenes with houses in disrepair and ragged children, industrial processes, full of steam and machinery, showing children at work. One in particular showed a child only a year or two older than

Dick. She thought the boy might have been used as a model, except the child in the painting was thin as a stick with wide, black-circled eyes and bare feet. He was kneeling beneath a huge loom, while an overseer stood over him with a whip. The pictures moved her almost to tears, which was no doubt what was intended. If they were exhibited, they might add fuel to the debate about poverty, but she doubted they would be a popular choice for buyers to hang on drawing-room walls.

'They are very different,' she said. 'Do you think a joint exhibition will show them to best advantage? Might not one detract from the other? I would have thought two venues would be better.'

'That's what I said,' Freddie put in. 'No gallery would put my work beside Joe's.'

'We shall see,' Richard said.

'What about you, Mr Harecroft?' she asked as Richard put the canvases back and they prepared to leave. 'Have you found a publisher for your work?'

'No, my efforts to find one have been unsuccessful so far. The subject matter is meant to stir consciences, but people do not like having their consciences disturbed.'

'What is your book about? I recall you said something about the plight of children.'

'So I did. It is a subject that needs addressing, but finding a publisher has not been easy, for the same reasons that Joe's work is rejected. It is not popular.'

'But you should not let that stop you. Publish yourself if you have to. Make a song and dance about it beforehand. Use Mr Harris's pictures to illustrate it. That way you would both benefit when it sells in thousands.'

'You might have an idea there, Diana, but I do not think I can afford to publish it myself. It is not the printing, so much as the marketing of it which would be horrendously dear.'

'Would your family not help you?'

His smile was a wry one. 'I would not ask. My father's views and mine do not coincide.'

'Politics?'

'That and other things.'

'He does not like the way you live with your friends?'

'I do not think he has ever spoken to them.'

'Not even Miss Standish?'

'No. She is an actress, not acceptable in the society my father inhabits and especially with Dick—' He stopped. Now was not the time.

'I hope you find a publisher soon,' she said, not wanting to talk about Dick. 'And a venue for all these lovely pictures.'

They left the young artist, who seemed to have forgotten their existence as he picked up a brush and dipped it in paint.

Once outside they fetched their horses and mounted, riding the rest of the way back to the stables at Borstead Hall.

It was late when they arrived and the stable lads had all gone into the kitchen for their dinner. Dismounting, Richard turned to help Diana and then set about unsaddling his mount and rubbing him down. Diana did likewise with Mayfly, smiling as the mare shivered with delight. They worked companionably, talking to the horses, not each other, and then led the animals into their respective stalls and gave them food and water.

'I must get back to the house, it must be nearly dinner time,' she said. 'Thank you for a pleasant afternoon.'

Richard found her sudden coolness inexplicable. Down by the water, she had looked at him with considerable warmth in those expressive smoky grey eyes, mesmerising him. For what seemed like minutes but could only have been seconds, he had been unable to move, struck dumb. He had never experienced that feeling with a woman before. Did she have that power over all men, or only over him? Did she know she had it? Was that how she had ensnared Stephen? He smiled at his own fancies, believing himself immune. 'My pleasure,' he said.

'Why are you laughing?'

He took her shoulders in his hands and turned her towards a trough of clear water where she could see her reflection. What she saw made her laugh herself. Her hat had fallen down her back, kept there by the veil which she had tied under her chin and there were wisps of straw, sticking in her hair, one coil of which had escaped its pins and hung to her shoulders. He lifted it and gently kissed the nape of her neck.

She felt the slight pressure of his lips and shivered uncontrollably. Her hands went up behind her head and found his face, whether to stop him or encourage him she could not have said. He took her hands in his own and kissed the palms one by one and then slowly turned her round to face him. Each searched the other's face, not speaking, then he bent his head and kissed her lips.

The feel of his mouth on hers sent shock waves right through her. Her knees began to tremble and would have buckled if he had not been supporting her, holding her so close against him she could feel his warmth turning her insides to liquid fire. She seemed to have left the ground, flying from all earthly things, all sensible thoughts. She wanted this man, she wanted the kiss to go on, to lead to other transports of delight she could only imagine. She clung to him, returning his kiss in full measure.

It was only then he realised what he was doing and released her. They stood facing each other, breathing heavily. Neither spoke. She did not condemn him; any sign of anger would be a pretence, and he must know it. Nor did he regret what he had done, though he did not know why he had done it, nor why a simple stolen kiss should have such a devastating effect on him. It had unnerved him. He opened his mouth, but no words came from his lips. 'Sorry' seemed inadequate. She was lovely and the temptation had been great, but that did not excuse him. Besides, he wasn't sorry.

Deliberately she turned her back on him and faced the water again and used it as a mirror to pick the straw out of her hair before pushing the heavy locks up under her hat and securing it with the veil. Then she turned towards him again. He had been holding his breath, but now he breathed out slowly and managed a rueful smile before going to the stable door and holding it open for her. Silently they walked side by side back to the house, where they parted, still without a word being spoken. Neither could think of anything to say.

Once in her room, Diana collapsed on her bed, surprised to find that her cheeks were wet, though she had not been aware she was crying. But she knew the reason for it. She had fallen in love with Richard Harecroft, head over heels, irrevocably. How and when had it happened? She tried to think back, to their first meeting, to his kindness in helping her father, the journey down from London, the acrimony since then, which, she realised, had been a direct result of her love for him, but there seemed to be no particular time when gratitude and tolerance had become love. It had crept up on her unawares. He already had a mistress and a child and lived openly with them, which did not seem to preclude him from kissing another woman. How could she love someone like that? But how could she not? If you loved someone, you loved them and nothing could change it.

How could she go on, day by day, knowing that when Richard came up to the house for dinner he was leaving afterwards to go back to Lucy and his child. She could not come between them. She must pull herself together and hide her feelings from everyone. It would be too humiliating if any of his family and particularly Richard himself were to find out how she felt about him. But how hard it was going to be!

One thing was certain; she must take the first opportunity to tell Stephen she could not marry him, though what the consequences of that would be she dare not conjecture. The prospect of searching for suitable employment again terrified her. And what reason could she give without revealing the truth? Her position at Borstead, difficult enough before, had become untenable. It was not fair on Stephen or Lady Harecroft or Miss Standish, come to that. First thing in the morning she would have to tell her ladyship that she had decided not to marry Stephen and under the circumstances it would be better if she left before he came down from London. Then she would go and see her father and tell him that she could not stay and she would not listen to his arguments. He would have to remain where he was until she had found accommodation for them both and a new job, but she could just about manage it for a week or two. Now the decision had been made, all she had to do was find the strength to carry it through.

She heard the first dinner gong, telling her she had half an hour to change and go down. It would be an ordeal to sit down to dinner with them all, but it must be done. Making excuses to stay in her room would invite curiosity and solicitous enquiries about her health. She could not bear that. Slowly she left the bed and went to the wardrobe to select something to wear.

She was tempted to put on the embroidered green gown that her ladyship had admired; after all, she would not be wearing it to the party now, but to wear it might cause comment. Tonight must appear to be an ordinary evening, as if nothing were amiss. She chose a blue silk she had made over from one of her mother's, arranged her hair in a severe style and wore a string of colourful beads, purchased in India. The second gong went as she was slipping into her shoes and she went down to the drawing room just in time to follow the family in to dinner.

Lord Harecroft was in a jovial mood and asked Diana what she thought of the stables and his horses. She was glad of the opportunity to talk to him and thank him for showing her round and added the tale of the kingfisher, but she was careful not to look at Richard when she spoke, knowing that looking into those blue eyes of his would totally unnerve her. 'We went into the chapel,' she added, then wondered if she should have mentioned that, but his lordship did not appear concerned.

'Oh, yes, I believe Richard's friends keep their works of art there. What did you think of them?'

'Very good indeed.'

He turned to address his grandson. 'Are you any nearer to finding a permanent home for them?'

'A little,' he said, helping himself to vegetables from a tureen a servant had placed at his elbow. 'I have an appointment with the owner of a gallery in the Burlington Arcade tomorrow afternoon. Something may come of it.'

'Burlington Arcade,' Diana repeated. 'You mean you are going to London?'

'Yes, didn't I say?'

'No.'

'I am leaving first thing in the morning. I also have other errands which I hope to conclude in good time to return for Great-Grandmama's party.'

'Will you come back with John and Stephen?' his grandmother asked him, while Diana digested the information that she would not see him again. She would be gone before he returned. Perhaps it was for the best, but, oh, how miserable it made her!

'No, because I shall take Great-Grandmama's carriage and Papa will not leave before close of business on Friday night. I would like to be back before that.'

'You will stay at Harecroft House, though?'

'Yes, of course.'

'Then will you tell your father to put business second for once,' Lady Harecroft said. 'If they travel after dark, who knows what might happen. They might be delayed and if they are late for my party I shall be most displeased. Tell them to make an early start.'

'I will tell them, but I cannot guarantee they will take any notice. You know Father's reluctance to miss a minute's profitable trading.' He turned to Diana before her ladyship could reply to that. 'Have you any messages for Stephen? I am sure he would like to know you are waiting impatiently for his arrival.'

She felt the colour flare in her face as she realised he was baiting her. She took her time to find an answer. 'I am sure he knows that already,' she said slowly.

He noticed her heightened colour and wondered if she were thinking of what had happened that afternoon. He had embarrassed her, but then he had embarrassed himself and he wished heartily he had not given in to the temptation to kiss that lovely neck. It had aroused in him a physical ache and a strange longing that a second and more protracted kiss had not assuaged. It had left him hungrier than ever. He was not a rake, whatever the world might think; he did not go about kissing young ladies just because the fancy took him to do so. She must think he did. Mentioning Stephen was a way of reminding himself that his brother had proposed and, as far as he was aware, she intended to accept. Otherwise, why had she come to Borstead to attend the party? And her measured reply had confirmed that. In a way he was glad to be going away, to have something useful to do that might take his mind off her.

He was relieved when the meal came to an end and his great-grandmother asked him to take her back to her room. They had the talk she had been promising him and it left him so bemused, instead of returning to the drawing room to join the others for tea, he left to go to the dower house, where he entered into a lively discussion with his boarders about what constituted a work of art.

Richard had left by the time Diana rose next morning. She dressed in her grey working dress and after breakfast went with Alicia to look at the ballroom and decide how many tables and chairs would be needed and where the flowers should be put. The servants had already lifted the huge carpet and were busy polishing the floor ready for dancing. 'How many extra footmen do you think we shall need for serving?' Alicia asked. 'There will be glasses of wine and cordial to be taken round throughout the evening as well as supper to be served. I thought about a dozen.'

'I am sure you know best. I know nothing about hiring staff. My mother saw to that when she was alive and afterwards we did not need servants.' She did not add that they could not afford them.

'I think we had better see how many tables and chairs we can rustle up ourselves before hiring any extra,' Alicia went on. 'The attics are full of old furniture. Shall we go and explore?'

They went up the stairs, along a corridor and then up another flight of stairs, this time with hard-wearing jute carpet. There were rows of doors evenly spaced along a corridor. 'The indoor servants' sleeping quarters,' Alicia explained, leading the way up another flight, this time with no carpet at all and their footsteps echoed. This led to rooms under the pitched roof, unoccupied except for discarded items which no one had a use for but that none could bear to throw away. There were old beds, tables, chairs, stools, mirrors, trunks full of antiquated clothes, dusty books, pictures stacked against the walls, astronomical instruments, the accoutrements from a soldier's uniform. A sword hung in its scabbard from one rafter decorated with a finely woven spider's web.

'I have brought a piece of chalk,' Alicia said. 'We will put a cross on everything we think will be useful and then send some of the men up to bring it all down and clean it up. We do not want the heavy stuff. Ah,' she added, darting forward. 'Card tables. We shall need those.' And she marked them with a cross.

Diana followed, too intrigued by her surroundings to be of much help. Here was the story of a family's life through goodness knew how many years. This was part of the history of the Harecrofts. There was one picture that intrigued her. It showed a young woman sitting on a garden seat under an oak tree, surrounded by her children, two boys and a girl. A man, presumably her husband and the father of the children, stood behind her with a bejewelled hand lightly on the back of her chair. And though the picture was dirty, she could see they were all dressed in the colourful fashion of the previous century. All, except the man who was dark, had hair the colour of ripe corn with just a hint of a red, as if the dying sun had streaked it.

The elder boy, who reminded Diana of Richard, had the bluest eyes, bright and knowing. He was about sixteen, she guessed and stood beside his mama in an almost arrogant pose, as if to proclaim himself the heir. The next had eyes of a paler blue and was perhaps two years younger. He looked as though he was there on sufferance and longed to be away playing. The little girl was much younger, only just big enough to stand, which she did, clinging on to her mama's skirts.

'That's me,' Alicia said when she noticed Diana's interest.

'Is it? Then that must be the dowager Lady Harecroft and your papa.'

'Yes.' She pointed to the older boy. 'That's William, the present Lord Harecroft, and the other is my brother James. They were both much older than me. There were other children between us, but either my mother miscarried or the babies died in infancy. I am only a few years older than my nephew, John.'

'I did not realise you had another brother.'

'He was a soldier and was killed in the American Wars. I hardly remember him. My mother had the picture brought up here after that. She could not bear to look at it.'

'How sad.'

'Yes. We do not talk of him. Now, how many chairs have you counted?'

Diana had not counted any at all and set to work remedying the omission. Then they went back downstairs and Alicia gave instructions to the servants. That done they had luncheon and after that Lady Harecroft and Alicia went to take their afternoon nap. Diana was left to do whatever she wanted. Now was the time to put her plans into action. The first thing was to see her father.

Making her way along the woodland path, mentally rehearsing the words she would use, she came upon Dick, curled up at the foot of a tree fast asleep. There was no sign of an adult. Gently she woke him. 'Dick, what are you doing here without your mama?'

He rubbed his fists into his eyes and looked about him. 'Mama.'

'I expect she is at home.' She picked him up. 'She will be looking for you. Let us go and find her, shall we?'

Trustingly he nestled his head into her shoulder and sucked his thumb. His little body was plump and warm against her breast and though he was heavy, the burden of his weight was nothing to the burden she carried in her heart. She gulped to stop herself crying and murmured reassuring words as she hurried towards the dower house.

At the gate she was met by a distraught Lucy. 'Thank God,' she said, relieving Diana of the lighter of her burdens. 'We have been searching everywhere for him. Where did you find him?'

'Fast asleep under a tree in the wood.'

'I do not know how he got out, I always keep the gate shut.'

'Perhaps one of the others left it open.'

'Perhaps. Richard left very early but I know he would not leave it open. Freddie went off to the chapel afterwards. It might have been him. He does not understand about small boys and how adventurous they can be. Thank you for bringing him home.'

'It is a good thing I was passing, otherwise he might have woken and found himself alone. It would have been frightening for the poor little fellow.'

'Yes. I was talking to him about his papa and saying he would soon come back and we should see him again and I suppose he thought he would go and look out for him.' She paused. 'Will you come in for a moment?'

'No, thank you. I must be on my way.'

'Thank you again.'

Diana left Lucy, shutting the gate firmly. She dare not look back lest she choke. The memory of the woman with the little boy's arms clinging tightly about her neck was something that would live with her for ever. She was all the more determined to leave.

Her father was in a difficult mood and telling him that she was turning her back on the Harecroft family and returning to London was not easy. He did not seem to understand. 'Papa, I cannot marry Stephen,' she reiterated, sitting in the garden with him, while Toby sat at their feet. She would have to leave the dog with the stable hands at the Hall until she was settled. 'And it is not seemly that I should stay under the circumstances.'

'What circumstances?'

'I am going to turn him down. They will all say I have taken advantage of their generosity when I had no intention of accepting him.'

'Why must you turn him down?'

'I do not love him. I respect him and admire him, but I am not in love with him.'

'Bah! Sentimental rubbish.'

'Papa, how can you say that? You have told me over and over again how much you loved Mama and how much she loved you. Am I not to be allowed the same happiness?'

'You will find it.'

'I do not think so, not at Borstead Hall, not with Mr Stephen Harecroft and his overbearing family.'

'But they *are* a family.'

'Yes, but a disjointed one. And that means nothing if I cannot be happy with Stephen.'

'How do you know you cannot?'

'I just do. Papa, please allow me to know my own mind

on this. I will find work and a home and we shall be like we were before.'

'I do not want be like we were before. I do not want to go back to poky rooms and evil-tongued landladies and bad food…'

'Neither do I. I will find something better.'

'Better to stay here. If you cannot bring yourself to marry Stephen, then marry Richard. I like him and he will be Lord Harecroft himself one day and inherit everything.'

'Papa, it is not a question of accepting one or the other,' she said, fighting back tears. 'Mr Richard Harecroft has not asked me to marry him. He lives with his mistress and little son. Do you think I would even consider coming between them, even if he did propose? And no wife worth her salt would turn a blind eye to what he makes no attempt to hide.' She stood up, tired of arguing. 'I am going to London to search for work and rooms.'

'And what will happen to me? I will be turned out if you upset the Harecrofts.'

'I have saved a little of my wages and can keep you here for a week or two if that happens, but I do not think they are so vindictive. I shall explain everything to Lady Harecroft.'

He sighed heavily. 'I need a drink.'

It was almost moral blackmail, implying he would only behave if she gave in. It took all her resolve not to do so. She might have capitulated if she had not reminded herself of Lucy and Dick and the hopelessness of her situation. 'I am afraid that will not make me change my mind,' she said, knowing that the matron would not give in to him and he could not go and find liquor for himself. 'I will write as soon as I find somewhere to stay and let you know when you can join me.' And before he could say another word, she put a hand on his arm, bent to kiss his cheek and left before he could start arguing again.

Chapter Eight

Back in her room, Diana sat on the bed and wondered how to tell the dowager and Miss Harecroft of her decision. No doubt they would give her similar arguments to her father's and probably find their own means of blackmail. She could not bear it. She sat at an escritoire that stood close to the light from the window and pulled out pen and paper. Writing her resignation would be more formal, more a sign that she meant it, than trying to tell her ladyship to her face and being quizzed on the reason for her abrupt departure. She could not tell her the real reason and the old lady was astute enough to know when she was being fobbed off.

The trouble was the words would not come. They were blocked by images of Richard kissing the top of Dick's head; Dick snuggling into the arms of his mother; Richard kissing her in the gloom of the stable and the realisation that he was unscrupulous when it came to women. Was Lucy content with her situation, or only pretending? She must love Richard very much to tolerate it. But so did she! The paper in front of her was blotched with tears. She screwed it up, threw it down and began on another. 'Dear Lady Harecroft...' She got no further before a paroxysm of weeping overcame her. And that was how Alicia found her.

Diana scrubbed at her face, but her first startled look as a light knock was followed by Alicia, calling, 'May I come in?' followed by her entrance, gave her away.

'Oh, my dear, whatever is wrong?' Alicia asked, hurrying forward to put her arm about Diana's shoulders. 'Are you not happy here? Has someone been unkind to you?'

'No one has been unkind,' she murmured, sniffing back the tears. 'You have all been very kind. That is the trouble.'

'I do not understand you.'

'If you had not been so good to me, asking me down here when you really did not need any help, paying for my father's convalescence, treating me as one of the family...' She gulped, determined to go on. 'I cannot go on.'

'Why ever not?'

'I came on the understanding that I would consider marrying Mr Stephen.' She was feeling stronger now and her words were clearer. 'I cannot marry him.'

'As I recall, you did not promise you would.'

'He thinks I will and so does your mother. I do not know why I was invited in the first place; I have nothing to offer Stephen. I am sure your mother has mistaken me for someone else, someone worthy of Stephen. Mr Rich—' She gulped over the name. 'Mr Richard said he was sure we had met before and I am sure we have not. I have been mistaken for someone else and should never have come. It is all a mistake.'

Alicia looked hard at her, wondering what was behind this sudden deluge of tears and doubts. 'Stephen will be disappointed if you turn him down,' she said evenly. 'But he will get over it. And whether you accept or reject him, I am quite sure my mother will not let you go.'

'Who does she think I am?'

'Why, Miss Diana Bywater, who else? Now, dry your eyes and cheer up. Mama will be very upset to see you have been crying.'

'I cannot face her. It is cowardly, I know, but I must leave. I am sorry I have done so little towards the party, but I do not think you truly need me.'

'Yes, we do.' Alicia smiled suddenly—there was more to this than Diana was prepared to tell her and she had a fair idea of what it was. 'I have a plan.'

'To make me stay? You will not succeed.'

'I cannot make you stay against your will, but I think perhaps you need to get away for a day or two, then you might see things more clearly….'

'Everything is very clear to me.'

'Then humour me. I have ordered a birthday present for my mother from a shop in Staines that needs collecting. You could fetch it for me. It is only a small thing, not heavy at all. If my mother asks where you have gone, I shall tell her you are on an errand to do with her party. If you still want to leave after that, then I will try to make it right with her.' She paused, putting her hand on Diana's arm. 'What do you say? It will save me a journey.'

'I…I don't know…'

'Do it to please me. I have friends in Staines, a Mr and Mrs Proudfoot who will put you up. They are coming to my mother's party so you could return with them, unless you choose to come back earlier. I will give you a letter to take to them.'

Diana found it impossible to refuse. Miss Harecroft had been kind to her and very understanding and what difference would it make in the long run? 'Very well.'

'Good. Now Richard has taken my mother's carriage and I think my sister-in-law is using the family coach. There is a gig. I could ask Soames…'

'Please do not go to the trouble. There must be a stage.'

'Yes, there is. Apart from the mail which goes at a pro-digiously early hour to get to the capital by the start of the day's business, there are two local stages every day from Ascot, one in the morning at quarter past ten and the other at a quarter to three in the afternoon. It is too late to catch that today, but I could ask Soames to take you to Ascot in the gig tomorrow morning in time to catch the morning one. Will that do?'

She had not planned to stay a single night longer, but as Richard had gone to London and would not be back before the end of the week, she would not be tormented by his presence. 'Yes, of course.'

'Good. Now dry your eyes and have a rest before it is time to change for dinner. We will say nothing about this little jaunt to anyone tonight. Agreed?'

Diana smiled wanly. 'Yes, and thank you for your under-standing.'

After Miss Harecroft had left, Diana sank on to the bed and stared at the ceiling. The cornice was finely carved with cherubs and angels, every one of whom seemed to have the look of Master Dick. Hurriedly she scrambled off the bed, washed and changed her dress and went down for dinner, wondering whose task it was to carry the dowager down when Richard was absent. She did not learn the answer to that as her ladyship decided to have her supper in her room. Diana dined with Lord and Lady Harecroft and Miss Harecroft. It was a quiet meal without dissension. Now and again, Alicia looked at Diana and smiled reassuringly.

Next morning, with a letter addressed to Mrs and Mrs Proud-foot and a few guineas in her purse, she climbed into the gig beside Soames and left Borstead. She did not intend to return.

* * *

Richard watched the countryside rushing past the carriage window, impatient to be home again. They were building a railway along part of the way and he supposed that before long it would go the whole way from London to the West Country. He fell to wondering how much faster than a carriage it would be. Could a galloping horse beat an engine? For a short distance, he surmised, it might, but over a longer distance, flesh, bone and muscle would be outstripped by iron and steam.

His trip to the capital had been partially successful. He had shown some of what he had written to several publishers, but they were reluctant to handle it. 'Too inflammatory,' they said. It was by chance he had met Henry Hunt, known by the populace as Orator Hunt, and had told him of his dilemma. Hunt had told him of an obscure publisher who might tackle it. He had business premises in Southwark, near where Diana had lived.

Going back there had brought her to mind most forcefully. His head was filled with images of her: caring for her father and trying to hide his shame; angry at him for going to her father behind her back, a move he bitterly regretted; dressed for the ball at Almack's, breathtakingly beautiful; the feel of her in his arms, especially the feel of her in his arms; the pressure of her hands cradling his face as he kissed her. He should never have done that. But it had shown him another side of her character. Did a seemingly virtuous young lady dally with someone else when she was supposed to be considering a proposal from his brother? He had thought about telling Stephen, but decided against it. It would have sounded like crowing over him and would certainly not improve their fragile relationship. And it could lead to heaven knew how many more complications.

Life was complicated enough what with Great-Grandmama's determination to get at the truth. Truth once carefully buried was hard to come by, but he did have some news for her. James Bywater had spent all his early years at the Foundling Hospital, taken there by his mother when he was less than a month old. 'She said she was a widow,' the principal had told him after consulting their meticulous records. 'She said she would return for him when her late husband's affairs had been sorted out, but she never came back. It is not unusual—bastard children are often abandoned here. We make no difference between them and those genuinely orphaned.'

'You do not think she was telling the truth about being a widow?'

The man had smiled. 'I doubt it. I never met her, of course, it was many years ago, but the fact that she did not return seems to confirm it.'

'What about her son?'

'He grew up here, was diligent at his studies and we were able to arrange for him to go into the navy when he reached his thirteenth birthday. Our records go no further.'

He thanked the man and left, wondering what his great-grandmother would make of that. Was it what she had been expecting? How much did Diana know? Would it make any difference to Stephen? If Stephen withdrew his proposal on the grounds of her father's bastardy, it would be a terrible blow to her and hypercritical of him. It would be better if she decided not to accept Stephen and then none of it need come to light. He hoped most profoundly that his great-grandmother was not going to make an announcement at her party. He would have to dissuade her from doing any such thing. It was the thought uppermost in his mind as his great-grandmother's comfortable carriage carried him to Borstead. He wanted to see Diana again, to satisfy himself that she was ev-

erything he remembered about her, warm and compassionate, beautiful and proud. He did not want that pride dinted by
anything he had discovered.

As soon as the carriage rolled to a stop outside the stables,
he left it to the care of the coachman and grooms and hurried
indoors. There was no one about. He supposed his grandfather was at the racing stables and his grandmother was out
paying calls. He went to find the dowager.

'So you are back,' she commented from the winged chair
by the window of her boudoir. 'You wasted no time. What did
you find out?'

'It is as you expected. James Bywater's mother was Susan
Bywater. The Principal of the Foundling Hospital was sure
she was not married.'

'Aah…' The old lady sat back in her chair with a sigh of
satisfaction. 'At last.'

'What difference does it make? He is what he is and it
is not fair to Diana to expose him. She does not deserve to
have the ignominy heaped upon her. She has been through
enough already.'

She looked sharply at him. 'I would not dream of doing
so.'

'I had supposed that was what your party was all about.'

'Then you supposed wrong. I did not know who she was
when I first thought of the party. And it was Stephen who
asked me to include her.'

'Ah, Stephen. What do you think he'll make of it?'

'Have you spoken to him about it?'

'No, it is up to you to decide whether anyone should be
told. It might be better to let sleeping dogs lie.'

'I do not think that is possible now.'

He supposed not. 'Why did you decide to hold the party?'

'Why should I not? I am coming to the end of a long life and I thought what a pity I would not be alive to see the reaction of my family on the reading of my will, and so I shall implement it before I die and have some fun watching my off-spring making use of their inheritance.'

'You are a wicked old woman, Great-Grandmama,' he said, laughing.

'You are not to say a word.'

'I won't. But what about Diana?'

'Go and find her, send her to me. I will tell her everything myself.'

'Be careful of her,' he said. 'It will be a great shock and I am not sure how she will react. Leave her with some pride.'

'I do not need a lesson in tact from you, boy. Now, off with you.'

He took his leave and went in search of Diana. She was nowhere to be found. Going out to the stables to see if she had taken Mayfly out, he was told by Soames that he had that morning taken her to Ascot to catch the stage to Staines.

'What has she gone there for?' he asked, remembering he had passed the Staines coach on the road. If only he had known she was in it!

'It is not my place to ask questions of that nature, sir,' Soames said. 'You had better ask Miss Harecroft.'

He found his great-aunt supervising the servants polishing the ballroom floor. 'Why has Diana gone to Staines?' he demanded, forgetting the usual courtesy of a greeting.

'I sent her to fetch Mama's birthday present. She will stay with the Proudfoots.'

'You could have sent a servant to do that.'

'I could, but as she was intent on leaving…'

'Why? Had someone upset her?'

'I rather think you might have.'

'Me?' Even though he feigned astonishment, he was reminded of that stolen kiss. Was it his shame or her own she was worried about?

'Yes. Can't you see what has happened? She came to Borstead to consider Stephen's proposal and finds herself in love with you.'

'In love with me?' He was astonished. Was she such a simpleton as to think one kiss constituted love? 'Did she tell you that?'

'No, of course not. I guessed. She said she was here under false pretences and had been mistaken for someone else.'

'I hope you told her that was not the case.'

'Of course I did, but, without betraying Mother's interest, I could not convince her.'

He looked startled. 'How did you know about that?'

'Mama told me. So what did you discover?'

He repeated what he had told the dowager. 'Do you think Diana will come back?'

Alicia shrugged. 'She might. It depends.'

'On what?'

'On what you do about it.'

'Me?' He looked searchingly at her. Was he expected to go rushing after her and persuade her to stay? But wouldn't it be better if she were not at Borstead when Stephen came down? He had said all along the marriage was a bad idea. Would that not solve the problem? But would it? Great-Grandmama had set her heart on welcoming Diana into the family. Irrespective of whether she married Stephen, being part of the family would mean the end of her penury, the need to earn a living for herself and her father, the terrible living conditions—Great-Grandmama would see to that. And what had her father said about wanting a family for her. At that moment his concern for her overrode his consideration of his brother. He had talked to Stephen long and hard when he was in London, though whether his words had had any effect he was not sure. All he could think of was that he had to go to Diana and stop her doing something irrevocable.

His hesitation was only momentary. 'I will leave you to tell Great-Grandmama I could not find her and why,' he said. Then he turned about, went to the stables, where, to Soames's annoyance, he had fresh horses put to the coach and ten minutes later, with young Archie Sadler on the driving seat, they were careering down the drive.

Diana looked out of the window of the coach, but she hardly saw what was passing in front of her: the villages with churches, houses and cottages straddling the road, the cattle grazing in meadows, the River Thames glimpsed now and again between the willows that lined its banks, the undulating countryside dotted with farms, and here and there the mansions of the rich, though not one of them was equal in size to Borstead Hall. She had left Borstead, she told herself, for ever, but she had left her heart behind. It was in someone else's keeping.

As if in sympathy with her dismal thoughts, the weather had changed. The sun, which had been scorching everything, had disappeared and dark clouds rolled up from the southwest, presaging rain. She hoped it would hold off until she had done what she intended to do, because she had not brought wet-weather clothing with her. To have packed more clothes than would be needed for a stay of one night would have made Miss Harecroft suspicious. She would have to send for the rest of her belongings when she came back for her father.

When the coach drew up at the Bells in the market square at Staines, she was down almost as soon as the wheels had stopped turning and, after asking directions, hurried to find the shop where Miss Harecroft's gift was waiting for collection. It was only a very tiny parcel and would have cost very little to send by mail; the whole errand was, as she suspected, a ruse to keep her. It made her feel a little better about what she was going to do, but only a little. She would write later and explain.

Her next stop was the home of Mr and Mrs Proudfoot where, instead of producing the letter Alicia had given her, she introduced herself as a friend of Miss Harecroft who had asked her to pick up her mother's birthday gift and to ask them if they would be kind enough to take it with them when they went to the party on Saturday afternoon. They were an elderly couple and anxious to please and did not question the truth of what she said. She handed over the parcel, thanked them and returned to the Bells. She was a free woman again. But her freedom had been purchased at a terrible price. And now it was raining. By the time she was back at the inn, she was drenched. She bought a ticket to London and then, too nervous to go into the inn alone, sheltered beneath the overhanging eaves to wait for the coach to arrive.

She spent the time mentally making plans. Her first task when she arrived in the capital must be to visit Harecroft's and tell Stephen her decision; she could not let him go all the way to Borstead in anticipation and not find her there. Then she would look for work, any work that provided her with enough for her and her father to live on. After that, she would know how much she could afford to pay for lodgings. It sounded easy listed like that, but she knew it would not be. Where would she ever get employment as congenial and well paid as Harecroft's? Sheltering from the rain, deep in thought she hardly noticed that the inn yard was full of people: drivers, guards, ostlers and passengers alighting from an incoming coach and those, like her, waiting for the London coach which was expected at any moment.

Richard left Archie with the coach at the Clarence Hotel and went to the home of Mr and Mrs Proudfoot, only to find Diana had been and gone again. 'She said she was going to London,' Mrs Proudfoot told him. 'She gave us a little parcel to take with us on Saturday, but now you are here, you might as well have it.' She fetched it from a drawer and handed it to him. He slipped it into his pocket and made for the Bells where he knew the London coaches called on their way from the west country, praying he was not too late. It was raining hard and he was glad that he had had the foresight to include his old army cloak in his bag when he left for London.

The inn yard was crowded but there was no mistaking that slim figure, those red-blonde tresses, now bedraggled, the proud carriage. She appeared to be making her way towards a coach that was then drawing into the yard. He hurried forward before she could escape him. 'Diana!'

She whirled round. 'Mr Harecroft!'

He doffed his hat and bowed, noticing the thin summer cape she wore and the rain dripping off the feather that curled about the edge of her bonnet. Some of it lay on her cheeks. She had never looked more lovely or more vulnerable. 'At your service, Miss Bywater.'

'What are you doing here?'

'Passing through,' he said. 'What about you?'

'Passing through,' she repeated his words. 'On my way to London.'

'Running away.'

'No, I am simply leaving.' She had left Borstead to escape him and instead had run straight into him. What imp of mischief had made that happen?

'Leaving?'

'Yes. I told you a long time ago that I meant to find lodgings for my father and myself in London. Now is as good a time as any to do it.'

'It is a very bad time,' he said. 'We cannot stand here in the rain; come inside and let us talk about it.' He took her bag with one hand and put the other under her elbow to steer her towards the inn.

'Mr Harecroft.' She tried to resist, to pull herself from his grasp, but he tightened his grip and, short of making a scene, she had to go with him.

The room was as crowded as the yard and there was nowhere to sit. He marched up to the landlord who was directing a waiter, and demanded a private room, handing him several coins, three of which she noticed were guineas. In no time at all they were conducted upstairs to a large bedroom where a servant lit the fire that was already laid in the grate.

'Sir, this is nothing short of abduction,' she protested, when the innkeeper and the servant had gone.

'You could have called for help.' He took off his cloak and threw it over a chair. 'You could still do so. I doubt mine host has reached the foot of the stairs.'

He was mocking her, playing with her like a cat with a mouse, and she was allowing it! Furiously she tried to regain her dignity. 'You have made me miss the coach and now I shall be stuck here for hours until the next one arrives.'

'Good.'

'How can you say so? Have you no care for my reputation?'

'At this moment, I care more for your health. Sitting in those wet clothes in a draughty coach could be the death of you and I cannot be held responsible for allowing it. Take off your hat and cape and your shoes.' He pointed down at them. 'You are making puddles on the carpet.'

She was very wet, having remained outside even when the drizzle turned to a downpour. And when he had spoken her name she had turned so suddenly she had put her foot into a puddle; she could feel the water squelching in her shoe. She looked down at her feet and then up at him. He was evidently not going to leave her in privacy. 'Don't be a fool, Diana,' he added when she made no move to divest herself of her damp outer garments. 'Now is not the time to climb on your high horse.' He reached forward and tugged at the ribbon that fastened her hat.

She made no move to stop him. Could not. His touch on her throat set her pulses racing, making her heart beat so hard and so fast she was sure he could hear it. This was not how it was meant to be. She was meant to be in control, but his gentle touch was throwing her insides into a spin while her body seemed melded to the spot where she stood. Even her hands had fallen uselessly to her sides.

He caught her hat as it fell back and put it on the table. 'Now that cape. I am surprised you should wear such a flimsy garment on a day like today.' He began undoing the row of buttons down the front of it. She wondered idly if undressing young ladies was something he did frequently; he did not seem to be finding it difficult.

'It was not raining when I left.'

'Why did you leave?' The garment undone, he helped her off with it and draped it over a chair near the fire, revealing a yellow-and-green striped gown with its mud-spattered skirt. Surely he would not insist she take that off as well? 'Did you fall out with Great-Grandmama or my great-aunt?'

She was indignant. 'I am not in the habit of falling out with people.'

In spite of her sharp tongue, he sensed her distress. 'Sit down.' He propelled her backward into a chair and then knelt on the carpet to take her foot in his hand. She held her breath. Surely not? But he was; he was gently removing her shoes and she was curling up inside and something extraordinary was happening in the pit of her stomach. 'Your feet are soaked. I suggest you remove your stockings too. There is a screen in the corner.'

She laughed to cover her confusion. 'And if I refuse, will you take those off as well?'

'You think I would not dare?' he queried, sitting back to look into her face.

She was taken aback. Their repartee to that point had been lively, just within the bounds of propriety, if being alone with a man in the bedroom of a inn could be called at all proper, but now she became alarmed and pulled her foot from his hand. 'No. I think you have audacity enough for anything.'

'Oh, I see. I kissed you. And you feel insulted. But let me remind you, there were two of us and—'

'I know,' she said miserably, reliving that kiss and breaking her heart over it. She scrambled to her feet and rushed behind a screen, which stood to one side of the hearth, to escape his searching look. Once out of his sight, she tried to calm herself.

'Then you must share the blame,' he said.

'You took me unawares. I was...surprised.'

'So was I,' he said. 'But if you are worried about what Stephen will say...'

'I am sure he will say that it was no more than he would expect of you.'

He acknowledged the truth of this and smiled ruefully. 'I shall not tell him.' He paused. 'You do not seem to be doing anything behind that screen,' he said, throwing a blanket over the top of it. 'Are you removing your stockings?'

'No.'

'Then hurry up and do so and your dress too. I ordered a meal and I am hungry, even if you are not.'

Glad that he had decided to stop quizzing her, she pulled off her stockings and dress, wrapped herself securely in the blanket and emerged from the screen with her clothing in her hand.

'Good,' he said, taking them from her and hanging the dress over another chair and the stockings from the mantelpiece, holding them there with a cracked vase and an ugly figurine of a cow. She watched this little piece of domesticity and her heart contracted with pain. To stop him seeing it in her face, she sat down and took a towel from a stand to rub her hair dry, hiding her head in its folds.

He watched her until her head of red-gold tresses emerged from the towel and he was suddenly filled with a great tenderness towards her. For all her hauteur, she was very young, little more than a wilful, exasperating, loveable chit. Did she really imagine she was in love with him? It was flattering, but he could not believe it was so; they did nothing but argue. Did she imagine he was in love with her just because he kissed her? He was wondering how to disabuse her of that idea when there was a knock on the door. Sighing, he went to open it to the waiter, who stood outside bearing a tray. He thanked him and took it from him, saying they could manage, before shutting the door on him.

'Mr Harecroft, that waiter was owl-eyed with curiosity. My reputation will be in shreds.' Her belated attempt to regain her dignity was only half-hearted. The damage was done.

'If your reputation is in danger, then it is you who have made it so. How can you have been so foolish as to try to leave alone and inadequately clothed? Surely you could have talked out your problem with my great-aunt.' He brought the tray to the table and set it down. The smell of bacon and coffee wafted to her nostrils and she suddenly realised that she was very hungry.

'I did. I told her I was at Borstead Hall under false pretences. I am a nobody, the daughter of a sea captain and a seamstress—why should someone like Stephen want to marry me, unless he is mistaken about who I am?'

'Do you still think that?'

'Yes. I can think of no other reason.'

'You underestimate yourself, my dear. And I do not think it is the only reason you are leaving.'

She looked into his eyes. They were searching her face, no longer full of amusement, but seriously considering her, as if he could read what was in her heart without her having to speak of it. But she must convince him. 'I must consider my father…'

'His revelations the day before yesterday were new to you, were they not?'

'Yes, and no doubt they have been conveyed to Lady Harecroft. I am leaving before I am sent away. I have my pride, Mr Harecroft.'

'I would not take that from you,' he said quietly. 'Without our pride, how could we carry on?'

He was talking about himself as well as her, she realised. It was his pride that kept him at the dower house, at arm's length from his father. 'You chose the path you took. I had no choice.'

'You are exercising a choice now, Diana.' It was said very quietly.

Her riposte that she had no choice died on her tongue. 'If I am, it is one that has been thrust on me.'

'Let us make a bargain,' he said. 'Let us eat and then take a turn into the town. I have some business to transact, but I will be no longer than I can help and then I shall be at your service.' He had no business but he knew she would not return to Borstead immediately and he had to think of a way to detain her until he could persuade her to go back willingly.

'For what purpose?'

'To escort you wherever you wish to go, of course. What else should I be offering?' She stared at him as he took a plate from the tray and loaded it with bacon and eggs, which he set before her. 'Eat.'

She was falling deeper into the mire with every minute. 'Mr Harecroft, I cannot impose on you…'

'It is my pleasure and my privilege. Now, I do not want to hear any more protests. Eat your meal and we will plan what is to be done.'

She obeyed him, while her wet clothes steamed before the fire. The food was hot and delicious and by the time she had eaten her fill, she was once again warm and dry and resigned to her fate, whatever that might be. It was in his hands, not hers.

He finished his own food, then poured himself another cup of coffee and sat regarding her quizzically. Her cheeks were pink from the warmth of the fire, but her smoky eyes were still troubled, making him long to take her in his arms to comfort her. But how could he? She was his brother's intended wife and he had scandalised her enough already. 'Diana…' he began slowly. 'If there is anything I can do to help, you have only to ask.'

Oh, how she longed to throw herself on his mercy, tell him everything, that she loved him, but he would undoubtedly be shocked and at that moment she was basking in the comfort his presence gave her and she wanted to savour it as long as she could. 'You have already offered to escort me—what other help should I need?'

'Only you know that, my dear. But whatever it is, please make use of me.'

'Mr Harecroft, I would not dream of making use of you.'

'Why not?'

'What sort of a person do you think I am?'

'At the moment, a troubled one.'

'If I am, it is because you dragged me up here.'

'Dragged you, Diana?'

'Yes. I protested, as you recall.'

'Only for your reputation, which you had already thrown away.'

'If you think so ill of me, why do you not abandon me? I can take the next coach out and we can pretend we never met.'

'I do not think we can do that,' he said softly, coming to stand before her. 'Can we?' And when she did not reply added, 'Can we forget we met, Diana?'

'No,' she whispered, all the stuffing gone out of her.

He reached out both hands to her and brought her to her feet. The blanket fell away, revealing a stiff white petticoat and a chemise. She made no effort to bend and retrieve the blanket, but stood in front of him and raised her smoky eyes to his. Neither spoke. Slowly he lifted her hands to his lips and kissed the inside of her wrists, one by one, looking into her face as he did so. She shivered, though it was not cold that made her do so. It would take so little to give in, to throw herself into his arms and confess the whole miserable truth. She was the daughter of a bastard, a nobody who had had the temerity to fall in love with him. But she held back. There was still a spark of the old Diana in her, still a little pride, and she would not let him play with her and torment her with kisses that he could not possibly mean seriously. She withdrew her hands. 'Mr Harecroft, I must dress.' She picked up her dry clothes and disappeared behind the screen.

He stood up and went to the window. He felt as though something within his grasp had been suddenly snatched away, a dream broken by the awakening, a longed-for pleasure denied him. He had never gone into his own motives too deeply, but the truth shocked him. He wanted to make love to her. And that was out of the question. He gave a deprecating smile. 'The rain has stopped and the sun has come out. We will venture forth and plan how to extricate you from this coil.' Coil was an apt description, he decided, for both of them. They were like springs, wound up so tight that sooner or later something would have to give.

'I am not in a coil,' she said, emerging from behind the screen, determined to stay in control, though how long she could keep it up, she did not know. As for escaping from him… Did she want to? The sensible side of her said yes, she did, the wanton side wanted to stay, to be whatever he wanted her to be.

'So be it.' He had regained control and would make sure he kept it. 'I have to make a call on a gentleman at the new literary and scientific institute. There is a coffee shop nearby. You may sit there and watch the world go by until I rejoin you. Then we will dine somewhere and talk and perhaps, if there is no more rain, take a promenade. Or you could, if you wish, wait here for me.'

She laughed a little crazily. 'Are you not afraid I will take the first coach out?'

'I do not think you will do that.'

'Why not?'

'You have not finished with me, Diana, just as I have not finished with you.'

'What do you mean?'

He looked at her with his head on one side, a faint smile playing about his lips, though it was one of irony, not of amusement. 'I mean I must take you back to Great-Grandmama. The rest is in the lap of the gods. Now what do you say? Come with me or stay here?'

'Come,' she said without hesitation.

She put on her shoes, dry now, and he helped her on with her cape and they left the inn.

The rain had been blown away on the wind and now the sun was shining in a sky where only one or two small clouds drifted. But it was wet underfoot and they had to pick their way carefully round the puddles and step smartly out of the way when vehicles splashed through them, throwing up a veritable cascade of water.

'You have returned from London very quickly,' she said, determined to stay calm. 'Did you go to the gallery in Burlington Arcade?'

'Yes. I took them some samples of Freddie and Joe's work. They liked Freddie's, but not Joe's.'

'Were you surprised by that? Most of it is very bleak.'

'No, but Joe will be disappointed and I am not sure I should accept if he is not included.'

'You are going to a great deal of trouble on behalf of your friends.'

'Isn't that what friends are for? They would do the same for me if our roles were reversed.'

She wondered if he were right, but did not express her doubts. 'I found Dick asleep under a tree in the wood yesterday. He had escaped from the garden and was all alone. I took him back to Miss Standish. She had been searching for him and was very worried.'

'Good God!'

'Miss Standish said he was looking for his papa.'

'He often does that.'

She waited for him to go on, but when he did not, she stopped walking, pretending to look into a shop window. It was cluttered with old books, pictures, pieces of jewellery and tiny carvings.

'There is something you could help me with, if you would.'

His sudden change of subject confirmed her worst fears. How could he be so mercurial? Was he simply playing with her, like a cat with a mouse that it had no intention devouring? Surely he knew she had mentioned his son in order to give him the opportunity to explain, but he evidently did not think he needed to enlarge upon what he had already told her. And he was right. It was nothing to do with her; she was on her way back to London to make a new beginning and would never see any of them again.

'If I can,' she answered automatically, hoping it had nothing to do with Lucy and her child.

'Would you help me choose a birthday gift for my great-grandmother?'

She breathed a sigh of relief. 'If I can. What had you in mind?'

'Nothing. She seems to have everything she needs.'

She looked idly at the collection in the window of the shop. Beside the tawdry pieces she spied some little carvings. They were all small, none more than a foot high and some only a matter of an inch or two. Some were marble, some stone, some almost perfect, others damaged; all were beautiful. 'What about something from here? A little carving perhaps.'

'But it is rubbish, not worth anything.'

'Surely it is not the price that matters to an old lady who is rich enough to buy anything she wants? It should be something that has some meaning.'

'You are right, of course, so let us see what there is on offer.' Anything to keep her by his side, he told himself as he ducked under the low lintel to enter the shop.

The bent old man who came to serve them fetched several

items from the window as Diana pointed to them. She picked them up one by one, could feel the life in the hands that had made them, the love and skill that went into their creation, and was almost moved to tears.

'They are Roman,' the shopkeeper said. 'Found near the old bridge when it was demolished six years ago to build the new one.'

'They are beautiful,' she said softly, wavering between the marble head of a horse six inches across but perfect in every detail and a tiny carving of a woman's head and shoulders in a creamy-coloured stone. It was beautifully done, every tress of hair, every fold of the dress was finely carved, the nose and mouth perfect, even though it was so small. 'They are both good, but I think perhaps the horse,' she said.

'The horse?' he queried in surprise. 'Not the little head?'

'The head is good, too, but this is even lovelier because it is so small. It did not come from a temple, it was done to please the sculptor, made as a private gift, perhaps, or a tribute to a special goddess, made with love. And it reminds me of North Wind, the way his nostrils flare and his mane flies out behind him. I think her ladyship would like the horse.'

'Then the horse it shall be.' He handed it to the shop-keeper to be wrapped. 'But I think I shall take the little head as well.'

Both pieces were paid for and the little piece of pale stone wrapped separately from the horse. Richard handed it to Diana. 'A gift to my particular goddess with my compliments,' he said, as they left the shop.

'Mr Harecroft, I did not expect you to buy this for me,' she said in dismay.

'Don't you like it?'

'Yes, it is exquisite, but I cannot accept it.'

'Good heavens, why not? It is only a piece of stone, not a

precious jewel, a small token of gratitude for helping me choose my great-grandmother's gift.'

'It is more than a piece of stone. Perhaps once, long ago, someone treasured it. Do you think they were unhappy when it was lost?'

'That is something we shall never know.'

'I like to think it was valued by whoever owned it, a memory perhaps of someone they loved and they were broken-hearted when it fell into the river and could not be found.'

He smiled at her romanticism. It was contrary to the capable clerk who kept Harecroft's books in such apple-pie order. 'And now it is yours.'

'Thank you. I shall treasure it because it is so beautiful. And a memento of my time in Borstead.'

He turned to look sharply at her, but she was concentrating on avoiding a puddle and did not look at him. 'Borstead? But you were running away from it.'

'I was not running away. I was, am, going to London to find lodgings.'

'And to see Stephen?' he queried, trying to elicit a confession from her.

'Yes.'

'But he is coming to Borstead on Friday. Are you so impatient to see him?'

'Yes.'

He gave up; Great-Aunt Alicia was wrong—Diana was not going to turn Stephen down and she had not fallen in love with him, but having accosted her and thrust himself on her, he could not leave her. And he admitted to himself he did not want to. It was stolen time, but he could not give it back. Indeed, he wanted to extend it if he could. Why he did not know—it would not change anything.

He stopped to buy her a posy of yellow roses from a flower girl who importuned him plaintively and in due course they arrived at the coffee shop. He waited until she was seated at a table where she could look out of the window, ordered a pot of coffee for her, then left her to have a look round the new literary and scientific institute, which he had been promising himself he would visit when he had time.

He was gone a long time; people came into the shop, sat a while over their coffee, read their newspapers, met friends and departed; and still she sat. Outside the sun made rainbows in the puddles and the population who had been sheltering indoors emerged on to the streets. Old and young, hale and sickly, passed where she sat. She heard the faint sound of an orchestra rehearsing in the assembly rooms nearby and wondered dreamily if Richard would take her there, if she asked him, though, naturally, she would do no such a thing.

Just when she was wondering where he had got to, he returned and dropped into the chair beside her. 'How did it go?' she asked.

'Well enough. Have you had sufficient coffee?'

'Yes, thank you.'

'Then let us go for a walk.'

They left the coffee house and explored the town. It consisted of one wide street with houses on either side and small streets branching off it. 'The town is very ancient,' he told her. 'A convenient crossing of the river for the Roman legions, who are believed to have had a station here. Now, with the new bridge, it is part of the highway from London to the West Country and a busy staging post, as you must have discovered.'

'Yes, I have,' she said, wondering when the next coach left for London and whether she ought not to be making her way back to the inn, but deciding to let the thought go. To be with Richard for these last few hours was something she would treasure along with the tiny gift he had given her.

Having seen all there was to see, they returned to the Bells and he ushered her inside. 'Mr Harecroft,' she said, suddenly realising how foolish she was being. 'I thank you for a pleasant afternoon, but I can take up no more of your time.'

'Now you have disappointed me,' he said. 'I have been told there is a dance at the Assembly Rooms tonight. I was hoping you would agree to let me escort you.'

She was beginning to feel the effects of everything that had happened—the journey and her reason for it, her sleepless night, the encounter at the Bells earlier that day and the long walk—but even as her mind started searching around for objections, she knew that she wanted to go, to experience again that strange oneness with the man who was looking at her now with his head tilted a little to the side and a slight smile on his lips. If he had said fly to the moon with me, she would have put her hand in his and gone willingly. She pulled herself together. 'Much as I would like to accept, I cannot. I must find out the time of the next coach to London.'

'I thought we had agreed we would return to Borstead together?'

'I do not remember agreeing to that.'

'Didn't you?' he murmured. 'I must have misheard you. But there is no coach to the capital until the mail passes through in the early hours.'

She was appalled. 'Mr Harecroft, if you think I care so little for my virtue—' She stopped as she was confronted with the prospect of being forced to spend the night with him. Had he planned it? Was that how Dick came to be born? He was a rake of the worst order.

He saw the changing expressions cross her face: horror and

embarrassment and something akin to fear. He could not help laughing. 'Oh, Diana, surely you did not think…?' He stopped and surveyed her, in that penetrating way he had, making the colour flare in her face. 'Oh, my dear, not even I would stoop so low as to compromise my brother's intended bride.'

'You already have. And you are playing games with me and I only wish I knew the reason why.'

'I am not playing games. I asked you to attend a dance with me, that is all. I will go back to the Clarence and I will call for you at eight o'clock.'

'How can I possibly go to a dance? I only have the clothes I am wearing and they are more than a little bedraggled.'

He turned to look at her and laughed. 'That dress looks perfectly suitable to me. After all, we are not in London, it is only a country hop. I am sure the innkeeper's wife can do something with it between now and eight o'clock.'

She was as weak as water, she told herself as she watched him leave, but, oh, how she wanted to prolong their time together, knowing that this day and this night would be all they would have. And she could still catch the mail after the dance was over.

Chapter Nine

It was only after he had gone and she had made her way up to the room she had occupied earlier and put her roses in a tumbler of water, that she started to think about the dress she was wearing. It was an afternoon dress of yellow-and-green striped muslin. She took it off, shook it out and hung it up, then flung herself on the bed, not knowing whether to laugh or cry. Where would it end? She was courting disaster. She unwrapped the little bust and studied it carefully. 'A gift to my particular goddess,' he had said. And she had promised to treasure it as a memory of her time in Borstead. It was not Borstead she wanted to remember, but today. And it was not over yet. She smiled as fatigue claimed her and she slept until she was woken by a servant bringing hot water.

'This came for you,' the maid said, holding out a large flat box. 'Just delivered.'

'For me?' Diana sat up to find she was still clutching the little carving. She put it down carefully. 'There must be some mistake. I am not expecting anything.'

'The gentleman who brought it said to put it into your hands myself and to say you are to wear it tonight.'

Diana took the box and lifted the lid. Wrapped in tissue was a shimmering gown in a blue that reminded her of forget-me-nots and summer skies and fields of flax. She scrambled off the bed and held it against herself. She ought to refuse it, she ought to send it back with a polite note and put on the muslin. She ought not to be going dancing with him at all, and she certainly should not be looking forward to it with such pleasure. In any case, the gown might not fit.

'He said I was to help you dress,' the maid said, eyes shining. Such a romantic thing to do and him so handsome. She wished her young man thought of things like that. She sighed; he did not have money for such luxuries. But the guinea the gentleman had given her would go towards the wedding they had been saving for.

When Diana had washed and allowed the maid to help her on with the dress, she realised it fitted as if it had been made for her. And it was lovely. It had a slim bodice with a dual row of tiny pearl buttons from shoulder to waist from which the six-gored skirt swirled out over her hips to the floor. Each gored seam was embroidered with silver thread. Its beauty lay in the material, the clever cut and the way the silver shone as she moved. She could not bear to take it off again.

She brushed her hair, pinning it up in coils and twisting a blue ribbon through it, then surveyed herself in the mirror. Her cheeks were unusually pink, her eyes almost feverishly bright, but was that any wonder, considering the day she had had? And there was more to come.

Richard arrived in Lady Harecroft's carriage promptly at eight o'clock. As was his wont, he stood and appraised her from head to toe. 'Lovely,' he said. 'That colour suits you. It makes your eyes seem almost as blue as Great-Grandmama's.'

She wondered why he had mentioned the dowager,

perhaps to make her feel guilty. But she had had no choice but to leave, whatever Richard said, and this evening was only a snatched few hours of happiness, of unreality before the real world claimed her again. 'How did you know my size?' she asked, as she followed him out to the carriage.

He laughed. 'Oh, I know everything about you.'

'Everything?'

'Almost everything.'

The dance was just getting underway as they arrived. It was not a venue likely to be frequented by the *haut monde* and the strict codes of London society, where a gentleman would not think of asking an unmarried lady to dance more than twice unless he wanted to set the tongues wagging. They danced almost every dance together and when they were not dancing they were promenading, though she knew the matrons on the sidelines were whispering, she did not care. They did not know who she was; word would not reach the ears of anyone who mattered.

'We could not do this at Almack's,' she said, as they danced a waltz. 'Everyone would be whispering and asking, "Who is that? She cannot be a lady, a well-brought-up lady would know how to behave."'

'But you are a lady. After all, what is it that makes a lady?'

'Breeding.'

'That is an answer I might have expected from Mama or Great-Grandmama, not you. I think a lady is known by the sweetness of her temperament, by her compassion for those less fortunate, her innate good manners—I do not mean the superficial niceties that go by the name of manners these days. To me, you qualify on every count.'

Her face was flaming. The trouble was not that she could not rebuff him, but that she did not want to. 'Thank you, kind sir.'

He laughed and whirled her round.

* * *

For three whole hours she was as happy as she had ever been. He was charming, amusing and attentive. She forgot the reason she was in Staines, forgot she was supposed to be marrying Stephen and still had the task of telling him she would not, forgot all about Lady Harecroft's party. Tonight was hers and Richard's, to be enjoyed to the full. There would be time enough on the morrow to worry about the future. When they were exhausted with the dancing they went and sat in the supper room, though both were too full of emotion to want to eat.

He was elated. Nothing else seemed to matter when he had Diana Bywater in his sight, looking radiant in a gown that he had known was perfect for her the moment he had seen it draped over a chair in a dressmaker's window. He had realised that she was special when he first set eyes on her at Harecroft's, that she was different from the typical run of young ladies he had met and not because of her unusual choice of employment. Now he knew the reason; it came upon him like a shaft of sudden light that almost blinded him. He had fallen head over heels in love with her, had been in love with her almost from the day they met. He had teased her and argued with her, but that had been a front to stop himself from admitting it. He could not tell her that, not yet, perhaps not ever. She was very astute, had always been quick at understanding him and he wondered how long it would be before she guessed. Not that it would help; even if she decided to reject Stephen, he could not suddenly step into his brother's shoes. Stephen would undoubtedly think he had planned it to thwart him, knowing he was not in favour of the marriage in the first place. He told himself, not altógether truthfully, that he would have given her up to his brother if Stephen had been sincerely in love with her, but he was doubtful of that. Stephen's heart was elsewhere.

He stood up so suddenly she was startled. 'What is the matter?'

'Nothing. It is late and you are tired. I think we should find our beds.' It was said flatly as if he would brook no contradiction. 'I will call up the carriage.'

It took a few minutes for the coachman to be found and given instructions, but less than a quarter of an hour later, they were sitting side by side in the gloom of the carriage being carried to the Bells. Neither spoke. She had found his sudden change of mood disconcerting. If he had asked her politely if she were tired, enquired if she would like to retire, she might have said yes. But his bluntness, his silence since then, made her ask herself what she had said or done to vex him. They had been talking normally and then, poof! It was as if some hidden mesmerist had snapped his fingers and brought him out of a trance and he had found himself somewhere he did not want to be. What had they been talking about? What had she said to bring on his ill humour?

'I shall call for you tomorrow morning,' he said, when the carriage drew up outside the inn.

'No, sir.' Her voice was as tightly controlled as his. 'I shall make my own way, thank you.'

'You will not. My great-grandmother would skin me alive if she thought I had allowed it. I am taking you back to Borstead and you will face whatever it was caused you to leave. Running away is the coward's way.'

'I am not a coward!'

'Then you will return with me.'

She did not argue, there was no point.

After a sleepless night when she veered from hope to despair, from wanting to hang on to what little they had, to a firm resolution to turn her back on the whole Harecroft family, she rose next morning with a heavy heart. She would dearly have liked to stay in bed, but she could not do that in a public inn; besides, Richard would come and demand to know what was wrong. In one thing he had been right—she had to face her demons. But not with him at her side; he made matters worse, simply by being there.

So many times the previous evening she had almost let him see how much she longed for him, especially as his behaviour had led her, in the euphoria of the moment, to wonder if her feelings might, after all, be returned. But then she thought of Lucy and Dick and knew it was out of the question. He was playing with her, tormenting her and she could not endure it. Alicia had said a little time away might help her to think clearly; the only thing that was clear to her was that she must keep to her original intention to leave.

She began to laugh. It went on and on, crazily, hysterically, while the tears ran down her face and dripped off her chin. And then the laughter turned to tears. It was as if floodgates had opened inside her and let out all the misery and anger and the sense of helplessness she had felt ever since Stephen had taken her away from her lodgings.

Her limbs felt heavy as lead as she dressed and her head ached. She told herself sternly that she had consumed too much wine the evening before, but she had drunk very little; it was not wine that had caused the elation while they danced, nor the lethargy she felt this morning. But the day had to be faced and she must be gone before Richard came for her.

She could not manage breakfast, but she had a cup of hot chocolate and when she heard the London coach drawing up, she picked up her bag and went out to the yard. Glancing round quickly and seeing no sign of her tormentor, she bought her ticket and boarded it. It was not full; there was a very thin

man in a coat with a collar high enough to scratch his hollow
cheeks, a young woman with a boy of six or seven and an old
lady in widow's weeds. The door had been shut and they were
just about to move off, when it was wrenched open again and
Richard put his head inside. 'My dear, you are in the wrong
coach,' he said sweetly for the benefit of the other passengers.
'You will be carried off to London in this one.' He held out
his hand.

Realising that he would not be averse to pulling her out
ignominiously if she resisted, she smiled at the other occupants as if to say, 'Silly me' and put her hand in his. He
helped her down, tucked her hand under his arm and he held
it there to lead her to where his great-grandmother's coach
was being readied for the journey to Borstead. She did not
speak. What was it about him that reduced her to a quivering
jelly, unable to stand up for herself?

'You did not really intend to go to London, did you?' he
queried, when they were on their way. 'You cannot have
meant to disappoint Great-Grandmama, and Great-Aunt
Alicia and your father by running away and absenting
yourself from the party.' It was as if he had forgotten they had
had almost the same conversation the day before. Or perhaps
he thought taking her to the dance might have made her
change her mind. If he'd hoped she would rise to the bait and
argue with him, he would be disappointed. She stared out of
the window and would not look at him. He gave up and
settled back in his seat.

She knew she ought to be thinking of what to say to the
dowager when she arrived, but her head was so woolly and
her eyes so heavy, she could not put her mind to anything. In
spite of all her efforts, her eyes began to close and her head
lolled. He smiled and eased his arm around her shoulders to
make her more comfortable.

* * *

'Wake up. Wake up, my dear.' The voice was low and insistent. 'We are here.'

Diana stirred, opened her eyes and blinked, wondering for a moment where she was. She could feel an arm about her and warm breath on her cheek and sat up to discover she had fallen asleep cradled in Richard Harecroft's arm. 'Oh dear, I did not mean…I am sorry…' she said, trying to straighten her bonnet, which had slipped over one eye.

He smiled. 'It is I who am sorry that our journey has come to an end.'

They turned in at the gates and the horses slowed as they rounded the curve in the drive and came in sight of the house. As soon as they stopped she scrambled down, intending to make her own way into the house, but found herself face to face with Alicia, who had heard the coach and was coming down the steps to greet them.

Diana's head felt so thick she could hardly think straight. 'I do not think Miss Bywater is feeling quite the thing,' Richard told his great-aunt, after she had kissed them both.

'Oh, dear, you do look a little pale,' Alicia said, tilting her head to one side to survey Diana. Richard returned to the coach to be carried off to the stables. 'What is the matter? Are you ill?'

'No, I have a headache, that is all.'

'Poor dear, you must go straight to bed. I will ask Mrs Evans for one of her herbal remedies. A dose of that and you will be right as ninepence in no time, I guarantee it.' She bustled away to give orders for the tisane and, once she had seen Diana settled in bed, went in search of Richard.

He was with his great-grandmother. His visit to Staines had convinced him of what he knew already. He loved Diana

Bywater to distraction. He had very nearly spoken about it in the coach coming back and might very well have done so if she had not fallen asleep. Oh, the pleasure and the anguish of having her head nestling on his shoulder! But it could not be. Not unless Stephen withdrew his offer or she rejected it, and he did not think either was likely. He was arguing with her about how Diana should be told when Alicia bustled into the room.

'Richard, what happened in Staines?' she demanded.

'Nothing. We ate and walked and I took her to a dance and then we parted. This morning I stopped her just as she was getting into the London coach and more or less forced her to return, but I am not sure I should have done so. I am sure Great-Grandmama has mischief up her sleeve.'

'You wanted her to come back, did you not?' Alicia queried.

'Yes,' he admitted. 'But I think we are all being a little selfish over this and not considering how Diana might feel. To be thrust upon the family…'

'I said I would talk to her beforehand,' the old lady said, a trifle truculently. 'It is not my fault she disappeared when she did.'

'And her father,' he added.

'Has he recovered? Is he capable of taking it in?'

'I am sure he is. I intend to visit him tomorrow to see how he is. I think he will be glad I brought his daughter back. He is in favour of her marriage to Stephen. He thinks it will take the burden of having to look after him from her shoulders.'

'Is he putting pressure on her? Is that part of her problem?'

'I do not know, but it is no more than Papa is putting on Stephen.' He paused. 'Does Papa know the truth about Diana?'

'Not unless he has guessed.'

'I think he might have done,' he said thoughtfully. 'Otherwise, why is he so keen for Stephen to marry her? Assuming there is money involved, he would want to keep her even more firmly in the family.' He paused. 'Is there money?'

'Some,' she said enigmatically. 'Now go away, both of you. I have to think.'

Cook's remedy, which had tasted foul, sent Diana into a deep, dreamless sleep. She did not wake until the first dinner gong echoed through the house. Alicia, dressed for dinner, came to see how she did.

'I am quite well,' she reassured her.

'Thank goodness for that. Richard said you were caught out in the rain yesterday. We feared you might have taken a chill.'

She felt the colour rise to her cheeks at the memory of what had happened in the room at the Bells. How much had Richard told his great-aunt? 'Yes, but I was soon dry again.'

'Richard said you did not stay with Mr and Mrs Proudfoot.'

'No, I did not want to impose upon them. They are elderly and were not prepared for company. I did well enough at the inn.'

'And do you feel better for your little trip away?'

'Nothing has changed.'

'But you are not leaving before the party, are you? If you are determined to turn down Stephen's proposal, you can tell him when he comes down. I promise you no one will hold it against you.'

'I do not deserve your kindness.'

'Of course you do. Now, would you like some supper sent up to you on a tray? Then you can go back to sleep. We cannot have you ill just before the party.'

Not wanting to meet any of the family, afraid that they would all know she had tried to run away and been brought back like a truanting schoolboy, she agreed. She would face them tomorrow when she felt stronger and when Richard had gone back to the dower house and his mistress and son.

She rose next day, loins girded to stand up for herself, but that was easier decided than done, simply because there was no one about when she went downstairs. The dowager had not emerged from her room and Alicia had gone to see the florist. There was no message about what she should be doing and so she set off to see her father.

The rain had passed and the sun was warm on her back. She strode down the drive purposefully, intending to take the long route to avoid the dower house. Turning onto the lane leading to the village, she heard the sound of a horse and carriage behind her and turned to see Lucy driving a pony and trap, with Dick beside her. The other two lodgers were mounted and riding alongside. Diana stepped aside and waited for them to pass.

Lucy pulled up and so did the horsemen. 'Miss Bywater, good day to you,' Lucy called. 'May I offer you a lift?'

'Thank you, but I am only going into the village.'

'We are going that way.' Lucy held the trap door open for her.

Diana stepped up and settled herself on the seat opposite Dick. The little boy gave her a wide grin that tore at her heart strings, but she had made up her mind to keep tight hold of her emotions and not mind too much that the man she loved was not, could not, be for her. It was a fact of life and if she told herself often enough that he was a rake, the black sheep his father had painted him, and that he liked to flirt, then perhaps she could cope. She might even manage to feel sorry for Lucy and her little boy.

'I did not thank you properly for bringing Dick back to me the other day,' Lucy said. 'I was so thankful to see him safe and well, I was perhaps a little brusque with you.'

'Not at all. You were worried and that is understandable. I am sure if he had been mine I would have been out of my mind.'

'We are off to the races to see North Wind run,' Freddie said, riding alongside. 'Would you like to come with us?'

'That is very kind of you, but I am going to visit my father.'

'He could come too,' Freddie suggested. 'There is plenty of room in the trap and he might appreciate a change of scenery.'

'I don't know,' she said doubtfully. 'He might not feel up to it.'

'Why don't you go and ask him? We could wait on the green for you.'

'Please do,' Lucy said.

Diana could not understand why Lucy was so friendly towards her; in her shoes she would have found it difficult. Was she so naïve she did not know that Richard liked to flirt or was she so sure of him that she did not mind? On the other hand, if she had been told Diana was destined for Stephen, why would she mind? 'I will ask him,' she said, wondering why she persisted in tormenting herself.

When she arrived at the home, she was told her father was in the garden. She stepped outside and realised he was not alone; sitting on the bench beside him was Richard Harecroft and they were deep in conversation. She almost turned on her heel and went away again, but scolded herself she had no reason to avoid the young man. She walked forward, a smile on her lips. 'Papa, you have a visitor, I see.'

Richard turned at the sound of her voice. 'Diana, are you well?'

'Yes, thank you.'

'I feared the dampness in Staines had made you ill.'

'It might have done if you had not done your best to

prevent it,' she said, colouring at the memory. 'As it is I feel so much better, I decided to come and see my father.'

'You did not go to London after all,' James said. 'Have you changed your mind about not marrying Stephen?'

She caught Richard's look of surprise and managed a ghost of a smile. 'No, Papa, I have not.'

'You did not tell me that yesterday,' Richard exclaimed. 'You let me think…'

She took a deep breath. 'Was there any reason why I should? Do you not keep back things about yourself you would rather not talk about? And it makes no difference, does it?'

In spite of the flushed cheeks, she sounded cool and in control. It was as if she had used up all her emotion in Staines and had wiped out the happiness they had enjoyed in each other's company and was determined to keep him at a distance. Had he imagined that coiled spring, a spring that drew them together with such devastating strength and could as easily fling them asunder, if they should let go of it? Had she let go? Was it time he did? 'Not a mite of difference,' he answered.

'Pity,' James said.

They both looked at him, wondering if he meant it was a pity she was not going to marry Stephen or a pity it made no difference.

'Your friends are outside,' Diana told Richard when the silence became unbearable. 'They are off to Ascot races and have asked if Papa and I would like to go with them.'

'Capital idea,' Richard said. 'I wonder I did not think of it myself. What do you say, Mr Bywater?'

James's eyes lit up at the prospect and he shambled into the house to fetch his coat and tell the matron he was going out. It was only when they left the grounds by a side gate that Diana noticed Thunderer tethered and realised Richard had arrived on horseback and had always intended to go with them. It was too late to change her mind, Diana told herself, but in company, they would not be close to each other, certainly not close enough to feel warm breath on their cheeks, hear the other's heartbeats as she had done coming back in the coach the day before, or look into each other's eyes. Nor would they be able to taunt each other with barbed words. And it would disappoint her father if she changed her mind. It would be self-torture, she knew, but perhaps seeing Richard with his mistress and child might cure her of her affliction, for affliction it was. She could almost compare it with her father's longing for a drink when he knew that giving in to it might be the death of him.

The little cavalcade was waiting on the green. Diana and her father climbed into the trap with Lucy and Dick and they all set off in high spirits, even if Diana was a little subdued. It was not easy to make conversation while they were on the move, but once they had arrived in Ascot and found a good place to view the races, they were able to talk. Diana had stationed herself between Mr Somers and Mr Harris, leaving Richard to hoist Dick on his shoulders and stand beside Lucy.

Freddie was enthusiastic about North Wind's chances, considering the rain had softened the ground, and he was even more excited about the prospect of an exhibition of his work in London. 'Can't thank Richard enough,' he said.

'I did nothing,' Richard put in. 'I showed Mr Hatley the examples you gave me and they spoke for you.'

'What about you, Mr Harris?' Diana asked.

'No luck, I am afraid. No one wants my work.'

'Do not despair, my friend,' Richard said. 'You will make your mark, if you have patience.'

'That is all very well for you to say, Richard, you have

enough to live on without doing a stroke of work. I need to eat, and fame and fortune are a long while coming.'

'Perhaps you should choose subjects a little less disturbing,' Lucy said.

'That would be a betrayal of my principles.'

'What price your principles if you are starving?' Freddie put in.

'He is not starving, nor will he,' Richard said. 'He knows he is welcome to stay at the dower house as long as he likes.'

'Supposing the dowager wants it back or you marry? You are bound to do so one day and then you and your bride will need the house to yourselves.'

'I cannot see that happening,' Richard told him. 'I am a bachelor and likely to remain one.'

'How can you? You are the heir after your father, you will be expected to marry and carry on the line.'

'You are as bad as my parents, always worrying me to marry and settle down. I will choose my own bride and my own time. Let us say no more on the subject.'

Diana listened with growing dismay. How could he talk of marrying or not marrying when Lucy stood beside him, faithful, uncomplaining Lucy, and his son was perched on his shoulders? She never imagined him being worried by society's rules, but he evidently was. Unless it was Lucy who was holding back, to save him from the ignominy of being married to an actress. It was uncommonly unselfish of her if she was. And what about the child? Dick needed a father and in later years might he blame Richard for casting him in the role of bastard?

She moved a little away from the group to sit beside her father in the trap. 'I can see just as well from here,' he had told them when they arrived.

The crowds were thickening and noisy and Diana was

caught up in the excitement. She watched the first race, picking her favourite from the line up and jumping up excitedly when it won. 'I wish I had put a wager on it,' she told her father.

'See if you are clever enough to pick out the next one,' he said.

She studied the starters. 'What about Greek Goddess?'

'Very apt,' he said. 'It says here in the programme that her dam was Diana and her sire was Zeus, a winning combination if I ever heard one.'

'I did not know that.'

He took his purse from his coat pocket and extracted a guinea. 'Ask Mr Harecroft to put this on her for us.'

She took the money to Richard. 'Papa says would you put this on Greek Goddess for him.'

'Greek Goddess?' he queried with a smile. 'Why that one?'

'It is Papa's choice. He says her dam was Diana.'

He laughed. 'So she was. Perhaps I should back her myself. She has as good a chance as any.'

She opened her purse and took out a second coin. 'And will you back North Wind on the next race, too.'

He took the money, handed Dick to his mother, and he and Freddie went off to find a bookmaker.

'Greek Goddess is fifteen to one,' he said, when he returned. 'North Wind's odds have shortened, he is only five to one. I do not know how that came about.'

'It is because he is such a handsome fellow,' Diana said. 'And he looks all fired up to go.'

Greek Goddess galloped home by a head and North Wind justified Lord Harecroft's faith in him by romping home a clear winner. Diana was delighted, as was everyone in the party and Freddie, who had backed him heavily, decided to celebrate. He went off and came back with a bottle of champagne and a handful of glasses. Diana tried to refuse the bubbly wine not only for herself but for her father too, but he would have none of it.

'The young man wants to celebrate,' he said. 'And so do I.'

'But Papa, you know it will make you ill.'

'Nonsense. Champagne will not do me any harm. Come on, young fellow, pour a glass for me.' James was suddenly jovial. 'It is not every day I can toast my daughter's success. And I am blowed if I am going to deny myself.'

Freddie handed him a brimming glass and before Diana could do a thing to stop him, he had poured it down his throat and held out the glass for a refill. Luckily Freddie was busy filling glasses for everyone else and there was not much left in the bottle when he returned to James and poured what was left into his glass. Richard contrived to jog James's arm and the wine was spilled.

'Oh, I am sorry,' he said, with a rueful grin at Diana. 'Let me refill your glass.' But there was none left in the bottle and Diana gave him a grateful smile.

'Go and buy another bottle,' James said, fishing in his purse. 'Can't celebrate with only one bottle, can we?'

'I think it is time we returned home,' Richard said. 'Dick is nearly asleep. And we must not keep you out too long and overtire you. Matron will have something to say if we take you back the worse for wear.'

'Thank you,' Diana whispered to him as they prepared for the return journey. 'I could not have made him come away, especially if the others were prepared to stay.'

'Think nothing of it.'

James grumbled, but Richard, who rode alongside the trap, kept him in good spirits and teased Diana about her win on

Greek Goddess, so that no one else noticed, unless it was Lucy, who was driving the trap and could not but hear what was being said. If she guessed what the trouble was, she said nothing.

When they arrived back at the green, Diana said she would see her father safely indoors and walk back to Borstead Hall. She was worried. Always before when her father had gone a long time without alcohol and then was tempted to have one, saying one would do no harm, it was like a dam bursting. One was never enough, and was followed by one more and then more until he was so inebriated he could not stand without assistance. She dreaded it.

She was surprised that Richard had stayed behind as the others moved off and was walking on the other side of her father, his hand under the stump of his left arm. 'I will see him safely in his room and then escort you to the Hall,' he said.

'There is no need.'

'I think there is.'

James, still sober, was annoyed that his enjoyment had been brought to an abrupt end; he called Richard and Diana his jailers, and when Matron appeared to take charge of him, he called her his prison warder.

'Papa!' Diana remonstrated. 'It not like you to behave so discourteously.' She turned to the matron, who was looking fiercely at him. 'I am sorry. I think we must have overtired him.'

'Is he drunk?' the woman demanded.

'No, of course he is not,' Richard said. 'He needs his supper and bed, that should set him right.'

Diana kissed her father and Richard shook his hand and they left him to the mercy of the matron.

'I hope she is not unkind to him,' Diana said as they re-trieved Thunderer from the hedge he was nibbling and Richard walked alongside her, leading the horse.

'No, but she will be firm, firmer than you would be, I think.'

'It is difficult…'

'I know. He is your father and you love him, but sometimes you have to be cruel to be kind.'

'He has been so good for so long. I hoped he would not slip back into his old ways.' She paused. 'Now you see why I must take him back to London?'

'No, I do not. The temptation will be even greater there and you need someone to help you. A lady on her own, and a very young one at that, should not have to deal with him.'

'Until he had his seizure, I was managing very well.'

'I know and I admire you for it.'

'I did not want anyone to know, I felt so ashamed, not because of what he does but because I could not help him. I would still rather they did not know. It is so humiliating for him when he is sober.'

'No one will hear about it from me.'

As they approached the stables, they saw grooms at work on a carriage standing in the yard. 'Good Lord,' Richard said. 'I never thought they would be so early. They must have taken Great-Grandmama's message to heart. Or perhaps Stephen was impatient to see you again.'

Diana's heart began to beat rapidly. Mr and Mrs Harecroft and Stephen had arrived and the moment she had been dreading was almost upon her.

The family were gathered in the drawing room and had evidently been waiting for them to arrive. They had been talking, but fell silent and turned as one to face Richard and Diana when they entered. Diana felt uncomfortable under their steady gaze. It was as if they could read what was in her heart and thoroughly disapproved. The sooner she made her position clear, the better. 'There you are, at last,' Mrs Harecroft said.

'I am sorry we were not here when you arrived,' Richard said, kissing his mother's cheek. 'We did not expect you so early. I felt sure you would not leave before the end of the day's business.'

'You were the one to ask us to arrive early.'

'Because I asked him to,' the dowager put in. 'I was afraid you might be held up on the road.'

'Good afternoon, Mr Harecroft, Mrs Harecroft,' Diana said, giving Mrs Harecroft a courteous bend of the knee. She turned towards Stephen, who stood in front of the hearth beside his father, and was struck by how like him he was. It was not only his physique, but his stance, the way he held his head, the slight lifting of the chin, which made him seem to be looking down on everyone, the way his hair was parted, the way he put his hands behind his back under his tail coat. In a few years' time Stephen would be a mirror image of his father. 'Mr Stephen,' she greeted him.

'Hallo, Diana. We left early so as to arrive in good time for dinner. I was disappointed you were not here when we arrived.'

'I am sorry, if I had known what time you were coming, I would not have gone to the races. We went to see North Wind run…'

'No matter, you are here now.'

'How is your father?' Mrs Harecroft asked.

'He is progressing favourably. He came with us to Ascot. I think he enjoyed the day.'

'Good. It sounds as if he is recovering well.'

'I think so. He will be able to leave with me when I return to London after the party.'

'I shall look forward to having you back with me,' Stephen said.

Diana stole a glance at Richard, who grinned ruefully at her. Now his parents and Stephen were here, he wondered how firm she would stand in her resolve to turn his brother down. They would undoubtedly bring pressure to bear on her to say yes. He wished Stephen would voluntarily withdraw his proposal, but there was little hope of it; to do so would cause no end of a scandal and he would never risk that.

'You had better go and change for dinner,' Mrs Harecroft said, addressing Richard and Diana. 'We will have plenty of time to talk afterwards.'

They turned to leave the room and Stephen sprang to open the door for Diana, catching her hand as he did so and raising it to his lips. Richard noted it and his heart sank; the pressure was beginning already. 'Stephen, come and talk to me while I dress,' he said. 'We have some catching up to do.'

Diana decided to wear the dress Richard had bought her in Staines; he had adamantly refused to take it back to the shop when she suggested it. It was only a gesture on her part; she had not wanted to part with it. She had just finished dressing when Mathilde arrived and told her Lady Harecroft wanted to see her.

Her ladyship was wearing a blue dressing gown that matched the clear blue of her eyes and went well with her snow-white hair. She looked Diana up and down in the same disconcerting way Richard had; perhaps he had learned it from her. 'You look delightful,' she said. 'That gown is perfect for you. And your necklace is very pretty.'

'Thank you, my lady. It was once my mother's.'

'Have you recovered from your headache?'

'Yes, thank you. I took one of Mrs Evans's remedies and it worked very well.'

'Good. You are not thinking of disappearing again, are you?'

'No, my lady.'

'My daughter tells me you are set on refusing Stephen.'

'Yes, I am. I am sorry to disappoint you, my lady, but he is not for me and I am not for him.'

'I am not disappointed. The decision is yours and yours alone.'

'I shall tell him at the first opportunity.'

'But you will be at my party, won't you?'

'If you still wish it.'

'Of course I still wish it.'

'Then I will leave the day after. My father is almost fully recovered and we must find lodgings—'

'Bring him to the party. I should like to meet him.'

'That is kind of you, but I am not sure he is ready for company.'

'You have just said he is almost fully recovered.'

'Yes, but…'

The old lady leaned forward and patted her hand. 'Bring him, to please me.'

Diana was in a cleft stick. If her father went to the party, could he be trusted to stay sober? If she said nothing to him, her ladyship would soon learn he had not even been asked and would want to know why. 'I will see how he is tomorrow,' she said. 'If he is strong enough, perhaps he can come for a short time.'

'Thank you. I admire the way you have protected him and worked for him—not many young ladies would have done so.'

'But he is my father!'

'Of course, but you are young and have your own life to lead and I do not believe the young should be hamstrung by the old. As you shall see tomorrow.'

Before Diana could ask her what she meant, they were interrupted by the arrival of Richard. 'Not going down to dinner, Great-Grandmama?' he queried, seeing she was not dressed.

'No, I need to conserve my strength for tomorrow. I shall have my supper sent up here.'

'I believe Uncle Henry has arrived.'

'All the more reason to stay here. He will do nothing but grumble in that carrying voice of his and wear me out. Go on down, both of you. And, Diana, do not forget about your father.'

'What did she mean about your father?' he asked as they went downstairs together.

'She wants me to bring him to her party. I do not think I dare risk it.'

'Why not?'

'You, of all people, should know why not.'

'But you cannot keep him confined forever, Diana. You have to show him you trust him or he will never be cured. I will be here to help keep an eye on him.'

'I told her ladyship I would think about it.'

'What else did she say?'

'Oh, nothing very much. She said she did not believe the young should be hamstrung by the old.'

'Very enigmatic—anything else?'

'No.'

He did not comment, but he was disappointed. Great-Grandmama had promised to tell Diana her secret, but she had obviously balked at it. She really was a wicked old woman, but he loved her dearly.

Chapter Ten

When they entered the drawing room, they found the rest of the family had arrived. Henry was regaling the company with his opinion on the state of the roads. 'Potholes everywhere,' he said. 'It was a wonder the horses were not lamed. As for the springs of my carriage, I am sure they will never be the same again. Can you not have something done about them, Uncle William?'

'Me?' his lordship queried. 'I do not own the roads.'

'You own Borstead village.'

'Those roads are kept in good repair,' William insisted.

Henry turned and saw Diana, the blue gown falling in soft folds about her feet and her red-gold hair piled up in a becoming coronet. 'God in heaven, you startled me,' he said. 'I thought I was seeing a ghost.'

Stephen hurried forward to take her hand, detaching her from Richard. 'Uncle Henry, Aunt Anne, allow me to present Miss Diana Bywater,' he said, leading her forward. 'Diana, my uncle, Mr Henry Harecroft and Mrs Harecroft and these…' he pointed to a young man of perhaps eighteen and a girl a little younger, who was dressed in pale pink decorated with rows and rows of ribbon bows '…are my cousins, Cecil and Maryanne.'

Diana murmured, 'How do you do', wondering what the man had meant about seeing a ghost. Had she been right all along? Was she being mistaken for someone else?

The butler came to tell them dinner was served and they lined up to go into the dining room. Diana went in on Stephen's arm and Maryanne seized Richard's arm and hung on to it, leaving Cecil to escort Alicia.

Once they were all seated, the servants served the soup and then withdrew. For a minute or two there was silence, but Diana could feel the tension in the air, a certain wariness, and she began to wonder if she were the cause. Or was it that they were suspicious of all newcomers?

'Do you live in Borstead, Miss Bywater?' the younger Mrs Harecroft asked.

'No, she is staying here,' Stephen answered for her.

'I came to help Miss Harecroft with the arrangements for her ladyship's party,' Diana told her. 'Normally I work at Harecroft's Emporium. I am a clerk.'

'A clerk?' Henry queried. 'I thought you must be one of the family.'

'I hope one day she may be,' Stephen said, reaching across and putting his hand over Diana's. She hurriedly withdrew it to take a spoonful of soup.

'A wedding,' Maryanne exclaimed. 'I love weddings, all that champagne…'

'What do you know of champagne, miss?' her father snapped.

'I know everyone drinks it at weddings.' She paused. 'And birthday parties. I expect Great-Grandmama will have bottles and bottles of it for her party tomorrow.'

'And you will have none of it,' her mother said. 'Miss

Bywater, you must forgive my daughter. Her school is supposed to teach her to be a lady, but I can see no evidence of it. Do you enjoy your work at the shop?'

Diana was glad they had stopped talking about weddings. If only she had had time to see Stephen and talk to him before dinner, she could have saved them both a great deal of embarrassment. 'Yes, very much,' she said, catching sight of Stephen looking at her. She turned her attention to the food on her plate and made a pretence of eating it.

'It is a strange occupation for a lady,' Henry said.

'I do not see why it should be,' Diana said, determined not to let them intimidate her. 'It requires no strength, simply a head for figures and a neat hand.'

'Miss Bywater does it very well,' John told them.

'I thought she was a Harecroft,' Henry persisted. 'I noticed the likeness at once. Miss Bywater is exactly like that picture of Grandmother in her youth…'

'Which picture?' John queried.

'You know, the one on the staircase wall. I forget the name of the artist.'

'Sir Joshua Reynolds,' Richard murmured.

'Yes, that's the one. She'd have been about the same age as Miss Bywater. It was as if Grandmother had stepped out of the frame, as young as she used to be. Except for the gown, of course.' He turned to Diana. 'Are you related?'

'I do not think so,' Diana said, wishing they would change the subject. It was almost as if they were trying to catch her out in some misdemeanor, as if she had inveigled her way into their home on the strength of a likeness. She cast a beseeching look at Richard. He smiled encouragingly before addressing his uncle.

'If there were one, I am sure Great-Grandmama would know about it,' he said.

'Unless two branches of the family had a falling out,' Cecil added. 'And neither knew of the other's existence.'

'There was Uncle James,' Henry mused. 'Of course I do not remember him, but I remember Grandfather mentioning him when I was a boy. He was talking to Grandmama. I was not supposed to be listening, but it stuck in my memory.'

'What did he say?' Stephen asked, intrigued.

'He said he did not know how large the family was because he had no idea how many brats James had bequeathed to the nation.'

'Henry!' Alicia cried. 'I am sure he said no such thing.'

'He did, you know. Grandmama was furious with him. You ask her.'

'I certainly will not. James was a hero, killed fighting for king and country in the American Wars. Mother was heartbroken when he died.'

'I think you are embarrassing Miss Bywater,' Richard said, casting a meaningful look at Stephen. He had given him a lecture earlier that evening, which had resulted in Stephen becoming angry and telling him to mind his own business. Papa wanted him to marry Diana and he did not see why he should not do so. He had even accused Richard of being jealous, which he had denied, though it was true. He was jealous as hell!

'They say everyone has a double,' Cecil said. 'Someone as like as two peas in a pod, but with no connection at all.'

'That would demolish my theory and I had been weaving such a romantic tale of lost love,' Maryanne said, laughing. 'Secret elopements and being cut off without a penny. Wouldn't that be something?'

At a fearsome look from her mother, Maryanne subsided, much to Diana's relief. She had no answer to the suggestions they made; she could not give them chapter and verse of her family history as they undoubtedly could of theirs and she could see that Richard did not like the subject being aired; after all, he had himself sired a child out of wedlock.

'What are you doing with yourself these days, Richard?' his aunt asked him, as the soup dishes were cleared away and the next course of lamb cutlets and vegetables from the garden was brought in and left on the table for them to help themselves.

'Richard is writing a book,' Stephen put in. 'Though no one has seen it. It is just an excuse to live a life of idleness with his friends at the dower house.'

'Are they still there?' his mother asked. 'I thought you were going to get rid of them.'

'While they have nowhere to go, I cannot turn them out, Mama. Mr Somers has been offered an exhibition, which means he will be moving to London soon. Mr Harris is going to illustrate my book.'

'Poor man,' Stephen said. 'It will never see the light of day.'

'There you are wrong, brother. I have found a publisher.' Mr Waterson of Southwark had expressed an interest, it was true but he had not made a firm commitment. 'Well written,' he had said. 'But to make any impact on the public it needs illustrations.' It was then he had remembered Diana's suggestion. He had written to Mr Waterson to tell him he had the perfect illustrator. It meant rewriting some passages to introduce the pictures, but that would not take long and he had promised to deliver the new text and illustrations within a month.

'Have you indeed?' his father put in. 'I hope he is reputable.'

'Yes, small but respectable.'

'Then I shall look forward to seeing your work in print.'

'And the actress?' his mother queried. 'Is she still at the dower house?'

'Miss Standish is my housekeeper. And, yes, she is still there.'

'Housekeeper! I cannot imagine any bride worth her salt condoning her being there.'

'Neither can I, Mama,' he said with a rueful sigh. 'Neither can I.'

'Then do something about it.'

Diana was glad they were no longer quizzing her, but Mrs Harecroft's words made her wonder if the lady knew the real situation at the dower house, if she even knew about the little boy. Her grandchild. Or did she know, did they all know, and were all choosing not to acknowledge the inconvenience of his existence? Poor little Dick, poor long-suffering Lucy! She risked a glance at Richard and was disconcerted to find he was looking at her with that steady gaze of his. She looked away quickly and helped herself from the tureens on the table, though she was not in the least hungry. She was glad when the meal came to an end and the ladies withdrew to leave the men to port and cigars.

While Lady Harecroft supervised the dispensing of the tea in the drawing room, Diana found a quiet corner where she hoped to remain undisturbed until she could politely leave the company. When the gentlemen joined them, a discussion was begun as to how they might amuse themselves for the rest of the evening and Diana took the opportunity to escape. 'Please excuse me,' she said. 'I would like to see how my father has settled down after his day out. I fear we overtired him.'

'Then I will come with you,' Stephen said.

Diana went upstairs to change her shoes and put on a light shawl and a bonnet. When she came down again, she found both Stephen and Richard waiting for her.

'I am going to the old chapel to see Freddie,' Richard said. 'I left him there finishing off a painting. You do not mind if I come as far as the village path with you?'

'Not at all,' Diana said politely.

All three set off across the park. No one spoke. The

tension in the air was almost tangible. Richard had adopted an air of cheerfulness that did not deceive her for a minute and Stephen's jaw was rigid as if he was suppressing a great emotion that threatened to burst inside him. She began to tremble at the thought of what she must do. How would he react? With anger, misery or relief?

When they came to the parting of the ways, Richard doffed his hat. 'Goodnight, Miss Bywater.'

'Goodnight, Mr Harecroft.'

'I will see you later, at the dower house, Stephen. You know what you have to do, don't you?'

'Leave me alone,' was the angry answer.

'What did he mean?' Diana asked, when Richard had left them.

'Oh, nothing. He has a bee in his bonnet as usual. He thinks that because he is the elder he has a right to dictate to me what I do.'

'Perhaps he cares about you.'

'Then why can he not be happy for me? Anyone would think he was jealous.'

'Jealous?'

'Yes, because I have you. He would take you from me if he could.'

'Oh, that is silly. He does not want me. Whatever gave you that idea?'

'Oh, do not let's talk about him. It is a whole week since I saw you and it feels like an age.'

'It does to me, too, but it has given me time to ponder.' She paused to take a deep breath. 'Stephen, I am afraid I cannot marry you.'

He swung round towards her. 'Why not? Has Richard been talking—?'

'No, certainly not.' It was said swiftly.

'Then it must be because the family were so abominably rude at dinner. Take no notice of them. I know you have a superficial likeness to Great-Grandmama, but that is only the colour of your hair, and as for long-lost relations…' He laughed. 'That only happens in cheap novelettes.'

'It has nothing to do with that either. I cannot marry you because I do not love you and I think, if you are honest, you will admit you do not love me.'

'Love comes after marriage, when two people have learned to live together in harmony, so I have been told.'

'I do not subscribe to that,' she said, thinking how dull he made it sound. 'If I did, I might enter into a marriage simply to have a home for myself and my father and have the worry of making a living for us both lifted from me.'

'Then do it. I promise you—'

'No, Stephen. We would both regret it and make each other miserable.'

'Is that your last word?'

'I am afraid it is. As soon as the party is over I am taking my father back to London to find lodgings and a new job.'

He gave a cracked laugh. 'Where will you find one as good as the one you have at Harecroft's? Not everyone is as benign as my father, you know.'

'I do know and I appreciate it, but I trust he will not hold it against me and refuse me a good reference.'

'You will have what you deserve. I know he will be displeased and so will Great-Grandmama.'

'I am sorry, I am very fond of you and I am grateful to your family for all they have done, but that is my decision. Please accept it with my good wishes for your future happiness.'

'Very well. You will not mind if I do not come any farther, will you?' And with that he turned about and strode away. Diana continued alone, relief washing over her. It had been difficult, but she was glad it was done. He would get over his disappointment and now she must map out her future and that was going to be even more difficult and heart-rending because it meant saying goodbye to Richard. Why did she continue to love him in spite of what he was and what he had done? Why could she not convince herself he was a rogue?

She went up the steps of the nursing home and was admitted by one of the attendants. 'Miss Bywater, thank goodness.' She looked past Diana as if searching for someone. 'Where is he? Have you not brought him back?'

'You mean my father? He came back hours ago. I saw him in myself.'

'I know, but he must have gone out again.'

'Did he say where he was going?'

'No, not a word. Come and speak to Matron.'

Diana followed her along a corridor to the matron's sitting room, her spirits, already at a low ebb, falling even further. It was soon apparent that her father was missing and had been missing for two or three hours. 'I knew it was not a good idea to take him out this afternoon,' Matron said severely. 'You have upset his routine and routine is so important when a patient is convalescing. And I am sure he had been drinking, I smelled it on his breath.'

'He had one glass of champagne to celebrate a win at the races,' Diana said. 'That, surely, could have done him no harm.'

'I do not approve of gambling either. Now you have un-settled him and he has wandered off. We have searched the house and grounds and he is certainly not here. I was about to send up to the Hall to let Lady Harecroft know what has happened. I am not going to be blamed for this.'

It was obvious to Diana that she expected to be held re-sponsible by those at the big house to whom she was an-swerable for Mr Bywater's well-being. 'I am sure no one will blame you, Matron,' she said. 'Do not worry, I think I might know where to find him. I will fetch him back, there is no need to send up to the Hall.'

'Very well. I cannot think why he wanted to leave. He is given every consideration…'

'You have looked after him admirably,' Diana said sooth-ingly. 'I am sure he will tell you so himself when he returns. Now, if you excuse me, I will go and find him.'

Diana had a good idea where he father was and set off for the Borstead Arms. It was the larger of the two inns in the village and the better of the two in terms of cleanliness. She braced herself to enter and ask for her father, desperately hoping he had not disgraced himself, because in a small place like Borstead the news would soon spread. She could imagine the disgust of everyone at the Hall when it reached there. But what did it matter? she told herself. She was leaving first thing on Sunday and while she was here she might as well enquire about transport to London.

Her father was not in the parlour, though several locals sat enjoying a glass of beer, including, she noticed, Dawkins, one of Borstead Hall's footmen, and Soames. They stared at her with curiosity and Soames touched his hat to her, but neither spoke. She approached the innkeeper and requested the times of the coaches and whether she could hire a conveyance to take her to Ascot. She was told there was a regular carrier who also took passengers.

'Beggin' your pardon, miss.' Soames had heard her request and come to stand beside her. 'Did you say you was wanting to catch the London coach?'

She turned to face him. 'Yes, Mr Soames. I only came down for the party.'

'But I should be taking you. Her ladyship would be vexed to think you were making your own way.'

'I wanted to save you the trouble.'

'It ain't no trouble. It's what I'm paid for.'

'In that case, I will speak to her ladyship about it,' Diana said. 'Have you seen my father anywhere about the village? Would you know him if you saw him?'

'No, miss, I don't reckon I would.'

'He's been convalescing at the nursing home and came out for a walk, but he has been gone rather a long time...'

'What does he look like?'

'Do he hev only one arm?' Dawkins, curiosity aroused, had joined them.

'Yes, have you seen him?'

'He was in here earlier on, treating everyone he was. Said he'd had a win on the horses...'

'Do you know where he went when he left?'

'No. He didn't say.'

Diana thanked them and left. If Papa was drunk, his shame would be all round the village in no time. Why had he lapsed? Thanks to Richard he had had only one glass of champagne, but that must have been enough to set him off again. And she had had such high hopes that he was cured. It would make it all the more difficult for her to find a new job and suitable lodgings. 'Oh, Papa,' she murmured, 'why do you do this to me?'

Her next call was at the Travellers Rest. This was little more than a hedge tavern and was tucked into a space between the blacksmith's forge and a narrow lane leading to a small holding. Its doorway was so low that she had to duck her head to enter. There was only one bar and it was full of labourers who looked round in surprise to see her invading what they considered their preserve. In the middle of them, surrounded by empty glasses, sat her father. Her heart sank.

'Papa,' she said, 'I have been looking everywhere for you. What are you doing in here?'

'What's the matter with here?' someone demanded. 'Not good enough for him, is that it?'

She ignored the man and squatted down beside her father's chair. 'Papa, come away, please.'

'All in good time, my dear, all in good time. I'm celebrating with my friends.'

'They are not your friends, they are only after free drink.'

'Hey, miss, can't hev that,' said another man. 'If the gen'leman choose to treat us with his winnings, we in't about to turn him down, don' mean we're spongers.'

'You do not understand,' she said. 'My father has been ill. He is not supposed to drink.'

'A little drink never did anybody any harm,' the publican put in. 'Where'd I be if a man couldn't have a glass of ale when he wanted one?'

'I did not say that…'

'Petticoat government, who wants it?' another said. 'Jimmy, my friend, are you going to let a slip of a chit tell you what to do?'

'Papa, please,' she beseeched him. 'Don't listen to them.'

He half-rose as if to accompany her, but then sat down heavily again. She realised he was in a worse state than she feared and would have trouble walking back to the nursing home, especially as he had not fully recovered from his seizure. And what would Matron say when she saw him? She looked around for someone who might help her, but they were all looking aggressive.

'Get along home, gal, and wait for 'im to come back in his own good time,' said the first man. 'This in't no place for interferin' women.'

She left them, intending to wait outside, but the publican came to the door and waved her away. 'You standing there in't good for trade,' he said.

She walked back through the village, knowing there was only one person who could help her. She hoped he was still at the old chapel; she did not want to go to the dower house for him.

'Mr Hatley cannot fail to be impressed,' Richard told Freddie, as they worked together cataloguing the paintings.

'I could not have done it without your help. One day I will repay you.'

'Your recognition will be payment enough.'

They turned in unison as Diana almost burst through the door. She looked distraught and Richard realised at once that something was very wrong. She was breathless, her face was drawn and her lovely eyes troubled. He assumed Stephen's revelation had shocked her. Nevertheless he was wary. 'Diana, can I help you?'

'May I speak to you?' she asked, then added, with an apologetic look at Freddie, 'Privately.'

'Of course.' He took her arm and guided her outside. 'What has happened? Where is Stephen?'

'Stephen?' she queried, puzzled. That young man had been furthest from her thoughts. 'I have no idea. I assume he has gone back to the Hall. I need your help.'

'Anything,' he said, wondering what she and his brother had said to each other. 'You have only to ask.'

'Papa is in the Traveller's Rest and I cannot make him come out and they are making fun of him, taking advantage of his condition.'

'Good Lord! You never went in there, did you?'

'I had to. How else was I to extricate him? As it was they were most discourteous to me. I am afraid he made no effort to correct them. Please come, he might listen to you.'

'Of course.' He went back to the door of the chapel and

called, 'I'm going now, Freddie. I will see you back at the dower house.'

'I am afraid he is already past being able to walk properly,' she said as they set off for the village. 'Oh, how I wish Mr Somers had not given him that champagne.'

'Freddie was not to know.'

'No. Will it always be like that, do you suppose, people offering him drink because they do not know what ails him? I feel like hanging a card round his neck: "Please do not offer me alcohol."'

'You could not possibly do that.'

'No, of course not. But he has been so good and now he is as bad as ever, worse because he has not had a drink for so long. I cannot lock him up, can I, or watch him every minute of the day?'

'No. You must have help. I am sure something can be arranged.'

'I don't want to lay my troubles at anyone else's feet. I would not have asked you if I could have managed him myself.'

'My dear girl, ask me as often as you wish. I would be sad if I thought you could not come to me with your troubles.'

'You are very kind.'

'Not at all.' Kind was not what he wanted her to call him, nor gratitude what he wanted from her, but for the moment, he would accept that. Until he had discovered what had happened between her and Stephen, he could not ask for more.

'I dare not think what Matron will say when she sees him,' she said. 'She was disapproving enough this afternoon and he had only had one glass of champagne then.'

'We will have to sober him up first.' He stopped to consider. 'We will take him back to the chapel. Freddie will have gone. You can stay there with him while I go to the house and fetch hot coffee. I believe that has a sobering effect. And then we will take him for a walk in the fresh air.'

'He can hardly put one foot in front of the other,' she said in dismay. 'If we are seen…'

'Then I have a better idea. You go on. I will harness up the trap and catch up with you. If you arrive before I do, do not go back into that tavern, wait outside.' He sprinted away towards the Hall. Slowly she walked on. Why was her father like he was? It must be her fault, something she had done or not done. She only wished she knew what it was, then she might be able to put it right.

As she approached the tavern, she could hear tuneless singing and a great deal of uproarious laughter. Already almost running, she quickened her pace, but turned when she heard the sound of hooves. Richard was driving the trap towards her and it was swaying from side to side as he made the poor pony gallop. He drew up beside her and jumped down.

'Steady, sweetheart, don't go rushing in.' He put his hand on her arm to detain her. 'Leave it to me.'

Sweetheart he had called her. Even in the midst of her distress, her heart had leaped at the sound, but quickly settled again. It meant nothing, could mean nothing. She stopped, eyes full of tears. 'They are making sport of him, Richard. How can he have so little self-respect that he allows it?'

It was the first time she had slipped up and called him by his given name. It pleased him, but he did not comment. 'You stay with the trap. I will fetch him out.'

He handed her the reins, then made for the inn, ducking his head under the lintel before disappearing. The jollity in the inn was suddenly silenced. A minute or two later, he re-emerged with his arm about the shoulders of her father, holding him upright.

'Up into the trap with you,' he said, pushing James up from behind. 'We are going to take you for a little ride.'

He tumbled into one of the seats, Diana climbed in beside him and Richard, reins in hand, took the opposite seat.

'Where we goin'?' James asked thickly, as the little pony carried them away.

'I am going to show you something that might interest you,' Richard said.

A few minutes later they drew up at the chapel. There was no one about. Richard unlocked the door, then helped James inside and sat him in the wide stone of the window embra-sure. 'Mr Somers and Mr Harris use this old chapel for a workroom,' he told him. 'They are getting ready for an exhi-bition. I would value your opinion.' He fetched one or two of Joe's canvases. 'You show them to him, Diana, I am going up to the house to fetch coffee.'

'I'd rather have a c…cognac,' James said, with a hiccough.

Richard smiled. 'I am sure you would, but I think coffee, don't you? We can't have you ill on the day of her ladyship's party, can we? Great-Grandmother especially wants you to be there.' He turned to Diana. 'I will not be long.'

Diana showed him the paintings, trying to keep him from thinking about another drink. 'Gruesome,' he said.

'They are pictures of true scenes.'

'Don't alter the fact they turn my sh…shtomach.'

'I believe that is what they are meant to do.'

His attention was drawn to the canvas in the centre of the room and he got up and wobbled over to it. Diana was terri-fied he would knock against it and damage it and ran to take his arm. He shrugged her off and pulled the cloth off it. 'Now thash more the thing. Tha's the little boy, the one we took to the races. I forget his name.'

'Dick,' she said. 'I believe he is named for Mr Richard.'

He turned towards her suddenly. 'That why you're not going to marry the young fellow?'

'Because of Dick? No, of course not. What has he to do with it?'

'Quite a bit, I sh…should have thought. What else is there?' He began pulling other covers off.

'Oh, Papa, do come and sit down again. If you break anything…'

He ambled towards her and sat down again. 'It happens, you know, girl. Men are indish…creet, don't mean they won't make perfectly good hush…bands.'

Diana went about replacing the covers, unsettled by what he had said. 'Papa, I have already told Mr Stephen I will not marry him and that is the end of the matter.'

Before he could answer her, Richard returned, carrying a steaming jug and some cups. He lost no time in pouring a cup of coffee for James. 'Drink that, it will make you feel better.'

Diana expected an argument; Papa did not like being told what to do, which was hardly surprising when for years he had been issuing orders to his crew. And even at home, his word had been law. But his disability and his drunkenness had made him almost childlike and Richard's was now the voice of authority. He gulped down the hot liquid, only to be faced with another full cup. 'Go on, drink it,' the younger man said when he hesitated.

After he had downed three cups, Richard hoisted him to his feet. 'Now for a walk.'

'Oh, Richard, not in the grounds, please,' Diana pleaded. 'We will be seen.'

'Very well, we will go up on to the heath.'

He guided James out and helped him into the trap and they set off again. It was growing dark by now, but the pony was sure-footed and they were soon climbing the lane that led to Borstead Heath, where they stopped. The pony was tethered, James was helped out and all three set off to walk across the grass. 'It used to be a great spot for highwaymen,' Richard said, putting his hand under James's only elbow to steady him. 'No carriage dared stop. Now all we see are a few beggars and people passing by on horseback or in carriages.'

Diana was grateful for his down-to-earth manner and for a few minutes they spoke of horses and the Harecroft stables, while supporting James between them and almost forcing him to walk. After a little while, he seemed steadier and they turned to retrace their steps.

'I told her,' James said, when they were nearly back to the trap. 'I told her a man's early indiscretions should not be held against him when it comes to matrimony.'

'That depends on the indiscretion and its consequences,' Richard said, after some consideration during which Diana began to think he did not mean to reply. 'And the character of the bride and what the lady wanted out of the marriage.'

She was reminded of his answer to his mother's comment about the actress at the dower house. He evidently did not expect his indiscretions to be overlooked by his bride, but why did he flaunt his mistress so openly? Surely discretion meant keeping her at some distance from his home and not being seen with her so openly? That part of his character did not sit well beside the compassionate, thoughtful man she believed him to be.

'This particular lady wants nothing,' she snapped. 'And now if you have finished philosophising, we will go back to the nursing home. It has been a very long day.'

James managed to step up into the trap himself followed

by Diana and Richard. All were silent. James's head nodded, as if he were falling asleep, and Diana knew he would have a dreadful headache the following morning. Would he be fit to go to the party and could she trust him? She doubted it.

When they arrived, Richard went into the home with them and placated Matron, a service Diana was very glad of, then they returned to the trap and, with hardly a word being spoken, drove back to Borstead Hall.

The sky was full of stars and a full moon hung low in the sky, throwing deep shadows over the house and the huddle of buildings surrounding it. 'It looks different in the dark,' she said. 'Ghostly, almost.'

'You are not afraid of ghosts, are you?'

'Are there ghosts?'

'One, so they say. One of the nuns from the priory was supposed to have thrown herself in the brook and drowned on account of breaking her vows.'

'What had she done?'

'Succumbed to the love of a man,' he said. 'Now her tormented spirit roams the bank dripping with water, her head festooned in weeds, crying for forgiveness.'

'Surely you do not believe it?'

He laughed. 'Of course not.' He drew the pony up at the stables, jumped down and turned to hand her down. She was standing beside the trap with her hand in his, when Stephen burst from the house and rushed over to them. Before either of them could speak or even move apart, he had landed a punch on Richard's jaw that sent him stumbling back against the trap and down between its wheels. The startled pony reared up, lifting the wheel off the ground. Diana stuffed her hand into her open mouth to stop herself screaming.

Somehow Richard managed to roll out of the way and

hauled himself to his feet, wiping the blood from his nose. 'I suppose you are going to tell me the reason for that?' he asked calmly.

'I should have thought it was obvious.' Stephen stood, feet apart, fists raised. 'Anything I have ever wanted you have taken from me and made your own. It has always been the same. Whatever I did, you did it better. Whatever I had, toys, books, pets, you coveted them. You took Lucy from me and now you have turned Diana against me.'

'No!' Diana cried.

He went on as if she had not spoken. 'You knew I had asked her to marry me, so you had to set your cap at her and take her from me—'

'Stop it,' Diana cried out. 'Stop it. It is not true…'

He turned on her. 'And you are nearly as bad as he is, allowing yourself to be seduced.'

She stared at him, unable to find words in her own defence. Far from getting over his disappointment, Stephen had brooded on it until he had worked up such a sense of grievance he could not even think coherently. But even so, a part of her brain was wondering just how true his words were. Had Richard taken Lucy from him? Were they both, she and Lucy, pawns in the deadly game the brothers played with each other? She turned and fled.

Chapter Eleven

The day of the party dawned bright and sunny. The kitchen staff had been supplemented by hired servants and for days there had been a great roasting of fowls, boiling of hams and making of pastry and puddings. Cook was red-faced and agitated, issuing instructions and countermanding them for others until Diana began to wonder if the plump woman would have a fit and throw the whole lot into the air. But now all was ready and huge platters of food and two barrels of beer were carried over to the barn, where the men of the village were setting out tables and chairs. An even more sumptuous repast was being prepared for the house guests who would eat in the grand dining room.

Diana had slept badly and could not concentrate on what she was supposed to be doing. On one thing she was determined. On Sunday morning she would turn her back on Borstead and the whole Harecroft family, but until then she would do the work for which she had been hired and when it came to the party, she would go to the barn and celebrate with the servants because that was where she would feel most at home.

The ballroom floor had been polished to a mirror shine and a dais set up at one end for the musicians. The florist arrived during the morning with a cartload of flowers, which, with the help of Alicia, he proceeded to arrange all over the house. The birthday gifts, which had been arriving for several days, were set out on a table in the corner. Diana, who had begun by wondering if it would be presumptuous of her to give a present, then later had put off doing anything about it because she had decided not to stay, realised that she should have bought something. It was too late now.

When everything was ready, she went up to her room to finish packing her bag ready to leave. She was kneeling on the floor putting her clothes in it, when she came across the little figurine wrapped in tissue in the folds of the dress Richard had bought for her. She sat heavily on the bed with the dress draped across her knees and the little figure clasped in her hands. Her own words came back to her: 'I shall treasure it as a memento of my time in Borstead.' She heard again his voice saying, 'It is only a piece of stone, not a precious jewel, a small token of gratitude for helping me choose my great-grandmother's gift.'

Again and again she went over everything that happened between them in the last week and could not believe it was so short a time. They had begun warily; she had been convinced he did not think she was good enough for his brother, and then by being amiable and helpful, making her sympathise with him over the loss of his dog and his estrangement from his parents, he had wormed his way into her heart. She could not change that, he was there for ever, but it had been the most humiliating experience of her life to realise he had only been using her in his vendetta with Stephen. Poor Stephen, her rejection of him must have hurt him badly, considering he had suffered it before.

And yet… She sat there for a long time, turning the little figure over in her hand and stroking the soft silk of the gown, her emotions going from anger to despair and back again. She had been manipulated by everyone, even her father, who, in some ways, was the most manipulative of them all. It was time she reasserted herself. She stood up and hung the gown in the wardrobe where it would stay to be found by chambermaids after she had gone. The little carving she slipped into her pocket to return to the giver. Then she set off for the nursing home, wondering, with some trepidation, what she would find there.

Her father was sitting on the bench in the garden. Newly shaved, he was in his best suit of clothes and looking very smart. 'Papa,' she said, bending to kiss him, noting that there was no smell of alcohol on his breath. 'How are you?'

'Sorry,' he said. 'Very sorry.'

'Papa, you have said that before, many times.'

'I mean it this time. Yesterday—'

'Yesterday you disgraced me and yourself. Now the whole village knows what you are. It is a good thing we are leaving. You must pull yourself together and help me. I am sure if you stayed sober you could find work for yourself.'

He turned to her, ready to protest as he always had, to tell her that she had no right to speak to him in that fashion, but the words died on his lips. 'Yesterday,' he went on as if she had not spoken, 'was the last time, the very last time. I could not help it. I had had a shock.'

'What shock? You do not mean because I turned Stephen down?'

'No, that does not matter now. I had a visitor…'

'Visitor? You mean Richard?'

'No, Miss Alicia Harecroft.' He gave her one of his lopsided grins. 'She came after you had left me last night. She said it was about time she met me and invited me to her mother's party. You were not going to tell me I had been invited, were you?'

'I was not sure I could trust you.'

'I know. I am a terrible burden to you, but no longer, not ever again. I will stay as sober as a judge, I promise you. They are going to send the coachman with the pony and trap to fetch me, it is all arranged.'

It was just one more indication of how they were being manipulated and the anger she had felt earlier returned in full measure. 'Then it can be unarranged. We are not going to the party, either of us. We are going to take the carrier to Ascot to catch the stage.'

'But we cannot do that,' he protested. 'We are expected.'

'We can and we will. Now I suggest you pack your bags. I am going back to the Hall to fetch my own and I shall tell them exactly what I think of their scheming.'

'You will live to regret it,' he called after her as she marched to the door.

She was too incensed to answer him and hurried back to the Hall, almost at a run. She even forgot to avoid the dower house and was passing the gate when she heard her name being called and turned to see Richard in the garden with Dick. He sent the child indoors and came over to her. 'How is your father this morning, Diana?'

He spoke as if there had never been that dreadful quarrel with his brother over her, but it had happened, as a bruise on his cheek bore witness. Seeing it, she wanted to reach up and touch it tenderly and ask him if it hurt, then berated herself for her stupidity. 'My father is well,' she answered coldly. 'Well enough to travel with me when I leave, which I shall do this afternoon.'

'This afternoon!'

'Yes, I am tired of being used.'

'Used—whatever do you mean? Who has done that?'

'All of you. Every one of you. Do the Harecrofts never think of anyone but themselves?'

'You are disappointed with Stephen?'

'No more than with the rest of you.' She paused. 'Why did you mention Stephen?'

His spirits rose, then plummeted again. 'He did not tell you, then?'

'Tell me what? That he had discovered I was a nobody, after all, and not fit to marry one of the mighty Harecrofts?'

'Good Lord, no! If anyone has given you that impression, Diana, I am sorry for it,' he said. 'Nothing could be further from the truth. You are too good for any of us.'

'Ha!' She was scornful. 'If you think flattery will bring me round, you could not be more wrong.' She delved into her pocket and pulled out the little figure he had given her. 'And you may have this back.' She held it out to him.

He recoiled, refusing to take it. 'Why, Diana? What have I done to displease you?'

'If you do not know, then you must be even more insensitive than I took you for. I bid you goodday, sir.' And with that, she left him.

He stared after her, then looked down at the little carving which had somehow got into his hand, though he did not remember taking it. Not since the day Pal had died, had he felt so consumed by dark despair.

As soon as she entered the house, Diana was swept up in the final preparations for the party, being appealed to by Cook and Dawkins to settle a dispute over the cleanliness of the silver, and then going to look for Catchpole, whose job it was to oversee the footmen's work. She handed the problem over to him and was on the way up to her room, when she was met by Mathilde. 'Miss Bywater, I was coming to find you. Her ladyship wants to see you.'

'Now?'

'Yes, if you please.'

Diana took a very deep breath to calm herself and tapped on the dowager's door, Receiving the command to enter, she went in to find her ladyship dressed, ready to receive her guests. Her gown was of cream satin embroidered with silver thread and seed pearls and she wore a small diamond tiara on her white hair. Mathilde had made up her face very discreetly and she looked much younger than her ninety years. Her blue eyes were sparkling.

'You wanted to see me?' Diana asked.

'Yes. Come in and sit down.' She waved at a stool close to her feet.

Diana perched herself on the edge of it and waited.

'You are still wearing that old grey dress, Diana. I expected you to be dressed for the party before now.'

'I am not going to stay for the party, my lady. My father and I are leaving almost at once to take the carrier into Ascot to catch the stage. I know you have spent money on Papa's convalescence and I am sorry for that, but somehow I shall find a way of repaying it.'

'My dear child, what nonsense is this? I thought you were happy here.'

'I should never have been asked. It was a great mistake on my part to accept. Mr Henry Harecroft seemed to think I was a relation and I think you thought it too and that is why…'

'Did you never wonder about it yourself?'

'No, of course not. I know Mr Richard thought I was using a superficial likeness to the family to worm my way into favour, but it is not true, I swear it. It never entered my head.'

'Did Richard really say that?'

'No, but he implied it.'

'Then he is a bigger dolt than I took him for. I knew you were a Harecroft the minute I set eyes on you in John's office. The trouble was proving it. Everyone was bound to say I was becoming senile if I told them. The only one I could trust was Richard.'

'I don't understand.'

'Listen to me for a minute while I explain.' She paused to collect her thoughts. 'Out of the six children I had, three grew into adulthood—William, James and Alicia.'

'Yes, I saw the portrait in the attic and Miss Harecroft told me who everyone was.'

'James was a handsome devil and all the young débutantes fell in love with him; he could have married any one of them with our blessing. Instead, he fell in love with a young woman called Susan Bywater, who was the daughter of a seamstress.'

'Bywater?'

'Yes, my dear. He wanted to marry her, but naturally, his father did not approve and, to my shame, I agreed with him. We did our best to dissuade him against the marriage. My husband even went so far as to threaten to cut off his allowance and disinherit him if he married her. They were both stubborn and neither would give an inch. In the end, James went off and joined the army, saying it was the only way he could be independent. A little like Richard, I suppose, though Richard did come back, thank God.

'We did not hear of James for over a year and then came the news that he had been killed in action in the Americas. It broke my heart that he had died without becoming reconciled with us. I wanted to find Susan, thinking that he must have married her and, whether we had approved or not, she was our daughter-in-law and there might be a child, but my husband was adamant. He said he had cut him off and that meant he had cut off his wife and any progeny he might have had. He would not listen to my pleading and it was not until after he died several years later, that I felt able to begin my search.

'I discovered from a fellow officer that James had been going to marry but he did not think he had done so before he was sent off to America. He had no idea what had happened to Miss Bywater. He said she might have been expecting a child but he could not be sure. After that the trail went cold.

'In spite of that, I have always been convinced there was a child and I kept trying to imagine what he or she would be like. If the child was a boy, was he handsome and good, or if a girl, was she clever and pretty? I tended to think that everyone who was the right age and bore a superficial likeness to the Harecrofts must be my grandchild. But I was always disappointed. When I met you, all my old hopes and frustrations surfaced again. I would have renewed my search as soon as I met you, but Alicia persuaded me it would only lead to another dead end. It was when Stephen asked if you might come to my party, that I really began to think about it again. This time I am sure.'

Diana had been mesmerised by the story, easily relating it to what she knew of her father. And he was called James! She stared at the old lady who was smiling at her, as if expecting her to welcome the news. 'You are saying that Miss Bywater was my father's mother?'

'Yes and what is more to the point my son, James, was your grandfather.'

'Are you sure? Can you prove what you are saying?'

'Yes, I think so. The Foundling Hospital has a reputation for placing orphans in the navy and when I learned that your father was a naval man and you told us he had been brought up in an orphanage, I asked Richard to make enquiries there. Their records of when your father arrived in their care and the date of his birth given to them by the woman who brought him there, coincided with the little I knew.'

'What happened to her?'

'No one knows. According to the hospital records, she said she would return for him, but she never did.'

'How do you know she was Miss Bywater? She could have been anyone.'

'I had met her once and the description fitted. And there was more tangible evidence. As a token of her intention to return, she gave the director of the orphanage a necklace, one James had given her, telling them it was to be used for his welfare if she did not. When he left the hospital, it was given to him.' She paused. 'I have seen you wearing it.'

Diana stared at her. 'I cannot take it in. Does my father know?'

'Alicia went to see him yesterday and told him.'

'He never said a word to me.'

'No doubt he could not take it in either.'

'I think it is more likely he would not like to think he was a bastard, born out of a young woman's shame. He would not want to tell me that. Does Stephen know?'

'No one does, except Alicia and Richard.'

'No wonder he did not want me to marry Stephen.'

'He had his own reasons for that and it is nothing to do with who you are.'

She was too full of the Dowager's revelations to wonder what they could be. And he did not seem to be the kind of man to condemn the child for the sins of its parents—in her case, grandparents. After all, there was Dick. 'Why did he not tell me?'

'Because I asked him not to. I have had so many disappointments I wanted to be sure. And I wanted to be the one to tell you.' She reached out and put a hand on Diana's. 'You are without doubt my great-granddaughter.'

Diana was silent for a long time, trying to digest what she had been told. 'I do not know what to say,' she said at last. 'My father is your grandson, cousin to Mr John and Mr Henry. And Richard and Stephen, Cecil and Maryanne are my second cousins, once removed. Is that right?'

'Something like that.'

'Do they know?'

The old lady smiled. 'Richard does, of course, and Alicia, and I think John might have guessed, but the others…no, I do not think so. I was tempted to welcome you into the family at the party, to watch everyone's reactions, but I realised you might find it humiliating and embarrassing, so that is why I asked you to come and see me now.'

'But you are going to tell them?'

'Yes, but not to cause a stir…'

'It will certainly do that.'

The old lady smiled. 'Yes, but I do so want you to be recognised as one of the family. I have waited so long.' She paused and there was a catch in her voice. 'You are not going to run away from me now, are you? Not when I have only just found you. You belong here.'

'Papa?'

'He will be fetched. I want so very much to meet him. And do not worry, Alicia has had a long talk with him; he is her nephew, after all, and he has promised to be good.'

'But you do not know… Unless Richard…'

'Richard said nothing. Your father confessed his problem to Alicia, explained how it came about because of his frustration and helplessness and the poverty in which you found yourselves. Now there is no reason for it. My husband could not quite carry out his threat to cut James off and he never changed his will. The money left to James has been accruing interest over the years and it belongs to your father. He is a wealthy man. It is sad to think you need not have suffered the hardships you have had to endure, but all that is over now.'

'Miss Harecroft told him all this?'

'Yes.'

'No wonder he felt he needed a drink. Celebrating, he said he was.'

'Do you blame him?' It was said with a rueful smile. 'I want him here, to acknowledge him for what he is, my grandson, the child of the boy I gave birth to and always loved. Do not deny me that pleasure. It would be the best birthday present you could give me.'

'I would be a churlish daughter if I denied my father the family he has always wanted.'

'Then go and change for the party.'

In the face of pleading like that, Diana gave in. How the revelation would affect her future, she did not know, but there would be time enough to consider that after the party was over. She kissed the old lady, called her Great-Grandmama and left her to change into her mother's green gown. She had no sooner reached her room than Mathilde came and offered to help her dress and do her hair. She was glad of the help; her hands were shaking so much she could not have done up the buttons or arranged her hair. Her brain was numb.

Later in the evening she found herself standing in the crowded drawing room surrounded by guests, their conversation a hum of noise that made no sense. The family had been told who she was at dinner before the other guests arrived. Henry had said he was not at all surprised, Stephen had gone very pink about the ears, and his mother had kissed her and welcomed her into the family very coolly. Diana smiled to herself; their disgust at her father's bastardy was mixed with the knowledge that he was probably the wealthiest of them all, barring Lord Harecroft, and they were unsure how they ought to react. It was amusing to see them struggling with their so-called finer feelings, wondering what to do for the best. But while the old lady presided over them, they were prepared to welcome Diana. They had yet to meet her father.

She wanted to talk to him, to find out how he felt, to make sure he stayed sober, but since he had arrived, he had been closeted with the old lady. She wanted to speak to Richard, too, but she did not think he would want to have anything more to do with her. She had been scathing to him and had practically thrown his gift back in his face. Well, he deserved it. Whatever her new status, it did not alter the fact that he had humiliated her. She was well aware that she was being inconsistent, but she could not help it. The images of Lucy and Dick always came between her and any thought of reconciliation with him. As for Stephen, she did not know what to think. She ought to have asked the old lady why he had been encouraged to offer her marriage, but in her confusion she had not thought if it.

No one came to speak to her; though she felt thoroughly uncomfortable, she refused to show it, standing tall and proud with a fixed smile on her face. She had nothing to be ashamed of and neither had her father, except for his love of alcohol— perhaps Lady Harecroft was right and his joy at finding himself with a family might effect a cure. She decided to make her way to the barn and see how the party was going there; after all, she had helped to arrange it and it was part of her duties to see that it was running smoothly.

Halfway there she noticed the chapel door was open and

went to investigate. Richard was standing in the middle of the room dressed in an impeccably tailored evening suit, a white shirt and a blue cravat, almost the exact colour of his eyes. For a moment he did not speak, he was engrossed taking in the sight of her: the flushed face, the smoky blue eyes, the red-gold hair, glinting in a shaft of the dying sun coming through one of the windows, the soft folds of the embroidered dress that emphasised a perfect figure. Oh, how he loved her!

'I am sorry,' she said. 'I saw the door was open. I did not mean to intrude.'

'You are not intruding. I was just locking up.'

'You said once you knew almost everything about me. I did not realise at the time that you knew even more than I did myself. You could have warned me.'

'I wanted to, but the old lady was adamant that she would tell you herself. She is a mischievous old dear and wanted to keep the suspense going as long as she could while everyone speculated about your identity. Please forgive me.'

'I do. I wish I had not been so hard on you when you have been so kind to me. I am sorry I made you take back your gift; it was unpardonably churlish of me.'

'Will you accept it, if I give it back to you?'

'Yes, of course.'

He took her shoulders in his hands and looked down into her face. The anger had gone, but she was still not happy. 'Diana—' He stopped suddenly.

She looked up into his face alerted by his tone and held her breath. He smiled ruefully. There were other issues to be resolved before he could declare himself. 'I think we should return to the party, don't you?'

She moved away from him, wondering what he had really intended to say. Whatever it was, he had balked at saying it. She found herself looking down at the portrait of the child, whose red-gold curls and blue eyes told their own story. If Richard married anyone, it ought to be the mother of his child. She could never come between them. 'Yes,' she said, knowing nothing had been resolved and probably never would be.

When they entered the ballroom, they soon realised that the dowager was present with James. He was laughing, his face was flushed and his blue eyes were unusually bright. 'Oh, no,' she murmured, hurrying to join him. 'Papa, how are you?'

He looked at her and grinned. 'As sober as a judge.' He looked up and saw Richard behind her. 'Good evening, young fellow.'

'Good evening, sir. Welcome to the family.'

'Thank you. What a shock it was! But now I have what I most wanted for Diana, a real family of her own. Aside from a good husband, that is. She tells me the wedding is off.'

'It never was on,' Diana said, squirming with embarrassment.

'Does not matter now, does it?'

'No.' She looked up as Lord Harecroft approached them. 'James, I have a new filly in the stables. Would you like to look her over?'

'I do not know anything about horses, except they have a head and four legs,' James said. 'I am a naval man, not a soldier. Give me a ship of the line and I will soon tell you her worth.'

'Oh, then we shall have to educate you,' William answered cheerfully.

James excused himself and followed his host through the crowds to the door. 'Do you think he will be all right?' Diana asked.

'Oh, I think you may stop worrying now, my dear.'

My dear, he had said, and he had once called her sweetheart. Did it mean anything at all to him? Did he not realise, that a new-found family and wealth meant nothing when her heart was in a thousand pieces? She was about to move away from him when a footman came hurrying towards them.

'Mr Richard,' he said, 'there is a young lady at the kitchen door. I believe she has come from the dower house. She asks to speak to you most urgently. She says her little boy has run off and she cannot find him.'

'The little terror! Tell her I will be there directly. Do you know where Mr Stephen is?'

'I am not sure, sir. I think he was in the garden.'

'Find him and tell him to join me at the dower house.' He turned to Diana. 'Please excuse me.' And with that he was gone.

Diana stood looking after him with a heavy heart. There was no doubt who had first call on him in any situation, and whoever married him would have to accept that. She turned to find John standing beside her. 'Where have Richard and Stephen gone?' he asked. 'I haven't seen either of them all evening.'

'I do not know where Stephen is. Richard was here a moment ago, but left. He was needed at the dower house. The little boy has disappeared and he has gone to help look for him.'

'I am surprised at Richard allowing that woman to take over his life as she has,' he said. 'I am glad Stephen is more sensible.'

'Mr Harecroft,' she began. 'I expect Stephen has told you—'

'That you have turned him down. Yes, he has, and I must say I am disappointed. We all are. You would make him an excellent wife and with our pooled resources…'

'I am sorry, I do not know what you mean.'

'My dear, your father is a wealthy man, able to give you a generous dowry; with that and your talent for business, we could have expanded even further. We could be one of the largest concerns in the city.'

She was shocked by his mercenary attitude. 'Mr Harecroft, how long have you know who I really am?'

'I guessed almost from the beginning. My grandmother was so adamant that you must be taken on, I knew there was something behind it. I had heard the story about the missing Harecroft when I was a boy; I remember Grandmother talking to my father about him and it stuck in my mind. I decided to make my own enquiries. After all, if you were one of the family, it made sense to encourage Stephen to marry you. Not,' he added quickly, 'that he needed encouragement.' He paused. 'I hope you will change your mind and accept him after all.'

She was astounded and angry. Just how much more would she discover today? 'I am sorry you are disappointed, sir, but I shall definitely not change my mind. Now if you excuse me, I must look for my father.'

She hurried away. James had been with Lord Harecroft in the stables, she learned from a groom, but they had left some time before. She went to the barn where the sound of music and laughter told her that the lower orders were enjoying themselves. In spite of the hardships they had to endure, she envied them. She went in, looking for her father, pushing her way through the mêlée. Dawkins caught her by the wrist. 'Come to join us, have you?'

'I am looking for my father.'

'Again? He's a great one for slipping through yer fingers, ain't he?' He knew nothing of her new rank as one of the family and treated her like the superior servant he supposed her to be.

'Have you seen him?'

'No. No doubt he is enjoying himself somewhere. Let him be. Come on, dance with me?' He grabbed hold of her to drag her into the centre of the floor. She pulled herself away and fled.

Papa must be out here somewhere. He had probably taken a bottle to enjoy in privacy. But where? Desperately she searched the gardens and outbuildings, then tried the chapel, but Richard had locked the door to that. She set off towards the path through the woods. She needed to calm herself, to try to think. Just how much did her new status mean? Would it mean losing her independence? Did it make any difference to how she felt about Stephen and Richard? Did it make her feel any differently about Lucy Standish and the little boy? It did not. On the other hand, it would mean that her father would be looked after, watched over, eventually cured. Did you ever cure a love of alcohol? She had lived with the problem long enough to doubt it. If it was poverty and lone-liness and frustration that had brought it on, would wealth and being given something to do within the family see an end to it?

Although it was not yet dark, the woods were gloomy and there were strange noises and rustlings that reminded her of Richard's ghost story. She was glad when she found herself on the path beside the brook. Halfway across the bridge, she stopped to lean over the rail and look down into the water. The ghost story was nonsense; it would be difficult to drown oneself in so little water. A child might… Dear God! Dick! She looked about her. All was still, there was no sign of disturbance and surely he could not have come this far on his unstable little legs.

Then she heard the sound of a child's giggle and then a man's chuckle. Neither were ghostlike. She crossed the bridge and ran along the bank. Hidden by a hawthorn bush there was a gently sloping beach and there, sitting with their feet in the water, were her father and Dick. They were laughing at some paper boats James had made and set off along the sluggish current.

'Diana,' James called to her, speaking more clearly than he had done since he had had his seizure. 'Come and join us, we are racing our boats.'

'Papa, how could you?' She scrambled down beside them. 'Everyone is searching high and low for the little boy. His mother is worried to death about him. You should not have brought him here, especially without telling anyone.'

'I didn't bring him, I found him here.'

'Then why did you not take him straight home?'

'I did not know where home was. I joined him in his paddle to gain his confidence so he would tell me where he lived, but he doesn't talk much.'

'Of course he does not. He is only two years old.'

Her anger evaporated. She realized that although her father had seen the little boy when they went to the races, no one had mentioned where the child and his mother lived.

'Now where are his shoes and stockings?'

She looked about her and spied a pair of tiny stockings and one small shoe. 'Where is the other shoe?' she asked.

'I don't know. He had them off when I found him.'

She squatted down beside the boy. 'Dick, where is your shoe?'

'Paddle,' he said, giving her a wide smile.

'Yes, I know you like to paddle, but it is time to go home now.' She held the shoe out to him. 'Where is the other one?'

He pointed to the brook.

'In there?'

'Gone.'

She kicked off her own shoes, pulled her skirt up between

her legs and waded into the water. It was only a few inches deep, but the bottom was muddy and she was stirring it up with her feet. 'It's hopeless,' she said. Turning to go back, she tripped over something unseen in the mud and fell forward onto her knees. Spluttering angrily, she scrambled to her feet, while both her father and Dick, sitting together on the bank, burst into delighted laughter. She tried to wade towards them, overbalanced and sat down in the water. It was impossible to remain serious; she found herself doubled up with laughter and it was then her hand went out and connected with the lost shoe. She held it up and waved it in the air. 'I've got it.'

Her laughter stopped suddenly when she looked up and saw Richard and Stephen, accompanied by Lucy, crossing the bridge at a run towards them.

Lucy reached them first and scooped her son up into her arms. 'Just what do you think you are playing at?' she demanded. 'What have you done to him? If you have harmed a hair of his head, I'll…' Before anyone could do anything to stop her, she set the boy down and rushed at James and would have hit him if Stephen had not grabbed her arms and pinioned them to her sides.

'Stop it, Lucy, Dick is quite safe,' he said.

James looked bewildered. 'I have not harmed the boy,' he said. 'I found him here.'

'It's true!' Diana had scrambled from the water to defend her father. 'Dick might have fallen in the brook and drowned if my father had not come upon him.'

'Oh.' Though her anger had abated a little, it was too red hot to subside altogether.

'Yes. I was going to bring him back to you. When you arrived, I was looking for his shoe, which he had seen fit to throw into the water.' She thrust it into Lucy's hand, picked up her own shoes and ran back over the bridge and along the path, hampered by her wet clothes. Richard caught her up before she had gone very far, reaching out to take her by the shoulder and stop her.

'Where are you going?' He turned her to face him and held her at arm's length while he looked her up and down. The beautiful dress was ruined, covered in mud and weed. Her hair had come down and was wet and bedraggled. There were spots of mud on her face.

'Back to the house.'

'Like that?' He was smiling. 'Have you any idea what you look like?'

She resented his amusement, even though she had been laughing herself a moment before. 'Yes,' she retorted, 'a half-drowned rat.'

'Half-drowned perhaps, but not a rat, never a rat. A kitten, if you like. Or a water nymph, a green water nymph.'

'Oh, I am sick to death of your silly jests. Let me go. I shall have to creep into the house by the back way.' She stopped suddenly. 'Or shall I present myself in the ballroom like this? That would give them all something else to talk about, would it not?'

'Now you are being silly. Come back to the dower house. Lucy will find you hot water to wash and something to wear, before you return to the Hall. I want to talk to you.'

'There is nothing to talk about. We have said it all. Your son is safe and you should be grateful to my father, not grumble at him. And before you say a word, he is cold sober.'

'I was not going to say anything of the sort. Neither was I grumbling at him.'

'Lucy was.'

'She was distraught. Turn round and look.' He took her shoulders and, even though she resisted, turned her about. Stephen had Dick on his shoulder, steadying him with one hand while his other was about Lucy's shoulder, holding her close to his side.

She stared at the trio. 'I don't understand.'

'No, because you jumped to the same conclusion as everyone else and like everyone else you were wrong. I am not Dick's father, Stephen is.'

She felt like a deflated balloon, as if someone had punched her in the ribs and knocked all the breath out of her, and for a moment she could not speak. What was he saying? What did it mean? And then she was angry, very, very angry. 'You knew I had made a mistake,' she rounded on him. 'I even spoke to you of your son when I first arrived and you said not a word to correct me. That was wicked of you, downright wicked.' She broke away from him and tried to run, but, hampered by her wet skirt, she had not gone far when he grabbed her again.

'Come to the dower house and, after you have changed, I will tell you the whole sorry story.'

'No. Let me go. I have had enough revelations for one day.'

'I said I wanted to talk to you and I will talk to you, even if I have to tie you down to do it, but if we stay here much longer you will catch a chill.'

'Do you care?'

'Oh, my dear, how can you ask that?' He stroked her wet hair back from her face with gentle fingers. 'Of course I care. Can you doubt it?'

'You have given me no reason not to.' Even as she spoke, she knew that was not true. Some of the time he had been the only one who did care. He might have had a strange way of showing it, but it was there, all through their relationship, in London when she was visiting her father, on the journey down when he went to endless pains to make sure she was comfortable, fetching her father out of that dreadful tavern and keeping his shame a secret from everyone. He was good at keeping secrets, was Captain Richard Harecroft. Her anger still simmered but she was beginning to shiver with cold. He took off his jacket and put it round her shoulders, proving yet again that he cared.

'Why did you not tell me about Stephen and Lucy?' She allowed herself to be led away.

'I thought he ought to do it.'

'Why didn't he? If he loved Lucy so much, why propose to me?'

'Mama and Papa had been telling him for some time that he ought to settle down with a nice little wife who would be a helpmate in the business. He dare not tell them the truth; an actress would most definitely not be considered suitable. But I knew he loved her and, given enough encouragement and a reunion with Lucy, would stand up to Papa in the end, but I dreaded you accepting him.'

'Oh, I see.'

'No, you do not see. I care for my brother, just as I care for my parents and the dowager, I care for Lucy and Dick and everyone who is unhappy for whatever reason, but I care most of all for you. You are my life.'

'What do you mean?'

Still confused, she walked beside him back through the woods, dark as night now, but she did not hear the squeaking and rustling, only her own heartbeat and his murmured words. 'I mean I love you, Diana Bywater. Dry and wet, I love everything about you.'

Her joy was unbounded. He loved her, just as she loved him. But there were still so many questions and the only one she could think of was, 'You never said so.'

'I thought you might have guessed. When I kissed you. You must have felt something…'

'I did. I discovered I loved you.'

'You never said so,' he repeated her words.

'I could not come between you and Lucy.'

In front of them Stephen and Lucy walked with their son, behind them ambled her father, who had put on his own shoes. 'How did you know we would be down by the brook?' she asked suddenly.

'We searched for Dick everywhere, in the garden, the park, even the chapel, wondering if he had been shut in there accidentally. We searched the barn, where the party was just breaking up. We even went back to the Hall, though I could not imagine he would go up there. Lucy was convinced he had been kidnapped or worse, and when one of the villagers said he had seen a little boy with a man down by the river, you can imagine how she felt. I am sure she is sorry she shouted at your father.'

They had arrived at the dower house. She was ushered inside and conducted up to Lucy's bedroom where a bath was filled with hot water by Freddie and Joe. 'I am sorry I was so angry at your papa,' Lucy told her. 'I know he probably saved Dick's life. I have told him so and he is downstairs now, regaling the men with how it happened, drinking hot chocolate.' She went to a cupboard and brought out a simple gingham dress and from a drawer produced a set of clean underwear. 'Will these do? I think we are much the same size.'

'Very well, thank you.' Diana was already slipping out of her gown, grimacing at the state it was in.

Lucy picked it up. 'I might be able to do something about this. While I was working at the theatre we had to keep the costumes in good order and I learned a lot from my dresser.'

'Please do not go to the trouble—'

'Goodness, I owe you more than I can repay. Cleaning up a

muddy gown is nothing. Come down when you are ready. There will be hot chocolate for you, too, and Richard will be waiting.'

He smiled when he saw her in the gingham dress half an hour later. 'That's better. Now, drink this chocolate and I will take you back to the Hall.'

'You said you wanted to talk to me.'

'I most certainly do. We will talk as we walk.'

Twenty minutes later, they were strolling side by side along the path back to the Hall. 'It almost seems like history repeating itself,' he said after a silence while he marshalled his thoughts. 'Your grandfather, my Great-Uncle James, fell in love with someone the family did not approve of, and so did Stephen, when he fell headlong in love with Lucy, but, unlike Stephen, James stuck to his guns and left the family. Stephen toed the line. He was only nineteen years old at the time and anxious to do well in the business. He can perhaps be forgiven for wanting to keep his affair with Lucy a secret; she was an actress and he knew Papa and Mama would not approve. When she became pregnant she asked Stephen for help, but the only help he felt able to offer was a little money and not much of that. Papa has always kept him on short commons. According to my father, one must learn that money only comes with hard work. I was lucky I had my own inheritance from my maternal grandmother and could be independent.'

'But how did she come to be living at the dower house with you?'

'I was out with Freddie and Joe one evening, enjoying supper at Rules when she came in with some friends. We knew them vaguely and introductions were made. I did not know she had anything to do with Stephen at the time and we enjoyed the usual banter, but later she asked to speak to me alone and I escorted her to her lodgings. She told me about Stephen and the fact that she was pregnant. I was angry with Stephen for leaving her in such straits. When I saw the miserable lodgings she inhabited, I was appalled to think of a Harecroft being born there. It was soon after I had moved into the dower house and so I suggested she came to housekeep for me. I did not think it was quite proper for her to live there with no chaperon and I knew Freddie and Joe were looking for lodgings, so all three came to stay.'

'What did Stephen say to that?'

'He was angry with me and afraid of what our father would say and that worried him more than anything. I realised after Dick was born that everyone had assumed he was mine, but I let it go. I was already out of favour and it would make no difference...' He laughed. 'Give a dog a bad name and he will live up to it. I hoped when Stephen came down to Borstead and saw Lucy again he would realise he loved her enough to stand up to Papa and marry her. The trouble started when you came into our lives.'

'I know. Your father guessed who I really was when he saw how your great-grandmother reacted when she saw me. He told me tonight that he expected me to have a good dowry. It was all about money, Richard. I had no idea, I certainly never expected Stephen to propose.'

'I know and I apologise for doubting you. It was not you that was marrying for money but Stephen, though the poor fellow did not know it at the time. He only learned it tonight with everyone else. When he was so reluctant to tell you about Lucy and Dick, I began to wonder if he really loved Lucy, after all. I realised he did when Dick went missing; he was as distraught as Lucy. And you saw the result.'

'He accused you of taking Lucy from him.'

'That was only frustration and jealousy talking and meant nothing. Papa had just given him a jobation for letting you slip through his fingers and he had to take it out on someone.'

'You are very tolerant of him. I am not sure if I could have been. I am still angry at the way I have been used.'

'With me, Diana? How have I used you?'

She stopped to think and then laughed. 'No, I suppose in the light of what you have told me, you have not done so.'

'Then are we friends again?'

'Friends?' she queried, stopping and turning to look up at him with a mischievous smile. 'Is that all?'

'You know it is not or you would not be looking at me in that teasing way. I said I loved you and I meant it. Now and for ever. It would make me the happiest man in the world if you were to say you loved me too.'

'I already have.'

'Then say it again.'

'Oh, I do. I love you, but I dared not hope for anything when I thought you and Lucy were lovers and Dick was your son. Why do you think I wanted to leave? Why do you think I was so weak as to allow you to bring me back when I had made up my mind to go? Because I could not bear the thought of never seeing you again.'

'Oh, Diana.' He wrapped his arms about her and kissed her over and over again until she was breathless. 'Will you marry me? Can you bear to live in the dower house and be the wife of the black sheep?'

'Black sheep? I do not think you are that. On the contrary, you have done your best for everyone, sometimes with little gratitude.'

'That has not answered my question. Will you marry me?'

'Oh, yes, it is my dearest wish.' She stopped. 'But what about Miss Standish?'

'That will be up to Stephen. I have told him it is about time he stood up to Papa and I think he might.'

'It will be a dreadful shock to your father.'

'He will get over it. Lucy will make an excellent shop Harecroft when the family get over their antipathy towards an actress.'

'That is nothing to getting used to having a…' she hesitated '…a love child in the family.'

He laughed and hugged her and she reached on tiptoe and kissed him again, then arm in arm they returned to the Hall.

Everyone was out on the terrace, intent on watching the fireworks exploding in the sky in a myriad of colours. They crept behind them and in at a side entrance. He kissed her and gave her a little push towards the servants' stairs. 'Hurry back to me.'

She raced up to her room, stripped off Lucy's gingham and put on the blue gown Richard had bought her. Then she tied her hair back with a ribbon and went to join him. They watched the last of the fireworks and waited until most of the guests had gone and the family had congregated in the drawing room. They could hear a babble of voices as they approached. 'Do we really want to join them?' Diana asked.

'Not if you do not wish it. Our news can wait until the morning.'

The door opened and Alicia came out. 'Where have you two been?' she asked. 'We missed you.'

'Having adventures,' Richard said. 'Dick ran off. Diana's father found him paddling in the brook.'

'Good heavens, what was Miss Standish thinking of to let him out of her sight? I hope he was none the worse for it.'

'No. All's well that ends well.' He reached out and took

Diana's hand. 'We have come to an understanding, Diana and I.'

'About time, too. What about Stephen? Does he know?'

'Yes, but Stephen has rediscovered his own love. They are together at the dower house now.'

'I am glad to hear it. You took a great risk bringing Miss Standish there, Richard, but your gamble seems to have worked.'

'Yes, but it very nearly did not. I have resolved never again to interfere in anyone else's life. Diana has taught me that it does not pay.'

'But Stephen will need your support when he tells your parents,' Diana said. 'They are going to be shocked.'

'Not as shocked as you might think,' Alicia said. 'Mama spilled the beans tonight.'

'Great-Grandmother knew?' Diana asked in astonishment.

Alicia smiled. 'There is not much that gets past my mother.'

'What did Mama and Papa make of it?' Richard asked.

'They were bemused, but it was not the only revelation she made tonight and they had much to occupy their minds.'

'Oh, you mean about my father and me.'

'More than that. You should have been here.'

'I hope her ladyship was not too cross that we missed it.'

Alicia laughed. 'No, she seemed to derive a great deal of satisfaction from the fact that you had disappeared together, as if she meant it to happen.'

'She could not have predicted Dick would go missing or that I would fall into the water.'

'No, but she laid her plans well, set everyone's nerves on edge and then waited to see what would happen.'

'Isn't that just like Great-Grandmama?' Richard laughed. 'Put all the ingredients into the pot, give it a stir and wait for the bang.'

'Something like that, but Mama did have something else on her mind besides making you two come to your senses. She decided not only to reveal the contents of her will but to enact it straight away and not wait until she died. You could have heard a pin drop when she made the announcement.'

'Go on,' Richard said. 'What did she say? I know you are dying to tell us.'

'William already has the estate and the stud and there was nothing for him, but he expected that and was in complete agreement. There were gifts to the staff, of course. Henry was given a batch of shares Mama has been hanging on to for years, but, knowing Henry's luck on the 'Change, they will probably treble in value as soon as he has them in his hands. Cecil and Maryanne are to be given a sum of money provided they spend a year working at Harecroft's to earn it. It did not please them, but she told them Stephen had been working there for years and Diana had already done her year and she was treating them no differently. All are to receive an equal amount.'

'Me, too?' queried Diana.

'Yes, of course. You have equal status with the others. Your father is to have his inheritance and John is to have sole ownership of all the shops except the one in Bond Street. Stephen is to have that, so that he can have a measure of independence, provided he marries Miss Standish.'

'And you?' Richard asked.

'Enough money to secure my independence. Do you not want to know what she is giving you?'

'I have what I want. She has been instrumental in giving me Diana.' He squeezed her hand and smiled at her as he spoke.

'Nevertheless you are to have the dower house, until such time as you inherit Borstead Hall, which you will do in the fullness of time, and enough money to secure a seat in the Commons. She expects you to make a name for yourself as a Member of Parliament and a force for good.' She laughed suddenly. 'You should have seen your father's face when she said that. He could not have been more surprised.'

'Am I no longer the black sheep?'

'It seems not, though when he discovers your political stance, he might not be so pleased.' She paused, nodding towards the drawing room and the sound of indignant voices, Maryanne's loudest of all. 'Are you going in there to tell him your good news now?'

'Is Great-Grandmother in there?'

'No, she retired as soon as she had had her say.'

'Then we will leave it until tomorrow. I think that will be the time for Stephen and I to present a united front.' He leaned forward and kissed the old lady's cheek and then took Diana by the hand. 'I believe there is a moon tonight, sweetheart. Shall we go and look at it?'

They went out into the garden hand in hand. There was indeed a moon and they stood side by side, gazing up at it, then he turned and took her in his arms to kiss her. He had kissed her before: in anger, in frustration, wanting to hurt, to demonstrate his ability to control her, but never like this, never with such tenderness, such overflowing emotion. It was an emotion she returned in equal measure and he was left in no doubt that he was really loved. When they were breathless and the moon disappeared behind a cloud, they turned and walked slowly back into the house.

'Tomorrow,' he said, as he kissed her again at the foot of the stairs. 'Tomorrow we tell the world and make plans for a wedding. Goodnight, my dearest love.'

He was loath to part with her, even for one night, and held on to her hand as she moved away from him and started up the stairs. When she was at arm's length, he let go and blew her a kiss. 'Happy dreams, sweetheart.'

She looked down at him, one hand extended towards him, eyes shining with happy tears. 'See you in the morning, my love.' She climbed the stairs and at the top looked back. He was still there, one foot on the bottom step, one hand on the banister. It was the picture she carried to her bed with her, the heart of her dreams.

Church attendance was mandatory for both family and staff at Borstead Hall and only Mrs Evans and the kitchen maids were excused on the grounds that they were needed to cook dinner, which on that day was always served at one o'clock to allow the servants to have their meal afterwards and then have the rest of the day in which to do as they pleased. Diana wondered if Stephen would go and was slightly surprised when she and Richard arrived with Alicia and James to see him carrying Dick into church with Lucy walking beside him. It was a public statement and she wondered if his father had approved, or even knew he was going to do it. She glanced at Richard and noticed his wry smile. 'It might set the cat among the pigeons,' he whispered to her. 'But I am glad he has decided to face up to his responsibilities.'

They had already spoken to John about their own plans. Going down to breakfast, Diana had discovered Richard was already there and waiting for her. 'We will beard the lion together,' he whispered, taking her hand and leading her towards his father. 'Sir,' he said formally, making John look up in surprise from the coddled eggs he was eating. 'I have the honour to present my future wife.'

Diana stifled a giggle; it was too solemn a moment for that.

'Have you, indeed?' He looked Diana up and down. 'Well, I suppose it does not really matter which one of you she marries.'

'I hope you will give us your blessing,' Diana said diffidently.

'Yes, yes, of course. Glad to have you in the family.'

'Thank you,' she said.

'Now, I suppose I shall have to find myself a new clerk.' He sighed. 'Changes, nothing but changes. Stephen off on his own with the actress and Richard standing for Parliament and writing books. I wonder if Grandmother knows what she has done.'

'Oh, I know very well what I have done.' The old lady stood in the doorway, laughing. 'Shaken you all up, that's what I have done.'

'And I thank you for it,' Richard said, going forward to kiss her wrinkled cheek.

'And me.' Diana kissed her too.

'I expect you to be very happy in the dower house, where I can keep an eye on you,' she said. 'I intend to live for years yet to enjoy your company and see more great-great-grandchildren. Do not disappoint me.'

They had looked at each other and laughed and now Diana stood between Richard and her father, as the first banns were read for two weddings.

* * * * *

On sale 5th September 2008

THE STOLEN BRIDE
by Brenda Joyce

Betrothed to a man of honour…

Sean O'Neil was everything to Eleanor de Warenne, but when he disappeared and sent no word, Eleanor abandoned all hope and promised her hand to another. Then Sean reappears, just days before her wedding!

Yet her heart belongs to a traitor!

Weary and haunted, Sean is loath to endanger the beautiful, desirable Eleanor. But in a moment's passion they are forced on the run: Sean has stolen another man's bride – and Eleanor steals his heart…

The Masquerade "dances on slippered feet… Joyce's tale of the dangers and delights of passion fulfilled will enchant."
—*Publishers Weekly*

The Regency

LORDS & LADIES
COLLECTION

More Glittering Regency Love Affairs

Volume 24 – 1st August 2008
The Reluctant Marchioness by Anne Ashley
Nell by Elizabeth Bailey

Volume 25 – 5th September 2008
Kitty by Elizabeth Bailey
Major Chancellor's Mission by Paula Marshall

Volume 26 – 3rd October 2008
Lord Hadleigh's Rebellion by Paula Marshall
The Sweet Cheat by Meg Alexander

Volume 27 – 7th November 2008
Lady Sarah's Son by Gayle Wilson
Wedding Night Revenge by Mary Brendan

Volume 28 – 5th December 2008
Rake's Reward by Joanna Maitland
The Unknown Wife by Mary Brendan

Volume 29 – 2nd January 2009
Miss Verey's Proposal by Nicola Cornick
The Rebellious Débutante by Meg Alexander

Volume 30 – 6th February 2009
Dear Deceiver by Mary Nichols
The Matchmaker's Marriage by Meg Alexander

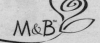